Books by K.M. Scott

Crash Into Me (Heart of Stone #1)

Fall Into Me (Heart of Stone #2)

Give In To Me (Heart of Stone #3)

The Heart of Stone Trilogy Box Set

Ever After (A Heart of Stone Novella)

A Heart of Stone Christmas

Unforgettable (A Heart of Stone Spinoff #1)

Temptation (Club X #1)

Surrender (Club X #2)

Possession (Club X #3)

Satisfaction (Club X #4)

SILK Volume One

SILK Volume Two

SILK Volume Three

SILK Volume Four

The SILK Box Set

Mike,
Thanks for being the
face of Unforgettable!
K. M.
Scott

UNFORGETTABLE

K.M. SCOTT

Grandma,
Another one to add to
the collection!
Lots of love,
Michael

Published in the United States
ISBN-10: 1-941594-34-4
ISBN-13: 978-1-941594-34-6

Cover Design: Cover Me, Darling

Adult Content: Contains graphic sexual content

UNFORGETTABLE

What do you do when the one you love is the one you can't have?

Gage Varo had accepted being alone for what he'd done. No one else should be hurt because of him. Then one day Jordan showed up and he fell hard for the beautiful blond who made him believe in love again. But his past returned with a vengeance and forced him to make the hardest choice of his life. He never stopped loving her, though, even as he watched her move on without him.

What do you do when the one you love is the one you shouldn't want?

Jordan Wright thought she found real love with Gage, but it all ended one night with a phone call. Now she's got a chance to have the life she's always wanted with a man who can give her everything. All she needs to do is forget about Gage and she can be happy. The problem is she can't forget the one man who loved her unlike anyone else ever had.

They'll have to put the past behind them if they ever want to have a future, but the past isn't going away that easy.

CHAPTER ONE

JORDAN

THE SOOTY SMELL OF A campfire fills my nose as I race through the woods toward the tent I'm sharing with my sister Kayla for the next week. It's a hot summer night, and the heaviness of the humidity hangs in the air, weighing me down, but I reach the tent safely and zip the flaps closed to a chorus of laughter from Kayla.

But I turn around and it isn't my sister sitting behind me but my mother. I shake my head in confusion and ask, "Why are you here? Where did Kayla go?"

Her expression turns serious, scaring me. She says nothing but points toward the outside of the tent, a look of terror filling her eyes.

"Mom, what's wrong? What's out there?"

"He's out there."

Her words come out in cryptic monosyllables as her look changes to sadness. I'm confused. Who's out there?

"Was Dad able to get off work and come with us?"

She just shakes her head. "He's out there."

I opened my eyes and struggled to remember the details

of the dream as I slowly eased back into consciousness. Reaching for my phone, I scrolled through my contacts to find my mother's number and called her. It was silly, but after having the same dream over and over for the past week, I figured I should mention it to her. Maybe she knew what my subconscious mind was up to.

"Jordan, is everything okay?" she asked in her usual sweet voice. "You didn't get mugged, did you? I worry about that with you living there."

"No, mom. I didn't get mugged," I said, stifling a yawn. "I just had a weird dream and wanted to know if dad's okay."

"Of course he's okay, honey. He already left for work, but he's fine. Why?"

I rubbed the sleep from my eyes as I thought about the dream and wondered why my father never appeared in it even though my mother kept saying he was out there. My mind clearly thought someone was out there, and if it wasn't my father, then who?

"No reason. I've just been having this strange dream where Kayla and I are camping and you show up saying that some guy is outside the tent. I ask you if it's dad and you say it isn't but you keep saying he's out there."

"It sounds more like a nightmare to me. Imagine me out in a tent in the middle of the woods. Just the thought of it makes me feel like bugs are crawling all over me. I did it once. No thanks."

Laughing, I sit up in bed. "I don't remember you ever going camping with us. That's why I was calling to ask about dad since he's the one we always go camping with."

My mother remained silent for a moment and then quietly said, "Well, I'm sure it's nothing. Nothing at all. You probably saw some show on TV that had camping in it and that's what's playing on your mind."

"Probably."

"Anything else new, honey?"

"Just the engagement party. I can't wait to see you two there. It's going to be great."

"Oh, I'm sure it will be, Jordan. We'll see you and Brock Saturday night. I'll tell your Dad you miss camping with him too. Maybe you two can get out to the woods before school begins again."

"I'd like that. Okay, I'm going to get moving with my day, Mom. I'll see you Saturday. I love you."

"Love you, honey. See you then."

I pressed END on my phone and set it down on the bed next to me, my mind occupied with the idea of what my mother's only time camping must have been like to ruin the experience for her forever. I wished I could remember, but I must have been only a baby then.

Maybe it was all that fresh air. She'd always been more of the air conditioning type.

THE MESS OF MY LIVING room stood as proof positive that I'd need to change my ways once I became Mrs. Brock Hannon. Mrs. Brock Hannon. I loved the way that sounded. Jordan Hannon. Not bad. Maybe something hyphenated would work. Jordan Wright-Hannon. That sounded pretty good too.

"Nina, which sounds better—Jordan Hannon or Jordan Wright-Hannon?"

Looking up from the magazine she was reading, a slow smile crept into Nina's usually placid expression. Tilting her head so her warm brown hair tumbled over her left shoulder, she said, "Well, I don't know. I've always liked your last name, so maybe the hyphenated one could work."

I pushed aside the pile of bridal magazines on the couch and plopped myself down. "I like that one too. Okay, it's settled. Hyphenated it is."

"Jordan, I can't believe you're getting married. It's still hasn't sunk in."

"I know. It's just so wild, isn't it? It's a nice feeling, though."

Nina stayed silent for a moment. "It is. I think it's great. I just thought…"

Curling my legs under me, I waited for her to finish her sentence. When she didn't, I asked, "What? You always thought what?"

She got a sheepish look on her face and I saw in her eyes she had something to say. Did she not like my future husband? "Nina, what is it?"

"I just always thought you'd marry someone else."

"Who? Have you been holding out on me? Does Tristan have another brother because you know I'd be open to that," I joked.

Knitting her brows, she shook her head. "No."

"Well, I was teasing anyway. I wouldn't just dump Brock that way, even for someone as great as Tristan."

Nina gave me a weak smile. "Jordan, I thought that you and Gage would end up together."

Her words landed like a flaming bag of shit right there in the middle of our conversation. Gage? Why the hell would she think I'd ever end up with him?

I crossed my arms and leveled my stare on her. "Why would you think that? The man broke up with me over the phone and never even bothered to call me when he came back here, assuming he came back and didn't hook up with some Hollywood tartlet instead."

"I know, but I guess I just always hoped that I got you together with the guy you'd end up with."

"Well, Gage lost out. His problem, not mine. We weren't very good together anyway. Not like Brock and I are. Now that I'm with someone like him, I see Gage and I could never have worked out."

Nina shifted her gaze down toward the magazine in her lap. "Oh."

"Oh what? Don't you like Brock? He's wealthy, smart, hot, and everything I've ever wanted. All Gage had going for him was hot."

"I don't think he was dumb, was he?" she said in defense of the man who'd broken my heart.

"No, but he wasn't Brock smart. He was just bodyguard smart."

"Oh, okay."

"Another oh? What is up with you? You don't like Brock, do you?"

She avoided my gaze and shook her head. "No, it's not

like that. I like him. I do. He's got everything a girl could want. Looks, money, intelligence, success…he's the whole package. I can definitely see why you'd be crazy about him."

Something in the way her voice sounded tentative told me that's not all she thought of the man I was set to become officially engaged to in just days. "Is there something you need to tell me, Nina? Did you have Tristan investigate him and you found out he's a serial killer or something? Tell me. You have to tell me! As my best friend, you can't let me marry someone who's a serial killer."

"No, I didn't have Tristan check him out. I don't know anything about Brock other than what you've told me and what I've seen in the times we've all hung out together. He seems perfectly nice. Just the kind of guy you deserve. I have no doubt that he'll make a fantastic husband."

"Okay. As long as he's not an ax murderer, we're all good," I said with a chuckle.

Leaning toward me, she got a playful look in her eyes and whispered, "You've never mentioned about the goods. How come?"

Nina never ceased to surprise me. No one would ever know to look at her, but she had the ability to see into someone in a way that other people couldn't. In truth, Brock's goods were…well, less than stellar. I'd never really talked about him that way because even though his skills in bed were definitely passable, the reality was that sex between us wasn't the best I'd ever had.

But then again, the best sex I'd ever had was with someone who thought so little of me he broke up with me over the phone and never called back.

"He's fine. You know. Everything is in working order and we have a great time together."

Wow. Even I knew that sounded lame.

"Oh. Well, that's good. Working order is definitely good."

Lots of goods. Except the ones we were talking about.

"Sex isn't everything in the world, Nina. We're not all as lucky as you are with Mr. Incredible Guy who has all any woman ever wanted."

That came out a whole lot more defensive than I'd intended.

Nina reached over and gave me a sympathetic arm squeeze. "I'm sorry. I didn't mean to say anything to upset you. I'm sure you and Brock will be very happy, Jordan. That's all I've ever wanted for you. If Brock's the one to give you all the happiness you deserve, then I'm his biggest fan."

"No biggie, honey. I know you love me and want to see me happy. I think Brock can do that—make me happy, you know? Maybe I'll get my happy ending like you did."

She tilted her head and smiled. "Definitely. So what kind of progress have you made on the wedding gown? You know, it's never too early."

I picked up one of the half dozen bridal magazines that sat between us and began to absentmindedly flip through the pages. I'd breezed through a bunch of them a few times, but nothing had jumped out at me. None of the dresses seemed right. I wasn't reed thin and tall like so many of the models or cute and shapely like Nina. I was too toned to wear the thin girl or the curvy girl dresses.

"None yet. I still have time."

Nina grabbed another of the magazines and turned to a page where she'd found one I might like. "What about this one? It's got great lines and with your body, it will look incredible."

I turned my head to look at a form-fitting white gown with a draped neckline and a body hugging cut. "Not horrible."

"It would be great on you. I could never wear that." Nina looked down her body and frowned. "Even before having triplets."

"Says the woman whose wedding gown nearly took her husband's breath away that day."

Nina blushed that cute way she always did when someone complimented her, and the apples of her cheeks turned pink. "Well, then we need to find you a gown that will do the same for your husband-to-be. Should I fold this page down?"

I glanced down at the dress again. "Yeah, it's fold-worthy."

"Good. We're making progress. I think if you can find ten fold-worthy dresses in this mass of glossy magazines you'll be in good shape."

"Nina, you know I'm only getting engaged in a few days. We're not getting married until next year. I think I have time."

She pointed at another magazine near my knee. "You can never be too early with the gown, according to an article I read in that one there."

"Well, the oracle has spoken then. Will twenty by Tuesday be okay with American Bride?" I joked.

Rolling her eyes, she made a clucking noise with her tongue. "You're not taking this seriously, Jordan. Brock is an important man. You're going to have a big wedding with lots of important people there. You can't leave the dress to chance."

The way Nina talked about my wedding made me queasy. I didn't really want a big wedding. I liked the way she and Tristan did it. Intimate and cozy with just a few close friends. The idea of some big shindig with hundreds of people who were little more than strangers surrounding me on my big day wasn't my style.

"Well, does that mean I can't have a wedding that's right for me? Does everything have to be right for him?"

Nina's blue eyes opened wide in surprise. "Is something going on that you haven't told me?"

I shrugged and waved away her concern. "No. I get that Brock is different than me. I'm all about shooting straight from the hip, and he's diplomatic and professional. I laugh out loud at funny things, and he can barely stand watching comedies. I get that. But shouldn't our wedding be a reflection of both of us and not just him?"

"Jordan, what's going on? Do you want to marry him?"

Her question hit a little too close to home, and I quickly answered, "Of course I do."

I couldn't answer that question as easily as I would have liked. I was crazy about Brock, no doubt. He'd swept me off my feet the very night we met. There I was standing outside school on the curb in the pouring rain deciding if I wanted to go home to my lonely apartment or stay in Manhattan for dinner by myself, and out of nowhere he pulled up and his limo drenched me with a puddle. Jumping out of the car, he ran to me and quickly stripped off his coat to try to dry me, like some fairytale hero.

But it was no use. I looked like a drowned rat. He gazed at me with those beautiful hazel eyes of his and introduced himself, and I thought maybe I was dreaming. When he offered to give me a ride home, I accepted, not even knowing his full name, and by the time we made it to Brooklyn, I hoped that one encounter wouldn't be our last.

He pursued me with a vengeance, sending gifts and calling me at all hours just to say he was thinking of me. By our third date, I knew we had something special. He doted on me like no man ever had, and for the first time in my life, I wanted to believe a relationship would last.

But for all that, something inside me made me worry that it would all go away as quickly as it came into my life, leaving me alone once again. This time that little voice inside me that always feared the worst seemed to be able to whisper louder than my positive side and its Good Things Happen To Good People mantra.

Now as we got ready to celebrate his asking me to marry him, my worries that something would make this all go away plagued me more than ever. What if I wasn't enough? I'd never been enough for anyone else. What if he woke up one day soon and realized that he wanted someone like him— wealthy, proper, and subdued.

Someone not like me.

I folded a glossy page with a long silk gown better suited to the type of woman Brock Hannon should probably be with. Needing to change the subject, I mumbled, "I had that same dream again."

"The one with your mother?"

Nodding, I looked up and pretended not to be frightened. I'd had the dream all week and still couldn't figure out what it meant, if it meant anything. But my gut told me it wasn't a good thing.

"Yeah. It's so weird because my mother wouldn't be caught dead camping," I joked.

Nina chuckled at the thought of my mother anywhere near the outdoors. My mother was the last person on Earth I'd expect to find camping or doing anything like that. In fact, the running joke in my family was that she was the inspiration for the giraffe from the Madagascar movie and his fear of nature.

"Your mother's a sweetheart, Jordan, but she's definitely not a woman who does the camping thing."

"I know! All those bugs and wild animals and no decent bedding. She'd crawl right out of her skin if she had to spend ten minutes in a tent."

"Was it the same dream as before?"

"Yep. She keeps saying some guy is out there. She never says who or if it's my father, even though it makes sense that she'd be talking about my dad since he's the one I've gone camping with for all my life."

Looking up toward the ceiling, Nina seemed to think

about it for a moment and shook her head. "I have no idea. Keep in mind that not all dreams mean things. It could just be that you miss going camping. Maybe you and Brock should take a weekend and spend it in the outdoors."

Now it was my turn to chuckle. "Brock and my mother are cut from the same cloth. He'd no more spend time in a tent camping than she would."

"Then maybe that's what it means! You love camping and because he's so much in love with you, Brock comes to see you out in the wilderness, even though he hates it."

I couldn't help but smile. "Always the romantic, huh? Well, if that's what it means, why don't I ever see him in my dream? And why does my mother keep saying he's out there instead of saying Brock's out there? She knows Brock's name."

Nina stood from the couch and leaned over to kiss me on the cheek. "I didn't say I had all the answers. I'll keep thinking about it, but I have to get back to the house. Cara and the kids will be back from the park by the time Jensen gets us home. When are you coming out to see them? Ever since they started walking they're even more fun to hang out with. I can grab Cara and we can take them to the zoo. They'd love that. What do you think?"

"Sure. We can do it before I go back to school. I still have a few weeks, so it's a date. Give them all a kiss for me, and be sure to tell Tristan I said hi."

Grabbing her purse, she turned toward the door. "Call me. I know we'll be seeing you Saturday night, but call me anyway. I get lonely for our talks out there."

I followed her to the door to see her out. "I will. Tell Jensen not to drive too fast, that maniac."

Nina rolled her eyes. "Jensen is no more a maniac than I am. We're all boring out in the country. Just think, that's going to be you in a few months."

I kissed her goodbye and as I closed the door, I thought about what she'd said. I didn't consider her and Tristan boring in any way, shape, or form. After all they'd gone through before they got married, they deserved some calm times. My life had always been pretty boring, though, until Brock.

Would that all change when we married?

✧   ✧   ✧

I STOOD IN THE LIVING room of Brock's penthouse apartment as he paced back and forth talking on the phone about some business issue that had come up just as we were set to leave for dinner. Dressed in his usual black suit, he looked every bit the businessman he was. The owner of a web startup company, he'd rocketed to the top of his field in just three short years. He'd branched out into other areas of business I had to admit I didn't know a lot about, but the main source of his income remained the internet startup.

It was that business that preoccupied him at the moment, making him rake his hands through his light blond hair in an obvious sign of stress. The frown on his face deepened with each pass by me, and I worried our night might be ruined by whatever bad news he was dealing with.

"Riley, I don't give a damn what you think. This needs to

happen and I expect it to happen this week. Do you understand me or do I need to explain it again? I assume you're bright enough to take care of this. Am I wrong in that assumption?"

The sharpness of Brock's tone made me feel sorry for poor Riley on the receiving end of his anger. For as sweet as he could be, my future husband had an edge to him that could cut anyone to the quick.

He passed me again, still grimacing, and bit out, "I'm going out tonight, and if I get back and find out this hasn't been handled, you're going to be out of a job. I don't think I can make this any clearer, Riley, so get it done."

And with that, he shut his phone off and stuffed it into his pocket.

Brock stopped in front of where I sat and looked down at me, the serious expression still on his face. "Jordan, I'm sorry that took so long. I had to take that call."

Looking up at him, I put on my sweetest smile. "I understand. It's no biggie."

He lifted my chin with his forefinger. "So sweet. Thank you."

"I did feel a little bad for poor Riley." Standing, I straightened his grey tie. "You gave him a pretty stern warning there."

"I understand," he said, his hazel eyes staring deeply into mine. "You're far nicer than I am. Riley probably wishes you were his boss. But sometimes you have to crack the whip."

"I'm sorry. I understand."

"No need to be sorry," he said sweetly. "So how hungry

are you because I'm starving."

I loved when he was like this—when he shed the serious businessman part of himself and just let himself be who he was with me.

"I'm famished. Where are we off to tonight?"

He tapped me on the tip of my nose and winked. "How about that Brick place near your apartment?"

"Wanting to slum it tonight, huh?" I joked. "Okay, I'm good for it."

Brock smiled and kissed me softly on the lips. "Good. Just let me change out of these clothes and we can go."

As he took off his business suit, I looked out the floor to ceiling window at the city below. For the first time ever, I felt like I'd really found someone who wanted me. Even though we were truly as different as night and day, we worked.

"Did I tell you Nina came over today to get me moving on the wedding gown?" I said loudly toward the bedroom.

He walked toward me dressed in jeans and a button down shirt, and I saw the slight frown that always seemed to come across his face whenever I spoke about Nina. They'd only spent a little time together and nothing of note had happened on any of those occasions, so I couldn't figure out why he wouldn't like my best friend.

"Nina? No, you didn't mention she came by to see you."

I encircled his neck with my arms and leaned in to kiss him, planting a tiny kiss on the center of his lips. "Yeah. She's coaching me on how I should be focusing on the dress since I'm marrying such an important man."

"An important man? Did she say that?" he asked.

"Yes, she did. She thinks I need to take the whole wedding gown issue far more seriously. I'm not having any luck finding the right one yet."

Brock turned away from me and walked over to the bar to pour himself a drink. "That's nice of her, but I wouldn't worry about that quite yet. We have time. We aren't even announcing our engagement until this weekend."

A hint of disgust hid just under his pleasant words, and I wondered if I should ask why he didn't like Nina. She and Tristan had never been anything but perfectly nice to him every time they'd be around him, so I was baffled. Nobody ever disliked Nina.

"Is everything okay, Brock? Nina doesn't mean any harm. She just wants to make sure our wedding goes as smoothly as can be."

Taking a sip of his bourbon, Brock shrugged. "No, everything's fine. I'm sure she's just trying to help. I just wish you'd come to me with any issues about our wedding instead of her."

I moved over to his side and shook my head. "No, there are no issues. Nina isn't trying to intrude, if that's what you're thinking. She's my best friend, so it's natural that she'd want to be involved in the happiest moment of my life."

He pressed a smile onto his lips. "I'd always thought that two people who want to be husband and wife would be best friends."

"I'm sorry, Brock. I didn't mean it that way. It's just that Nina and I have been like sisters since college. That doesn't mean she's more important to me than you are, though."

Instead of making things better, that only made them worse. "I certainly hope not. After we're married, I hope to move to Dallas so it's just going to be me and you then."

Something in the way he said that made the hairs on the back of my neck stand up. I'd been a New York girl for so long and near Nina since freshman year in college, and the thought of leaving the city I'd grown to call my own for a brand new one without a friend anywhere close made me uneasy.

I was just being silly. Brock offered me the world, and all I had to do was accept that I couldn't continue to live the life I'd lead as a single girl all these years. I'd wished for this for so long, and now all my dreams were coming true all because of this wonderful man.

So why did the mere mention of him taking me away terrify me so?

Brock reached out and took my hand in his, almost petting my skin. "I'm sorry. I didn't mean to be like that. It's my work and Riley's screw up. Let's just go to dinner and forget all this."

I smiled, even though his remark about leaving and it being just the two of us continued to echo in my mind. This was what my life was now. If I ever wanted to move out of that Brooklyn apartment and have nice things like Nina had with Tristan, I needed to be willing to make compromises. Brock could offer me everything a girl could want, if I could compromise.

No one got everything they wanted.

Right?

CHAPTER TWO

GAGE

FINISHING THE REPORTS FOR THE month, I clicked SEND to make sure my accountant had everything for July and sat back in my office chair to read over the letter that had kept me up most of the night before. I'd done exactly what they'd demanded every time they'd sent one, convinced that if I did they'd leave my life, but now they'd returned with more threats.

She still isn't safe, Gage.

I closed my eyes and swallowed hard at the thought of Jordan being hurt because of my failures. I'd left her with no explanation, making her think she was the reason I'd basically turned my back on her but willing to be that kind of bastard if she'd be safe.

The memory of the hurt in her voice that night when I broke up with her over the phone made me cringe now, months later. I couldn't give her a reason for leaving, knowing when I didn't that her imagination would take over and fill in the blanks.

I could be a real dick sometimes.

That I did it to protect her didn't matter when I heard

her quiet sobs and her pleas for some answer to why I could be so callous to her. If I told her, then she'd be in danger too, and I couldn't risk her life because I'd made one stupid mistake.

Since that day, I'd lived with the guilt of knowing the one woman I loved hated me and had good reason to. She'd gone on with her life, probably getting hooked up with some great guy through Nina. If I knew Nina, she found her friend a man with all the things I couldn't offer her.

Money. Power. All the things Jordan deserved and I'd never have to give her.

"Boss, we're off to the Becker party. You coming?"

I looked up from the letter and smiled at John, one of my workers at the tiny business I'd started from the money Tristan had given me after I'd returned to New York. Saving someone's life came in none too cheaply, and with the money I'd built Varo Security. Tristan had helped me by referring some clients too, so it didn't take long before I'd gotten back on my feet again.

"I'll be there. It's just a birthday party, so unless Becker has pissed someone off, it should be mostly making sure no one put their hands on him. The man has a real problem with people touching him. I told him I'd be stopping in after the party begins, but if you have any problems, just call my cell."

"Got it. See you there."

John left me sitting alone in my tiny office with my memories and my guilt. As I did every night, I typed in Jordan's name on my computer to search for any news of her. Not that anything would have changed since yesterday. I knew that, but it didn't stop my need to see if today was finally the day I'd learn that she'd moved on.

The usual came up on Google. A shopping trip with Nina. A picture of her with Nina and Tristan standing near their triplets on one of their days at the playground near the house in Dutchess County. An older picture of Jordan from college, her blond hair much longer but her eyes the same gorgeous, unforgettable green.

I'd seen all of these before, but it didn't matter. I had to make sure.

Not that I'd be able to do anything if one day I saw an engagement announcement with her name. The people blackmailing me had sworn that if I ever even tried to contact her again, they'd hurt her. I didn't doubt them either, so even if I wanted to do my best impression of the famous scene in The Graduate and try to stop her from marrying another man, I couldn't.

I couldn't risk them hurting her because of their hatred for me.

I sat there staring at the pictures of her on my laptop screen, my mind drifting back to the night when I first stopped over at her apartment in Brooklyn. That night I knew I'd fallen hard.

Jordan sat cross-legged on the couch wearing shorts that showed off her tanned, toned legs and a pink t-shirt, her long blond hair tied up in a messy ponytail. She had an All-American girl look that said the boys at the high school football games had watched her as she cheered on the sidelines each Friday night, every one of them secretly in love with the bubbly blond with the beautiful smile.

"I was a little surprised to see you at my door," she said quietly, her green eyes staring at me with a look that made me think she'd see right through any tough guy act I'd try to pull.

"Well, I was in the city, so I thought I'd stop in."

Not exactly the truth, but I wasn't about to tell her I'd been thinking about her for weeks and as I drove down the Taconic I'd finally decided to take a chance on whatever we could be instead of living in the past.

Her cheeks turned a deep pink color that only made her more beautiful, and she smiled. "I'm glad you did."

We sat there awkwardly trying to be cooler than either of us were about the obvious attraction between us. I'd fought it day and night when we'd lived together out at Tristan and Nina's house, convincing myself that being with her would be a conflict of interest. I couldn't let another client down because my attention was on my desires instead of their safety.

Jordan hadn't fought it then, though. Every evening, rain or shine, she'd pretend to walk around the grounds exercising, as if I didn't know exactly what time she worked out in the gym inside the house every morning before going to school. She'd wave and smile as she walked toward us, and I'd pretend I wasn't thrilled to see her there for me. Most nights I'd stand practically silent as she and West talked, but no matter how bad my day had been, just seeing her made it better every time.

"Do you miss living out at the house?" I asked, more nervous than a teenage boy on a first date. Christ, even my palms were sweaty!

Jordan looked around her small apartment and sighed. "In some ways, yeah. I miss living with Nina. We've lived as roommates for so long that it feels weird here without her. That was one good thing about living out in the sticks. And the gym Tristan has out there is first rate. I loved that! Now I have to haul my cookies eight blocks to get a decent workout. I definitely miss the gym."

"Eight blocks at the crack of dawn could be dangerous around here," I considered out loud, more than mildly concerned about her walking that far so early in the morning.

A sly smile spread across her lips. "Crack of dawn? How did you know when I worked out?"

"I…I just assumed since you work all day and you're probably exhausted after dealing with all those little kids all day."

Hopefully gorgeous women loved rambling because that's what I was offering at the moment.

"You knew when I worked out when I lived at the house, didn't you?"

I shrugged, attempting to be nonchalant. "I was security for the estate. I was supposed to know what was going on there."

"With Tristan and Nina, Gage. Not me."

"I was thorough."

"You knew when I worked out. You liked me."

I nodded, unsure of what to say. I had liked her, more than I wanted to admit at first and then much more, even as I tried to fight it.

"Why didn't you let me know you liked me? I was convinced all those times I tried to get you to talk to me that you didn't even like it when I came around."

"I didn't think I should start anything when I was watching Nina, Jordan. I didn't mean to make you think I didn't like it when you came around."

She gave me one of her gorgeous smiles and bit her lip lightly. "It's okay. I survived."

We sat there staring at one another, neither of us knowing what to say next. The beginning was always hard. Two people who've noticed they like the world a little more because the other person is in it realize they want to say all those things they've heard in songs but are too afraid to in case they've misread the signs.

Jordan stood from the couch and pointed toward the next room. "You thirsty? I'm going to grab a glass of soda or something. Want one?"

"Sure. Thanks."

I watched her walk to the kitchen and something inside me said it was now or never. Time to bite the bullet. If I didn't make a move now, we'd sit there in her living room talking around our attraction to one another by retelling stories of the one person we had in common. As much as I liked Nina, I didn't want to spend the entire night talking about her with Jordan.

Rounding the corner, I found her standing at the counter pouring a glass of soda. I watched her catch a drop as it slid down the side of the glass, smacking her lips as her finger touched her lips. She put the bottle of soda back in the refrigerator and stopped to look at herself in the glass front cabinet door next to the sink.

I walked up behind her and whispered, "You look beautiful."

As she spun around, her hands ran into my chest. Startled, she took a step back and hit the counter. "I didn't know you were standing there. I was just looking...getting the drinks."

"You look beautiful, Jordan."

She looked gorgeous. Her blond hair hung in long wisps around her face, escaping the confines of her hair tie that held her ponytail and making her look messy in a sexy way. She never wore much makeup, so her skin had a natural look to it, a glow that made her look healthy. Then there were those green eyes, a green unlike any I'd ever seen. They weren't dark like pine green or vivid like emerald or Kelly green. They were more like deep moss green, the kind of color you could get lost in trying to figure out where in the world you'd seen that exact shade before.

She blushed at my compliment and smiled up at me. "I never noticed how much taller you are than me. I guess since I was always in shoes, but I wore sneakers a lot, so—"

I stopped her talking with our first kiss, soft and unsure but thrilling nonetheless as I watched her eyes slowly close. Her lips yielded to mine, and she slipped her arms around my neck. Her touch against my skin sent chills up and down my spine. I'd waited for this moment for months, unsure I'd ever be able to go through with it and sure I'd fuck it up when the time finally came.

I didn't want to fuck this up like I'd fucked up with everyone else in the past.

Pulling back, I cupped her face in my hands and watched her as she kept her eyes closed. "Why won't you look at me?"

"Because you're so close and so right here that I'm afraid I'll open my eyes and see you don't like me as much as I want you to."

"Open them, Jordan." Still they remained closed. "Open your

eyes and look at me."

She took a deep breath and winced as if she was in pain. Then she slowly lifted her eyelids to show me those beautiful moss colored eyes looking up at me.

"Okay."

"I love it when you look up at me like you are right now. You did that the first time I met you. Did you know that?"

A tiny smile made her mouth turn up slightly and she shook her head. "No. I didn't know."

"I remember it. I remember wondering what it would feel like to have you give me that look if we were ever alone together. I told myself if the chance ever came around that I'd make sure I took it."

Her eyes grew wide as I spoke, like hearing the words made her want to see more of me. She looked away and began to speak, but I took her chin and made her look at me again. "It's okay. Don't look away."

"I think I should warn you. I don't have a good track record with men. It always starts out good, but then it always ends."

"My track record isn't great either, so I guess I should warn you too. At least we know going into this, right?"

She nodded. "Yeah. We gave each other fair warning. That's all anyone can ask for."

I kissed her again, loving the feel of her lips on mine. We stood there in her kitchen for hours talking and kissing as she sweetly scolded me for ignoring her the entire time she lived at the house and I teased her about how I thought for a while she might have liked old man West instead of me. The entire night was comfortable and easy, like we'd known each other forever and could tell one another anything.

I looked around my tiny office to see I'd been daydreaming about Jordan for an hour. I could have spent the rest of my night sitting there at my desk remembering how she made me feel, but Becker was expecting me, so I had to go.

Duty called.

"GAGE VARO, GOOD TO SEE you! How are you?" Mitch Becker asked as he ushered me into his Upper West Side penthouse. "Your guys are already here, so head out to the terrace and have a drink."

Mitch Becker looked like nearly every client Tristan sent me. Tall, lean, with perfect hair and perfect teeth and always wearing a suit, no matter the occasion. They all seemed to reek of inherited money, but unlike Tristan, most of them were insufferable. I could deal with Mitch, though. He acted more human than the others.

"Thanks, Mitch. Any problems I should know about?"

He flashed me a big toothy smile. "No. These people are mostly friends, so they know the rule about touching. You'll know if there's a problem."

"Got it. I'll circle back in a few, Mitch."

Backing away, he pointed toward the doors leading outside. "Sounds good. Tristan Stone and his wife are out on the terrace."

I smiled like this was good news, but seeing Nina and Tristan always brought back more memories and at that moment, I didn't want to think any more about Jordan. I couldn't avoid at least saying hello, though, and heading out to the terrace, I saw Nina wave her arms in the air to get my attention.

"Gage! I didn't know you'd be here!" she announced with a smile as she moved through the crowd toward me.

"How's my favorite power couple doing?" I asked, truly happy to see her and Tristan again, even if just the sight of them made me think of Jordan.

Nina hugged me and took me by the hand to join Tristan, who seemed to be enjoying the party as much as a trip to the dentist. Shaking his hand, I said, "It's good to see you again. How's life out in good old Dutchess County?"

He leaned in toward me and whispered, "Better than here. If I didn't have to attend parties like this, I'd much rather be sitting with the kids and Nina watching the Care Bears movie."

Nina beamed her happiness at hearing him say a night of cartoons was better than a swanky party in Manhattan, and I couldn't blame her. They'd been through so much they deserved a quiet life in the suburbs.

It wasn't what I'd want for my life, though.

"How's the security business going? I hope some of my references panned out."

"It's going well. Thanks for referrals. They've been working out great so far."

"That's wonderful, Gage," Nina said as she gave my wrist a sympathetic squeeze.

I knew what was coming next. Nina and Tristan knew

too. It always happened this way. Every time we saw each other, we made some small talk, and then there came the uncomfortable lull, which meant none of us wanted to mention the person we all had in common, even though we were all thinking about her. But Nina would end up saying something about her and I'd have to pretend just the mention of Jordan didn't hurt like hell.

This time I wanted to leave before any of that happened, though. "I need to get going, but it was nice seeing you guys again." I extended my hand to shake Tristan's again. "Keep those referrals coming."

"Always," he said in that genuine way I knew meant he'd keep on sending me work.

They both smiled as I turned away and I was sure I'd escaped before any mention of Jordan, but Nina caught up with me just as I walked back inside and took my hand. "Hey, Gage. I wanted to tell you that Jordan is—"

I looked down and saw sadness in Nina's eyes. Suddenly, terror raced through me. "What's wrong? Did something happen to her?"

Frowning, she said the words I'd dreaded hearing since I lost Jordan. "She's getting engaged. She and her fiancé are announcing it this Saturday. He owns a web startup company. I'm sorry, Gage. I just thought you should know."

In an instant, the room felt like someone had picked it up and shaken it like a snow globe. Everything seemed to float around me as Nina's news sank into my brain. Jordan getting engaged. I mumbled something about thanking her for letting me know and quickly made my way through the crowd of party guests to get outside. I needed to escape that world that had just taken the woman I loved away.

Jordan had moved on and in just a few days she'd be engaged to be married to another man. What I'd feared every day since I broke up with her had finally happened.

And it hurt even more than I ever thought it would.

I HEADED DOWN COLUMBUS AVENUE, unsure where I was going. I didn't want to go back to the office, but it didn't matter where I went. Everywhere in the city made me think of her. What the fuck had I been thinking when I moved back here?

My chest felt like someone had just hit me square with a sledgehammer. I tried to take a deep breath in, but I couldn't. Nina's news threatened to smother me right there in the middle of Manhattan. My legs continued to move, but my brain was preoccupied with one thought.

Jordan marrying another man.

A half hour later I was in a cab headed toward her apartment for the second time that week. I knew I couldn't talk to her or I'd risk putting her in danger, but maybe if I could see her as she left her apartment for the night I might not feel like my chest was being squeezed until I couldn't breathe.

Who was I kidding? Seeing her would only make this feeling worse, but I didn't care. At least if I saw her, even for just a fleeting moment, it could feel like I was still in her world and she was still in mine.

"Hey, slow down past these buildings," I ordered just as the cabbie turned onto Jordan's street. On the sidewalk, people stood talking and laughing, never knowing that for one guy in a cab he would have given the world to see the woman he loved for even a second.

The car slowed down to a crawl, and as we passed her building I looked up toward her windows. Dark, except for the light from the lamp in her living room she left on whenever she went out, it looked empty and lonely.

Like me.

She was probably out with her soon-to-be fiancé planning a life together. My chest contracted at the truth that finally Jordan had moved on. I'd promised myself that as long as my past put her in danger, I wouldn't try to be part of her life anymore, but the reality that come that Saturday she'd be officially engaged to another man made me want to forget all those promises I'd made to myself and finally tell her the truth of why I'd had to leave her.

I told the cabbie to take me back to my office as the hard truth settled into my brain. I couldn't tell her any of that if it meant she'd be in danger. So she'd get engaged and I'd remain what I'd always been since that first night at her apartment.

In love with her more than I thought it was possible for one person to love another.

CHAPTER THREE

JORDAN

JENSEN PULLED UP IN FRONT of my apartment at eleven sharp, and I headed down the stairs to join Nina for our noon mani/pedi appointment at our favorite spa, Roget's. A treat from Nina to celebrate my engagement, it was also a chance for us to spend time together like the old days.

"Nina, any chance we can stop for a coffee before we go to Roget's? I'm dragging without caffeine this morning," I said as I climbed into the back of the car. Turning to face the front seat, I tapped Jensen on the shoulder. "Hey, Jensen! How are you today?"

"Very good, Miss Jordan. It's good to see you again."

"It's good to see you too. Just like old times."

"Can you wait until we get to the spa? You know they have those delicious scones I love," Nina said as we pulled away from the curb.

"Any coffee shop will do," I pleaded. "I ran out of coffee yesterday and you know how I am without my morning nectar of the gods."

Giggling, Nina said, "I haven't forgotten all those mornings we lived together. Jensen, there's a Dunkin Donuts on the next block. Please stop there so Jordan can get some caffeine in her and become human again."

"Thank you. I promise once I get my coffee, I'll be the same old wonderful Jordan I always am."

Nina began talking about the day ahead of us, full of enthusiasm for our spa time and the final fitting for the gown I'd wear just two nights from then. I loved how excited she was for me and my big event. I just wished I felt as terrific about it as she did. It all felt like so much more than I was used to, but then again, I was marrying a successful man, so it was all new to me.

The car stopped and I jumped out to make a beeline for my morning go-go juice. Thankfully, the line was short and I only had to wait a few minutes to become human again. With coffee in hand, I climbed back into the car and we were off to Roget's for a day of pampering.

Bumper to bumper morning traffic into the city held us up, and as we sat waiting to move again, Nina said quietly, "I saw Gage last night at a party. He was working."

Just hearing his name made my heart skip a beat, and suddenly it felt like all the air had been sucked out of the car. Trying to act cool, I said in my best nonchalant voice, "Really? Who's he guarding now? The same teenager as before?"

"No. He's got his own security firm. I didn't tell you because I didn't want to upset you, but he's been back in the city for a while."

Back in the city for a while. So not only had he broken up with me over the phone, but he'd been back for a while and never bothered to even call me?

"Have you seen him before last night?"

"Yeah, a few times. The first time you were still pretty broken up over him so I didn't want to say anything. Then the other times you were already with Brock. Tristan sees him more than I do since he's been trying to help him get his business off the ground."

"Oh, well, that's nice," I said as all the pain of him leaving rushed back into my mind. "Nice to get his business off the ground."

Nina took my hand and squeezed it as if she'd just told me someone I loved had died. I didn't want sympathy. I wanted to forget Gage Varo, but every time I thought I'd finally put him out of my head, something reminded me of him and all those feelings came back with a vengeance.

God, I didn't want to feel that way anymore.

"I told him you were getting engaged, Jordan. He looked like he'd lost his best friend and then he left the party."

I turned away to look out the window so Nina couldn't see the tears in my eyes. "I don't know why he'd look like that. We were never friends. We were never much of anything by the way he could leave me with nothing more than a goodbye and never talk to me again."

"I'm sorry. I didn't know if I should tell you, but I figured since you're getting engaged to Brock, you wouldn't be upset like this. Jordan, what's going on?"

I wiped under my eyes and turned back to face her. "Nothing's going on."

"Then why are you so upset about me seeing Gage?"

"I'm not. Feel free to tell him I said hi the next time you see him."

Jensen stopped the car in front of Roget's and as I climbed out behind Nina, my entire world turned upside down. It was as if the universe was trying to hammer the idea that I needed to suffer into my head. There on the sidewalk in front of a boutique just two doors from the spa stood Gage with a stunning brunette in a red and white sundress. Nearly as tall as him, she looked like a wealthy debutante or super-model with her gold jewelry and designer purse draped over her arm.

My brain told my legs to move, to follow Nina, but I stood there watching him smile and laugh with the woman and felt as if my feet were encased in cement. For nearly a year, I'd promised myself if I ever saw him again, I'd tell him how shitty a person he was. I'd finally show him how I overcame what he did when he left me without even a word of explanation. But now that I saw him there just a few yards away, none of that was in my mind.

All I could think of was how much I'd missed him.

His dark hair seemed longer than the last time I'd seen him, just brushing up against his collar now. It still looked soft, though, and the feel of it against my cheek as we lay in bed on Sunday mornings, relaxing on the only day of the week we both had off work, rushed back into my head.

He looked good. I hated that he looked good. I wanted him to look like shit because he missed me so much, but I didn't have that kind of luck. No, he looked like he always had.

Masculine and strong. The kind of man who would protect the woman he loved.

I felt the tears well in my eyes. He hadn't protected me. He'd been the one to hurt me, and now he got to stand there smiling and joking around with some beautiful woman while I stood frozen on the spot desperately wishing I didn't fucking care about him anymore.

"Jordan, honey, you okay? What's wrong?"

I tried to speak but his name got caught in my throat. Swallowing hard, I whispered, "Gage."

Nina followed my gaze to where he stood and quickly pulled on my arm. "Oh, sweetie. Let's go inside."

I looked back at the car to see Jensen watching me with concern and I turned to face Nina. "I need to go. I can't do this now. Get me out of here, Nina."

She hurried me back into the car, ordering Jensen to drive away quickly. I sat there staring at Gage, needing to see his eyes. Those dark blue eyes I'd loved. All I needed to see were his eyes. If I saw his eyes and he looked happy, I'd have to admit to myself that whoever I'd been in love with hadn't loved me. But if I saw something in his eyes that told me he wasn't as happy as he looked, maybe I'd find some solace in that.

Maybe I could believe he missed me like I missed him.

As the car drove past him, I lowered the window and he turned to look at the car. For a moment, there was only him and me in the world. His gaze met mine and I saw he recognized me. Those blue eyes stared into the car, and I searched them for any shred of a chance that he still cared. I wanted to believe somewhere inside him he missed me like I missed him, but the man who looked at me now wasn't like me.

Everything in his eyes told me whatever love I'd felt hadn't been mine in return.

The moment ended and Jensen sped down the street, weaving in and out of traffic on his way to wherever Nina had ordered him to go. It didn't matter. Wherever we went, I'd still feel the same.

"Jordan, what's going on? What happened back there?"

Losing the battle against my tears, I hung my head, embarrassed as they began to roll down my cheeks. "I always thought the first time I saw him I'd be able to be cool about things, but just seeing him standing there with that woman laughing and joking was too much to handle."

"Sweetie, why do you care? You're getting engaged to another man in a few days. What does it matter who Gage is talking to?"

"I don't know. It's been months since he broke up with me and I thought when I met Brock that I'd gotten over Gage, but you mentioning him the other day when you said you thought I'd marry him brought all those feelings back. And then you said you told him I was getting engaged and he looked bothered. I guess I just hoped that when he saw me he'd look like he missed me."

"I think you're wrong, Jordan. Every time either Tristan or I mention your name, he gets a look on his face like he's fighting some kind of awful pain. But if you feel this way about Gage, what are you going to do about Brock?"

I wiped my tears away and straightened myself in the seat.

"Nothing. We'll get engaged this Saturday and then I'll begin planning a big society wedding just like he deserves to have."

Nina's face twisted into an expression of horror and confusion. "What do you mean nothing? You can't marry him! You still love Gage."

"Love has nothing to do with it, Nina. Brock can give me a good life. Gage obviously doesn't even care enough to tell me he's in the same fucking city as I am."

The car turned toward Brooklyn, and Nina leaned up against the front seat. "Jensen, please keep driving. We're not going back to Brooklyn just yet."

"Yes, we are, Jensen," I interjected, ready to go back to my bed and forget this day had ever happened.

"No, we aren't, Jordan. We need to talk."

"What's there to talk about? He doesn't care! End of discussion. Now poor Jensen can stop driving to random places and get me back to my apartment where I can crawl under the covers and call it a day."

"I'm talking about Brock. You can't seriously think you should say yes to marrying him if you're in love with another man. You'll be miserable."

Nina touched my shoulder and suddenly I couldn't stop myself from crying. I looked away and mumbled through my tears, "I'm already miserable. At least with Brock I'll be wealthy and miserable."

"Oh, honey. I don't want to see you miserable, and money won't make it any better."

"You don't understand, Nina. You have everything. A fabulous husband, three wonderful children, houses, cars, someone to drive you around wherever you want to go. You don't have anything to worry about."

"It hasn't always been that way, but I will admit I have a great life. I want that for you too, and I don't think Brock will give you that."

"Then I won't be getting it because other than Brock, no other guy has ever offered me much other than a few months and a quick goodbye."

"Is money that important?"

I couldn't help but look at her with disgust. "Spoken like someone who doesn't have to worry about money."

She sat back against the seat and sighed. "I could say that's not fair, but I see your point. But Tristan knows lots of wealthy, single men. You give me the word and I'll have him round them up."

"What does it matter? It will just end like it always does with me. What I want to know is why you don't like Brock and why you never told me before today."

Nina suddenly grew quiet and wouldn't look me in the eye, so I repeated my question and waited for some kind of answer. My best friend obviously didn't like the man I planned to marry, and I intended on finding out why.

"Well?"

"I don't know. I have a gut feeling about him and it's not good. There, I said it. The first time we met I felt it."

"That's because you're a diehard romantic and think I should be with someone else."

"I'm not going to lie. I like Gage. I always have, and I hoped you two would work out. But if you feel like you do and can't even see him without falling apart, why are you even thinking about marrying Brock?"

"Because I've never had a chance with someone like Brock, okay?" I screamed. I saw Jensen's look of surprise in the rearview mirror and lowered my voice. "I'm afraid if I don't take advantage of this I'm going to end up alone."

"Jordan, you're never going to be alone. Look at you. You're gorgeous. When we go places, men don't look at me. They look at you. The blond hair, the green eyes, the great body. You've got it all, and on top of all that, you're smart and funny. You're the whole package. Please don't sell yourself short and think you can't have any man you want."

"I can't," I said quietly, admitting a truth I'd tried so hard to avoid since that last time I heard Gage's voice tell me he basically didn't care enough to keep dating me.

"Why didn't you tell me you still cared for Gage? I could have invited the two of you out to the house and you could have had a chance to speak to him."

"Nina, he knows where I live. He's been back in the city for months and never once has he made the effort to see me. He doesn't want to speak to me. He never cared for me like I cared for him."

"I think you're wrong. I don't know why he hasn't called or come by, but I see the way he looks when I bring you up. He looks lost."

"Not lost enough to find me, though," I said, hanging my head.

We rode along in silence with the unavoidable truth there with us. If Gage had wanted to see me, he would have. It was that simple.

And since he hadn't, I had to accept that he didn't care about me anymore, if he ever really had, and I had a man who did care about me who wanted to marry me. All my romantic notions about Gage meant nothing compared to the reality that Brock loved me and had asked me to be his wife.

So he didn't make me feel like Gage did. So my best friend and the person I trusted more than anyone else in the world thought there was something hinky about him. That wasn't enough to throw away a chance at a good life with a man who could give me everything I'd ever dreamed of.

Especially not for a dream of someone who couldn't offer me anything the way Brock could.

"Jordan, please tell me you're going to reconsider this whole engagement thing."

I shook my head and took a deep breath. "No. Brock has asked me to marry him and I've said yes. On Saturday, he and I will be there with nearly a hundred people to celebrate our engagement. I hope you'll still be there."

Nina wrapped her arms around me and hugged me tightly to her. "Of course I'll be there. I just wish you'd think about this."

"There's nothing to think about."

She leaned back and sighed. "What about Brock? Do you think it's fair to him? How would you feel if he still loved someone else but was getting married to you?"

"Stop trying to make me feel bad. People get married to people they aren't madly in love with all the time. Not everyone gets the white knight like Tristan Stone. Some of us have to settle for a regular guy on a horse. Brock's more than just that regular guy, so all in all, I'm making out pretty well, if you think about it."

"Well, if you put it that way..."

"Sarcasm in my moment of need isn't what my best friend should be doing."

"Jordan, you talk about getting married like it's a negotiation. Marriage isn't like that. I'm afraid if you aren't crazy about Brock now, you're going to be forever unhappy. Why not just put off the whole engagement thing for a while? Tell him you need some time."

"No. I can't do that to him."

"Why? Is there some reason you have to get engaged now?"

"The party's all planned. It can't be changed. So we better get going to the spa and my dress fitting."

I didn't want to tell Nina that I was still uncertain about marrying Brock. When he asked me, I hesitated at first, unsure we should marry so quickly since we'd only known each other for a few months. His insistence on getting engaged as soon as possible because we loved each other reassured me, even if I wondered if we were rushing things. No one had ever wanted me enough to even consider marriage, though, so I said yes.

Did I love him? I wasn't sure, but he was the kind of man who could give me a life I'd dreamed of, so why shouldn't I marry him?

It wasn't fairy tale perfect, but it was real life pretty good and that was okay too.

CHAPTER FOUR

GAGE

BEFORE I HAD THE CHANCE to sink into my own head over Jordan's impending engagement, a call came in about a job and I dove into work. Anything to get my mind off the news I'd dreaded for months. The addition of an uptown party for the well-known socialite Janine Truman to my crew's schedule made the weekend a tight one, but thankfully my people were as eager to see Varo Security succeed as I was. At least I hoped they'd still feel that way when I told them about this late change to their Saturday plans on a Thursday morning.

Seated on the edge of my old oak desk, I braced myself for my staff's possible mutiny. The seven men and one woman in front of me chatted about their weekend plans and a Yankees doubleheader a few of them had snagged tickets for while I sipped the last of my morning coffee trying to think of a nice way to upend their days off.

There was no time like the present, so I cleared my throat and began.

"Okay, I've got good news. A new client contacted me last night and even sent over a check this morning, so we have a new job."

Casey Dawson, the only female with the company, smiled and gave me the thumbs up sign. Deceptively strong for her just over five feet height and at least as tough as any of the guys, she'd taken on the role of workplace cheerleader almost as soon as she started working for me. Casey often reminded me of those female gymnastics champions who barely weighed a hundred pounds but could throw a man halfway across the room if they had to. Behind the pretty brown hair and blue eyes, she had that kind of quiet spunk about her. Sometimes we got a drink after work, and the boss-employee relationship between us had gradually morphed into a friendship like I had with my sisters.

"But—"

"There's always a but, isn't there, boss?" Jack said from the back of the room.

One of my first hires, he was young and a bust ass, but he was right. Good news always seemed to come with a hitch.

"Yeah, and this one's a big but. She needs security for a party this Saturday."

I let the news sink in for a moment before I continued, and within a few seconds, the realization that their weekend plans had just been shot to hell came over the people in front of me and the happy faces that had just been smiling at me grew dark.

As they grumbled about bad timing and missing the Yankees beat up on the Red Sox, I held my hands up in surrender and nodded my understanding of all their complaints. "I know, I know. And I'm sorry, but I need everyone on this job. It's a big one."

Not that I truly understood having my weekend ruined by Janine Truman's party needs. All I ever did on Saturdays and Sundays was either sit in my office or sit at home watching TV, spending too much time in my head and no time out in the world the city offered.

"We understand, Gage," Casey said in her best sympathetic voice. "I can see the Yankees another time. I think everyone else agrees we signed on to Varo Security because we wanted to be a part of this company. Weekends come with the territory."

I looked around and saw the rest of the group nodding. "Thanks. I appreciate this, everyone. It's the Royale, so we're doing the big time now. It's a birthday party for Janine Truman, so unless she's the world's worst person, I'm not thinking we'll have much to really worry about. Just the usual issues with drunk party guests and the birthday party version of wedding crashers."

"What time does the fun begin?" Will, my newest hire, asked.

"We need to be at the Royale for five, and the party begins at seven. I'll be heading over there in a little while to meet with the hotel's security so we can coordinate our efforts."

"Boss, why does this lady need more security than what the Royale can offer? They've got a crack staff there, and they're used to high society parties and their problems."

I shook my head because I had no idea why Janine Truman had wanted to hire security, or why she'd wanted my company in particular. It must have been Tristan's influence, but it still seemed like overkill.

"No idea, Casey. I just know the lady wants us and she's willing to pay. Maybe Varo Security is getting a good name out there."

"Why not? We're the best!" she cheered in an effort to rally the troops.

"Alright, let's get going. We have work to do today before our big debut at the Royale."

THE GRAND BALLROOM OF THE Royale Hotel had been decorated to within an inch of its life with silver and white decorations, silver silk bunting, and enough burgundy to make it my new least favorite color. Wait staff buzzed around with armfuls of napkins in that very color followed by more staff with dishes and silverware for what looked like an army.

If this lady had enough people for all that at her birthday party, I could only imagine how popular she was. Money certainly talked in this city. I hadn't thought about it before, but as I watched the preparations continue around me while I checked out the nooks and crannies that could present issues during the party, I wondered if she was more than just some Upper West Side wealthy woman. She had to be someone important to warrant all this effort.

The sound of my crew coming into the ballroom distracted me from any more thoughts about Janine Truman's net worth and I turned to see them staring in awe at the room and all its decorations.

"Who is this woman, boss?" Casey asked, her eyes wide as she took in all the silver and burgundy surrounding her.

"Someone more important than us, Case. Try not to get blinded by the splendor of it all," I joked. "Let's check out where we all need to be stationed. The gift table appears to be over there in the corner of the room farthest away from the door, and other than that, there are all these archways and alcoves that could present us with issues if someone wants to cause trouble."

"You seem to know an awful lot about this kind of thing, Gage," Will said with a grin.

He wasn't wrong. I'd spent enough time with Angela at events even bigger and more impressive than this to know a thing or two about how the other half lived. Not that I ever felt comfortable in their world, but I knew enough to navigate through.

"Yeah, I've lived an exciting life," I said with a laugh. "Always a bridesmaid, never a bride. Time to get to work."

BY SEVEN O'CLOCK, MOST OF Janine Truman's guests had arrived, and I could tell this woman had some serious money. Her friends and family all had a telltale air of old New York penthouse wealthy to them. From my spot in one of the alcoves, I noticed the women all seemed to have tightly pulled faces like they'd had too many facelifts and Botox treatments. Or maybe that was what women born into money looked like. For their part, the men seemed looser in every respect, from the way they talked to the amount of alcohol they drank. The party had barely begun and more than a few already looked half in the bag.

Looking down at my black suit, shirt, and tie, I couldn't help but compare what I wore to the guests' clothes. Intended to make me as invisible as possible to the partygoers, my clothes gave me an almost funereal appearance compared to the women in their dresses of virtually every color and the men in their formal black tuxes and white shirts.

Not that I cared what I looked like. I was there to do a job. This wasn't a social event for me. It wasn't my style.

My style was a few beers at a neighborhood tavern with me in a pair of jeans and a t-shirt, and I definitely wouldn't be there with any of the women at this party.

As I watched for any trouble, out of the corner of my eye I caught a glimpse of a familiar face and turning, I saw Nina walk past the ballroom doors as a group of partygoers entered. Was she a friend of Janine Truman's? That would explain how Varo Security got the nod for this job.

I quickly made my way through the crowd and caught up with Nina as she began to walk away from the room. "Nina, the party's in here."

She spun around and her eyes opened wide. "Gage, what are you doing here?"

Gesturing toward the ballroom filled with Janine Truman's hundred or so closest friends, I explained, "I figure I got the job because you and Tristan are friends of the birthday girl. I'll have to thank him when he gets here. Where is he?"

Nina's face contorted into an expression that looked like she was in pain. "Oh, Gage, I'm sorry. I don't know how this happened, but we're not going to that party. We're going to…uh…to the one next door."

"Oh, no problem. I just figured Tristan was the reason I got this job," I explained with a shrug.

She frowned, as if what I'd said upset her, and as I opened my mouth to ask what was wrong, she said, "We're going to Jordan and Brock's engagement party in the main ballroom, Gage. I'm so sorry."

Suddenly, it felt like all the air had been sucked out of my lungs. Jordan was right there in the same building celebrating her engagement to another man. I quickly made sure my face didn't show how much Nina's news hurt and forced a smile. "Small world, huh? Well, please tell her I said congratulations. I better get back inside just in case any of the guests get out of hand."

Reaching out to squeeze my arm, Nina tried to be chipper as Tristan joined her. "I wish it wasn't like this."

"Gage, nice to see you again and so soon."

Nina shook her head quickly. "He's working a party right next to Jordan's, Tristan."

He looked at his wife and then at me with a curious expression. "Sorry, Gage. Hell of a coincidence."

"Yeah. I better get back in there. Have a nice night."

I got away before either one of the Stones could apologize again. I knew they meant well, but being pitied wasn't what I wanted at that moment. What I really wanted was to get the hell out of town and never look back.

The people attending Janine's party made me question why she'd even contacted me about extra security. Other than drinking more champagne than I'd ever seen anyone drink, they were a pretty calm group of middle-aged New Yorkers. The most excitement I saw in the next half hour came from her two twenty-something kids and their friends who decided to pretend like their mother's birthday was a good time to get hammered.

Casey joined me at my post after gently separating a few of the younger partiers who had gotten out of hand on the dance floor. As we watched for any more antics by Janine's kids, she nudged me and said, "So this is how the other half lives. I'll still take a few beers at the ballpark over this."

I nodded, wishing I was sitting behind home plate instead of anywhere near the Royale. "I hear that."

She continued to talk about the scene in front of us, but my mind was in the room next door where the woman I loved was announcing her engagement. I couldn't stop it, but that didn't mean I didn't hate it. I'd stayed away from Jordan for fear that if I didn't she'd get hurt, but we'd left everything between us unresolved. I always thought I'd get the chance to explain myself—or at least I'd always hoped I would.

Now that she was getting ready to marry another man, that chance was gone.

Casey gently elbowed me in the side. "Hey, boss, did you hear me?"

I looked to my right and saw her staring up at me. "No, sorry. I was a million miles away there for a moment. What's up?"

"I just said you look beat. You can leave, if you need to. We got this. I doubt this group will get much wilder than what we saw from those kids before."

"No, I'm good," I lied.

She looked me up and down and shook her head. "Gage, you don't look good. Maybe you're coming down with something. Whatever's going on, take the night off. I'll make sure everything is handled to your standards."

I knew I shouldn't leave the party, but the need to talk to Jordan one last time and at least try to explain why I'd done what I did pressed on me enough to take Casey up on her offer. Knowing I could trust her, I headed over to the ballroom next door and hoped I'd get the chance to set things right.

FOR AN HOUR I WATCHED as Jordan greeted guests and charmed them with her gorgeous smile and grace. She was the most beautiful woman in the room, and one of the best things about her was that she wasn't like these uptight society wives who looked like they had no idea how to have fun or be good people.

Her fiancé spent little time next to her, instead glad-handing and schmoozing the men in the room. He didn't bother to pay much attention to the woman who was supposed to share the evening with him, and it made me dislike him instantly. Not that I had a whole lot of love for him anyway. He had a cheap look about him, like some kind of millionaire who'd only gotten his money through winning the lottery.

I waited for Jordan to be alone after she'd finished greeting the long line of people dying to speak to her. All I needed was a few minutes to at least show her that letting her go hadn't been as easy or painless as she thought.

She finally came close to where I stood hiding in an alcove, and I took my chance. Grabbing her by the arm, I pulled her into a room off to the side and closed the door. But if I had thought she'd be happy to see me, the look of pain I saw in her eyes instantly told me otherwise.

"What are you doing here?" she asked, her voice full of sadness. "Why would you come to my engagement party?"

"I needed to talk to you, Jordan. I needed to see you."

"No! Why would you do this to me? I've finally found someone who actually cares about me and now you come back and act like I should want to talk to you?"

I held her gently by the shoulders, afraid if I didn't she'd leave and I'd miss my chance. "Jordan, please listen to me. I need you to forget what I did and hear me out."

Tears welled in her eyes. "I can't forget. I can't, so whatever you need to say to me, you should have said it back when you had me in your life. Now let me go."

She pushed me away and went for the door, but I grabbed her hand and squeezed. "I just want a chance to explain. I don't want to ruin anything for you. If you love this guy, I wish you nothing but happiness."

"You drag me into this room to tell me you want to explain? Explain what?"

"Why I broke up with you like I did."

Tears welled in her eyes, and she shook her head. "No! I won't let you do this to me again. I can't listen to this. Do you know how many nights I cried myself to sleep because of what you did? You broke my fucking heart, and now you think you can just make up for everything by explaining yourself? Go away, Gage. I finally got over you and found someone who really loves me."

"I still love you."

It felt as good as it always had to tell her that. Her response, on the other hand, made me feel like shit.

"Well, I don't love you. Go away and let me be happy."

"I just want you to listen to what I have to say."

I touched her arm and she yanked it away from my hold. "Don't touch me! You don't get to do that anymore."

Her rage surprised me. I'd expected anger, hurt, even sadness, but not the level of rage I felt coming at me. I couldn't let that deter me from telling her the whole truth, though.

"Jordan, you deserve to know what happened. I hope you'll hear me out."

"This is for you, Gage. Not me. If you wanted to do something for me, you would have done it that night you broke up with me over the phone and didn't call back. You would have done it on my birthday a month later when I waited for you to call to let me know you remembered me. You have done it when you returned to New York and lived close enough to see me whenever you wanted to. What truth am I supposed to know other than those?"

"I can't fix what I did. All I can do is tell you the reasons why I did those things."

"So now you want to tell me your excuse for breaking up with me over the phone like I never meant a damn thing to you? As I sat there and pleaded with you to tell me why you were doing this to me and all you said was it just wasn't working out for you."

"I couldn't tell you the truth. I never meant to hurt you. I didn't think I had a choice. All I was thinking of was keeping you safe."

Jordan closed her eyes, shutting me out, and said in a low, sad voice, "You always had a choice. Always."

"I didn't. Someone was threatening me and said they'd hurt you if I didn't stop seeing you."

She looked up at me with a complete look of disbelief in her eyes. "Really? This is what you expect me to buy as the reason you dumped me? Okay, I'll bite. Did he tell you to break up with me like a callous dick, Gage? Did he? Did he say to call me on the phone and act like I meant nothing to you? Did he tell you to give me nothing to go on so I'd naturally think you'd gone back to your ex-girlfriend the actress?"

"No. All I knew was if I didn't let you go, you could get hurt because of me. I couldn't let that happen."

"So you hurt me instead."

I wanted to look away, to avoid the indictment in her eyes as she stared at me with the purest hate I'd ever seen. I had hurt her, and as far as she was concerned, I was still hurting her.

"You just think I'd willingly hurt you?"

"Whether it was willingly or not, the end result was the same."

"Jordan, is it that you doubt how much I loved you or that you just will never be able to forgive me? Because at least if it's the first one, I can try to prove to you how I feel, but if you can never forgive me, I don't know what to do about that."

She shook her head and opened her mouth a few times to speak, but no words came out. Finally, she spoke, and I felt like someone had kicked me hard in the gut.

"It's both. I didn't realize until now, but it's both. I don't believe you loved me. You couldn't have and done what you did. And I don't know if I can forgive you, Gage. I don't know if I have it in me."

"I can't believe that."

"You can't believe that because you don't know how much it hurt when you broke up with me. Let me try to explain to you what it felt like to hear the man you loved tell you things just weren't working for him. To have him tell you that over the phone while he was three thousand miles away surrounded by women who already had made her insecure."

"You had no reason to be insecure, Jordan. You're more gorgeous than any of those Hollywood actresses I met guarding that kid."

"You knew how I wondered about your ex and you being in the same town, and you broke up with me with that vague bullshit line of things not working for you. What did you think I'd think?"

"I didn't. All I could think about was making sure you were safe. If I stopped dating you, then the person threatening me would go away. That's all I was trying to do. I never meant to hurt you."

"You keep saying that, but that's what happened! You called me up and over the phone broke up with me like we hadn't spent all that time together. Like we hadn't given each other everything we had inside ourselves. You knew more about me than even Nina did. I told you things I never told anyone else in the world."

She couldn't hold back the tears anymore, and as they rolled down her cheeks, she sobbed, "All those hours we lay in each other's arms after making love and all you could say was things weren't working for you?"

Christ, she was tearing my heart out. I wanted to take her in my arms and find a way to make up for all the hurt I'd caused her then and now. As she stood there sobbing, I tried to figure out a way to fix things.

"Jordan, I loved you. If they had done anything to you, I wouldn't have been able to go on."

"And then you never called back. It was as if I'd never meant a damn thing to you. You went on with life, and I could barely get out of bed. Then I went out to live at Nina and Tristan's and all those memories of you were there too. I couldn't go anywhere without seeing you or remembering something we did. All those months together suddenly meant nothing. And every time you said you loved me hurt like someone was carving into my chest."

"I couldn't call. If the person threatening me found out we were still together, you'd be in danger."

"You were three time zones away. How did you know I wasn't in danger?"

"I knew."

"How? How did you know I wasn't in danger?"

"I knew."

She wiped the tears from under her eyes and shook her head. "More stalking."

"It's not stalking if you're watching the woman you love."

"No, then it's worse. Then it's letting her believe you don't care anymore and seeing her fall apart and still doing nothing."

"In my defense, I wasn't watching you myself. I had a friend who also works security watch you until I knew you weren't in danger anymore."

Her expression twisted from disgust. "So what, did he take pictures of me, sort of an album of my falling apart after you left me?"

"It wasn't like that. He made sure you were safe and no one harmed you."

Jordan wiped the last few tears from her cheeks. "Well, since he didn't let you in on how I really was, let me tell you. For the first couple days, I didn't get out bed. I just laid there feeling like everything I loved had been taken away. My phone never left my side just in case you called. I was sure you'd call and say you were sorry or at least explain why you didn't want to see me anymore."

"Jordan, I never—"

"Yeah, you never meant to hurt me! I got that, Gage. But you did. So after those first few days when I felt like I wanted to crawl into a hole and die I hurt so bad, Nina brought me out to the house. All that did was bring back all those memories of when you lived there. I'd go for walks back near the carriage house and remember how you looked when you'd stand there like a stone while I flirted to get your attention.

Then I'd remember that first night you came to my apartment and we laughed about all those times I came to see you and you thought I might like West."

I wanted to tell her I remembered all those times too, and every day it felt like I was missing part of me. I wanted to tell her every night I'd lay in bed and think about her sitting on her couch in a pair of shorts and a t-shirt with her hair in a ponytail drinking her diet soda looking more beautiful than any woman I saw in LA.

I didn't say any of that. I just let her talk, knowing I deserved everything she threw at me.

"On my birthday—the day you and I had planned to meet at Brick Fire because that's where we had our first date after that night at my apartment—I waited for you to call. I sat in my apartment on my couch with my phone sitting on the coffee table and waited. I lied when Nina asked if I was okay and pretended my heart wasn't broken. I lied when my mother called to wish me happy birthday and told her I didn't sound good because I was getting over a cold. I sat there for hours waiting and you never called. You never even texted happy birthday. The day came and went and I ended my birthday alone crying myself to sleep."

"I'm sorry, Jordan."

Shaking her head, she held her hand up to stop me. "Save it. Want me to continue? My days and nights were basically the same for months. During the day, I pretended not to be so heartbroken all I wanted to do was die, and at night, I spent my time with the covers over my head wishing something could take all the pain away."

I didn't know which was worse—her anger or her sadness. Both cut me to the core.

"And then one day as I stood in the rain a man came into my life and for the first time I didn't hurt as much. Brock made me feel like I might be able to go on. He listened to me when I talked, took me wonderful places I'd only dreamed of before, and wanted to marry me. And then you showed up and ruined everything."

"We can still be what we were. I still love you."

Her mouth hung open in shock for a long moment and then she shook her head violently. "Are you out of your mind? You tear my heart out by breaking up with me over the phone and now you show up at my engagement party and claim you still love me after living in the same city for months without bothering to call me even once? Do you hear yourself? He loves me. He wants to marry me. You broke up with me long distance over the phone to go fuck around with Hollywood starlets! Who do you think I should go with?"

"I didn't break up with you to go with anyone. I had to. For you."

Jordan's eyebrows shot up in disbelief. "For me? You broke up with me for me? Are you high?"

I knew what this sounded like. I had to find some way to explain what I'd done without sounding like a madman.

"Please, just listen to me. I had to break up with you to make sure you didn't get hurt."

"Uh, I'd say you failed epically then because I got hurt. I got hurt bad, Gage. Now let me go and rejoin the party so I can celebrate my engagement to my future husband."

"That's not what I meant. I know it sounds bizarre, but I'd been getting letters threatening your life if I didn't leave you alone."

"Really? That's the best you can do? Some crazy story about letters threatening me unless you left me? And yet here you are endangering my life because you wanted to tell me you love me. I've heard enough. Goodbye, Gage. Have a good life."

She tugged her arm from my hold, but I couldn't let her go. Not with her finally standing right there in front of me after all those months. "Tell me you don't miss my touch. Leave here with me right now. I'll go anywhere with you, Jordan. Please."

Closing her eyes, she bit her lip in that way that never failed to make me want her. When she opened them, those beautiful green eyes were filled with pain. Pain I'd caused. "I don't miss you at all. You left me. Now I'll do you the same favor. Goodbye, Gage."

Her lips were so close I couldn't stop myself. I pulled her into me and kissed her long and deep, the way I'd fantasized I'd kiss her if I ever had the chance again. For a moment, she melted into my arms and all the feelings I'd kept bottled up began to surge through me after so long. She was my Jordan again.

But then she pushed me away and pointed her finger at me. "No! I won't let you do this to me. I won't! I have someone who loves me and wants to marry me."

"He doesn't love you like I do."

She flashed her enormous engagement ring in front of

me. "Really? He gave me this diamond ring because he doesn't love me?"

Looking down at the giant rock on her left hand, I felt my jealousy begin to overtake me, knowing full well I'd likely never be able to give her anything close. "Nice. Who wouldn't want a diamond the size of their fist?"

Jordan recoiled from my sarcasm and shook her head. "You had your chance, Gage. Goodbye."

I reached out to hold her there with me, but she turned and in a moment was gone from the room, leaving me to figure out how I'd convince her the man she planned to marry didn't love her as much as I did.

How was I going to make her see that no matter what I'd done, I was the man she should be with?

CHAPTER FIVE

JORDAN

I GOT THE HELL OUT of that room and away from Gage's accusations that Brock didn't love me as much as he did before I started to believe him. See, that was the problem. All it took was being close to him and one incredible, knee-buckling kiss and I wanted to believe every word that came out of his mouth.

At least my heart did. Thank God my brain still had some control over me or I'd really be a mess.

Making a beeline to Nina who stood next to Tristan alone in a corner of the ballroom, I apologized to him and pulled her aside, barely able to contain my shock at what had just happened. "Gage is here. He just pulled me into a room to tell me that Brock doesn't love me and that I should be with him."

Nina's blue eyes stared at me in stunned amazement. "What? Gage is here?"

I began to nod frantically, as if my head couldn't stop telling her he was there. "He is. He just pulled me into a room and tried to convince me to leave here with him because he's still in love with me. The man is insane!"

"Calm down, calm down. What did he say exactly?"

I took a deep breath in and let it out slowly. "He said that Brock doesn't love me like he does and that he left me because he was getting letters threatening my life. It's craziness, Nina. The man is crazy. Why would he do this to me on the night of my engagement party?"

"Hang on. Let me get Tristan." Nina pulled Tristan from his quiet corner and told him what I'd just told her. "Do you know what he's talking about?"

"No, but I only know Gage through his work for me. What did the letters say?"

I stared at Tristan in shock. Was he actually taking Gage's outrageous tale seriously? "I don't know. What does it matter? Letters or no letters, he broke up with me and never bothered to even come see me until tonight."

Nina tugged on her husband's arm the way she always did when she was excited about something. "Go find Gage and ask him what this is all about. Please. Find out what he's talking about."

Tristan looked at me for a moment and left before I could tell him to forget asking Gage anything. "Nina, why did you do that? Now Tristan is going to hear all about Brock not loving me as much and all of Gage's nonsense."

"Jordan, we have to find out what this is all about. Would you have rathered I go find Gage and leave you here with my husband?"

Sighing, I had to admit that would have made things worse. "No. Even on his best days Tristan says very little to me. I'm not in the mood for making small talk about the weather or how he looks in his tux at a time like this. That strong, silent type thing isn't what I need at the moment. I need someone to talk to now."

"See? There's method to my madness. So did anything else happen when you talked to him?"

I pressed my lips together to relive the memory of our kissing and looked around before I whispered, "He kissed me. I shouldn't have let him, but I did. I couldn't stop myself, Nina. Oh, God! Why did he have to come here tonight?"

"I told you he still cared! He wouldn't have kissed you if he didn't," she said with a huge smile. "Now you can't marry Brock. You got your wish. You know Gage still misses you. Call this whole thing off and get back with the man you love."

A few of the guests standing nearby turned to stare at us with a look of confusion on their faces. I forced a smile and pulled Nina away toward the next alcove. "Are you crazy? No! That man broke my heart and left me in pieces. You should know. You had to pick them up and put me back together how many times since then?"

"But you can't go through with it, Jordan. This was a sign. Don't try to ignore it."

"I'm going to start ignoring you if you don't stop with this craziness. You're as bad as Gage. So we kissed and it felt good. Well, actually great. So what? That doesn't compare to the chance at a life with someone like Brock."

Tristan returned and looked at me like he'd just heard all my deepest, darkest secrets. "I found him, and he says the letters began coming while he was in LA with the teenager he was guarding. He still doesn't know who they're from, but they stopped when he broke up with you. But recently he began getting them again."

"The man's insane! I don't care about what letters he's getting. This ship has sailed."

"He's worried, Jordan. I don't know Gage as well as you do, but I can see he's worried," Tristan said quietly. "He also seems genuine when he says he's still in love with you."

Nina tugged on my arm now. "See? He still loves you and you still love him."

"Honey, you two are starting to sound as mad as Gage. Brock loves me. It may not be the love story of the century, but he cares for me and I care for him. This whole thing is Gage's attempt to—"

I couldn't finish that sentence. I had no idea why Gage would show up at my engagement party. Did he really still care for me? Was this his way of trying to win me back?

No! I couldn't let myself think those kinds of things. He'd proven how little he cared for me by leaving me without even the most basic excuse and then letting me make up my own reasons why I wasn't good enough to stay with. And he'd lived in the same city as me for months, even seeing my closest friends, and never even bothered to try to see me. He didn't want me back. He just wanted to hurt me again.

"I have to go deal with my guests. My parents probably think I'm avoiding them. Don't worry about me."

Squeezing my arm, Nina said quietly, "You know you don't have to go through with any of this, Jordan. It's just an engagement party. There's still time to change your mind."

"I know, honey. I'm fine. All this nonsense from Gage made me a little nuts for a few minutes, but I'm fine. Enjoy the party, and be sure to stay until Brock and I make the official announcement."

Nina stopped me dead with the most serious look she'd ever given me. "Okay, but let me ask you one thing before you run off. Who are these people to you? The only people I recognize other than my husband and you are your parents. Where are your friends from school? Where is your sister? Why does it seem like everyone here is here for Brock and not you?"

I looked around the ballroom filled with strangers and saw what my best friend saw. Almost no one there had come for me. I'd let Brock handle the guest list, assuming he'd just include all the names I'd given him, but instead he'd packed our engagement party with his guests and invited only my parents and Nina and Tristan. Even my sister had been left out.

But I couldn't admit that without feeling foolish. So pressing a smile onto my face, I lied. "Kayla had to return to school early since she's a senior RA this year. It's no big deal. Like you said, it's just an engagement party. Everyone will be at the wedding. I have to go now, but please don't leave without saying goodbye."

Nina opened her mouth to speak, but I left to rejoin my guests and my future husband, standing by his side for the rest of the night. When Brock toasted to having the best woman in the world as his fiancée, I smiled and believed every word. Then out of the corner of my eye I saw Gage standing in the shadows of a far alcove toward the back of the room watching me and the look in his eyes wasn't the same as the one in the man I stood next to.

That sadness I'd looked for days before as Jensen drove us away from the spa was telegraphed as clear as day now as he stood there staring at me from behind a column. All that I'd needed to know every night and day for months I now saw in those dark blue eyes.

I remembered when I thought he'd be the man I could marry. All those dreams of a happily ever after and us riding off into the sunset to live together in married bliss were just that. Dreams. The harsh reality was that Gage Varo dismissed me with one phone call and never thought about me again until he found out I was happy and someone else wanted me.

The party wound down and people lined up to kiss me and Brock to wish us congratulations before leaving. Nina took me in her arms as Tristan wished Brock all the best and in my ear she whispered, "I'm only a call away at any time. I may be out at the house, but I can get into the city in no time or have you out to the house just as quick. If you need anything, call me."

I turned to look at Brock and smiled. "Thanks for coming both of you. It means so much to us that you were here to share this with us."

Nina leaned forward to hug Brock, who gave her a brief embrace before letting her go. "It was nice of you to join us. Thank you for being a part of our big night."

I saw in Tristan's eyes a slight disapproval for Brock now. Had Gage changed his mind about him? But always the gentleman, he extended his hand to shake Brock's and said, "It was a great party. Congratulations to the both of you."

"Remember, call me so we can talk more about your wedding dress. We need to get on that," Nina said with a forced smile as she pretended she didn't want me to call her to talk about Gage.

As they left, Tristan leaned in to kiss my cheek and whispered, "Let us know if you need anything."

I smiled as if he'd merely wished me well and moved on to thank the next guest for attending, but I couldn't help but think that the two people I was closest to in the world believed what Gage had said.

I couldn't, though. The hurt he'd caused me made it impossible.

✧　✧　✧

BROCK POURED HIMSELF A DRINK and stood by the window looking out at the city below. I waited for him to offer me one, but as usual he didn't, so I got myself a glass of bourbon since it was a special occasion. Gulping down a swallow, I felt its effect immediately as my body began to warm all over. Never much of a liquor drinker, I definitely understood why Brock drank this stuff.

I padded up behind him and pressed my cheek to his shoulder. Raising my glass, I offered a toast to our engagement. "To a wonderful night, don't you think?"

Instead of toasting us, he took the glass from my hand. "I don't like women who drink. You know that, Jordan."

"I just thought since it's a special night that we could share one. It's no big deal. I don't like drinking anyway."

Brock tipped his glass and swallowed the last inch or so of alcohol before pushing past me to fill up his drink. His coldness confused me. After such a wonderful celebration of our engagement, I couldn't understand why his demeanor had changed from the party.

I followed him over to the bar and wrapped my arms around him. "It was a lovely party, wasn't it?"

"It was. I saw you spending a lot of time speaking to your friends and family. You didn't think that was rude to the rest of our guests?"

"I didn't really know anyone else."

Staring straight ahead, he groaned. "Like I did?"

I stood there confused. The way he'd said it, he hadn't known most of the guests at our engagement party either. Weren't they all his business associates and friends?

"I don't understand, Brock. If they weren't there for you, then why did you invite them?"

He shrugged and took another gulp of his drink. "I didn't mean it that way. Nevermind."

"Nina and Tristan were the only people there for me other than my parents. I wanted to make sure they knew how happy I was to see them there for our big night."

Brock turned his head and glared at me. "I told you my feelings on them. You're going to have to remove yourself from them once we marry, so you might as well begin now. And what could you possibly need from Tristan Stone?"

I knew what he meant. He wanted to know why he'd said

to let them know if I needed anything. I quickly shrugged and tried to make it seem like I didn't know why he'd offer help as he and Nina left the party. "Nina and I will be shopping for my wedding dress soon. She says it's never too early. And there are a lot of plans that have to be made for the ceremony. He knows Nina wants to help."

Brock slowly spun around to face me, and I saw in his eyes I'd angered him with my answer. "You'll have a personal shopper for that, Jordan. There will be no need for Nina to accompany you as you look for your wedding gown."

"Nina's my best friend, Brock. She's going to be my matron of honor in the wedding. I have to have her with me," I said, practically in a panic. I hadn't taken his comments about weeding Nina out of my life seriously until that very moment and suddenly his behavior frightened me.

He let out a frustrated sigh and kissed me on the cheek. "We can have this discussion another time. I have a long day ahead of me tomorrow, so make sure to turn the lights out when you come to bed."

I wanted to say we'll have this conversation now because you need to know I'm not abandoning my best friend for you or any man. I wanted to say that, but I didn't. Instead, I put on my nice girl smile and played the role I knew I'd have to play for the rest of my life.

That didn't mean never seeing my best friend again, though. No matter what he said, Nina would be with me forever. We may not end up growing old together like we'd planned, two old ladies sitting on the front porch of the nursing home checking out the hot doctors, but she'd be part of my life until the day I died.

Friends like her you didn't just toss away, not even for a husband.

Brock left me standing there alone looking out at the city below and feeling especially lonely. I poured myself another drink as the memory of Gage and I kissing began to root around in my mind. I'd tried so hard to get rid of every trace of feeling I had for him, and on most days, I didn't think of him much at all. Maybe a passing thought if I heard a song that reminded me of something we'd done together or a faint yearning brought on by my seeing a place we'd gone to that faded as fast as it came.

Seeing him at my engagement party made every feeling, every longing for him rush back so I couldn't think of anything else. Why couldn't he just leave well enough alone? All those crazy things he'd said about Brock not loving me as much as he did and letters threatening me—who made those bizarre accusations? He hadn't backed any of them up with facts. They were just the ramblings of a crazy person.

I wanted to believe that because if I could, then I could dismiss him. I could dismiss that kiss that had taken my breath away just like when he'd kissed me the first time in my kitchen that night. I could dismiss the look of longing in his eyes that made me want to take him in my arms and whisper, "I forgive you."

Swallowing a gulp of bourbon, I felt a rush of warmth cover my arms and legs and knew I was getting buzzed. Not good. One of the reasons I didn't drink much anymore was alcohol always made me reminisce. It didn't take much for my mind to wander back to Gage, so instead I usually just remained sober. Better to avoid the temptation to take that walk down memory lane than feel the pain all over again.

God, I was truly a mess.

I didn't want to be this way. I'd been dumped before by boyfriends. Why did he make me feel like I'd lost everything when he went away?

Maybe Nina was right. Maybe tonight was a sign, and the fact that just one kiss made me want Gage all over again, even after he broke my heart, meant something. Or maybe she was just her overly romantic self, as usual, and I needed to forget all this nonsense from the past and focus on the present and the future.

A present that included a gorgeous wealthy man who wanted to marry me. A future that if only I could get my head out of the clouds could be what I'd always wanted.

I finished the last of the bourbon in my glass and poured myself another drink. If I could get drunk enough, maybe I'd pass out and all those thoughts of Gage and me rambling around my brain could go away.

There was just one problem with that idea.

I wasn't that kind of drunk. If anything, drinking made my brain kick into overdrive, so by the time I'd finished my second glass of bourbon I couldn't think of anything but the craziness Gage had dumped on me hours earlier. The story he told was so fantastic that I couldn't believe it.

Letters threatening me. What bullshit!

And if these letters did, in fact, exist, why did he feel perfectly fine endangering my life tonight, of all nights?

Jesus Christ! This was what Gage Varo did to me. He made me crazy and filled my head with nonsense. Flopping down on Brock's black leather couch, I reached for my phone and considered calling Nina before I did something incredibly stupid and called Gage.

But talking to Nina now would only mean more discussion of the person I was trying to forget.

Tossing my phone aside, I leaned back against the cool leather and breathed deeply, already feeling entirely too drunk from the bourbon. I hoped I wouldn't have to change that part about who I was when Brock and I got married. Then I remembered his admonition about not liking women who drank. No, I definitely wouldn't have to learn to handle my liquor.

Or wear jeans, which he hated on women.

Or hang out with my best friend because he disliked her and her husband.

It didn't sound like I'd be much of the Jordan I'd always been when I became Mrs. Brock Hannon. But who wanted to become a drunk anyway?

Lately, I wondered if he wasn't different from the person I'd met that rainy night. Now that I'd agreed to marry him, something had changed between us. At first, he'd showered me with flowers and gifts and complimented me all the time. But all Brock seemed to compliment me on these days was my blond hair. That he loved.

Gage had loved my blond hair too. Closing my eyes, I remembered the time he and I drove to Vermont on an impromptu ski weekend. Wet from a day on the slopes and nearly frozen to the bone, we made love and then lay in each other's arms in front of the fireplace as he played with my hair, telling me it was just one of the things about me he loved.

I shook my head violently to rid my brain of that and every other memory of him. Why did the mind only save the good stuff? Why couldn't I remember all the bad stuff about him so I never wanted to think of him again? Like how he often didn't say a word when I talked about work, instead just sitting there watching me as I talked. Who wanted that kind of guy?

Or the way he liked to sit around in that damn beat up Broncos jersey of his and drink beer while he watched football games on Sunday afternoons instead of visiting museums or going to see concerts in the park? What kind of woman would want that type of man?

Or how he broke up with me over the phone, not even giving me a decent reason why he didn't want to continue being with me. Who the fuck wanted that kind of boyfriend in her life?

CHAPTER SIX

JORDAN

I REACHED FOR MY PHONE and stared at it, debating whether I should do it or not. Should I finally call him and tell him what I thought of him and everything he'd done? If I didn't, I'd never be rid of him, and if I ever wanted a life with Brock, I needed to put Gage and that part of my life behind me. Unsure if I should do it, I went into my contacts and scrolled down until I found his number under the secret title I gave him when Brock and I began dating.

V.

Pressing my fingertip to his name, I put the phone to my ear and took a deep breath. I didn't have to think about what I would say. I'd rehearsed it in my mind a million times since that night he broke up with me.

I heard him say hello and felt like my stomach dropped inside my body, sending butterflies fluttering everywhere. Mustering every ounce of courage I had, and even some the bourbon had supplied me, I said quietly, "I'll never forgive you for trying to ruin my engagement party, Gage."

Not exactly the way I'd wanted to begin, but it worked for a start. I had more things to say, but then he spoke and so many of those things went to wherever those butterflies had gone.

"Jordan, I need to know you're okay. Tell me you're at your house and I can come over so we can talk."

"I was okay, or at least I was getting better at pretending I was okay until I saw you on the street the other day with that woman," I said suddenly unable to keep my emotions from spinning out of control like some goddamned whirling dervish.

"What woman? Where?"

"I know you saw me, Gage. Right outside of Roget's Day Spa. You were standing there with some gorgeous woman with a designer bag. Do you know so many women now that you can't figure out when I'm talking about?"

"Jordan, you know me well enough to know that describing her as someone with a designer bag doesn't help me. I don't notice those things. But I know when you mean. I did see you. Why didn't you come over?"

"And say what?" I asked too loudly and heard Brock stir in the next room. Lowering my voice, I moved toward the window and whispered, "And say what, Gage? Hey, what's new with the guy who dumped me and broke my damn heart?"

"Jordan, I'll be happy to explain myself if you tell me you're at your apartment and the doors are locked."

"No, I'm at Brock's apartment. He is my fiancé, Gage. It's not odd that I'd be with him after our engagement party."

"Then meet me somewhere. I'll go anywhere. Just pick a place."

"I will not. I'm happy with him and your story about whatever bullshit you were spewing earlier doesn't change that. Brock loves me and I love him. I just wanted you to know that."

I thought I heard his breath catch, and then there was a long silence before he finally said in a much quieter voice, "If you love him so much, why are you calling me on the night of your engagement party?"

I didn't have the answer to his question. All I knew was I needed him to know I'd moved on. If only I had. Looking toward the bedroom to make sure I hadn't awoken Brock, I sat down on the couch. "I have to go, Gage. I just wanted you to know I haven't forgiven you."

"Let me come get you and take you up to Nina's. Tristan has a solid security set up there, and you'll be safe. Tell me where you are."

I stood and began to pace, my drunkenness pushed away by the adrenaline pumping through my body. Who the hell did this guy think he was? Why would I ever go anywhere with him ever again?

"You're not hearing me, Gage. I'm not leaving Brock. He loves me, and if any of this threatening letter bullshit is even true, he'll protect me."

"Jordan, I'm not lying about the letters. They began when we were dating. I finally started to believe that the only way to keep you safe was to break up with you. I never meant to hurt you. I meant to protect you. And now that they've started coming again, I'm beginning to wonder if your fiancé has something to do with them."

This guy just never gave up, did he? "You're out of your mind. You just want to see me miserable and alone. I don't know what you think I ever did to you, but I don't deserve this. Goodbye, Gage."

He began to say something again about needing to believe him, but I clicked END and threw my phone away from me. All those months I'd waited for him to call me and say he missed me were all a waste of time. He'd never missed me. He'd never even cared about me, no matter what he claimed about loving me.

I willed the tears away, but they came anyway, and as they rolled down my cheeks, I hated myself. Why did he have such power over me? Dozens of boyfriends had come and go since I moved to New York, but only he still stayed in my mind. Why?

The worst part of all of this was the seed of doubt he'd planted in my mind. True, Brock and I weren't a perfect match, and no, he didn't light my world on fire. But Gage's claim that Brock didn't love me as much as he did made me look at my fiancé's behavior toward me in a new light, and what had just been concern that the people I cared about the most didn't like my future husband was quickly snowballing into my worrying that I was marrying him for all the wrong reasons.

What if what Gage claimed was really true? What if I was still in love with him and marrying Brock was a big mistake?

God, why was this happening now? Why couldn't he just leave well enough alone? It wasn't bad enough he'd broken my heart, but now he had to ruin the rest of my life too?

Gage had never been cruel. This wasn't like him.

Slumping onto the couch, I felt my stomach roil from the bourbon sloshing around in there as I couldn't stop myself from remembering when Gage and I had been happy and in love.

The evidence of our time together lay strewn around the room, like some path showing the progression of Gage's seduction of me hours before. His shirt and pants in a pile near the door. My t-shirt and pink bra hanging off the back of the chair in the corner. His boxer briefs and my pink lace panties beside the bed.

Not that I had been an unwilling participant. I'd loved him since that first night he came to see me at my apartment. Maybe I'd loved him since we all lived out at Tristan and Nina's house in the country. It didn't matter when I fell in love with him because once he came to me that night, he was all I could think of.

"I could stay here forever and be the happiest man on earth, you know that?" he said in a low voice as he nuzzled my neck.

Rolling him over, I straddled his hips and balanced myself on top of him with my hands on his chest. God, he was beautiful! Never before had I been with a man so masculine. His body seemed to be all hard muscle, from his strong shoulders to his carved abs. I slowly ran my fingertips over his soft skin covering all that hardness and couldn't help be impressed. Gage Varo was definitely the most gorgeous man I'd ever been with.

"I think we might get sick of each other if all we ever did was have sex," I said with a smile.

He lifted his hips off the bed, sliding his hard cock through my pussy. "I think we should see if that happens. I'm good for the next week, so that could be a good start."

Gage's hands roamed down my sides until they reached my waist. His touch tickled me, and I giggled as I said, "I don't have the next week. I have to be back by Monday or my students won't have anyone to teach them."

"Substitute teacher. Your students will love you for it. Kids love it when they walk into class and see a substitute."

I leaned down and pressed a tiny kiss onto his nose. "You promised me we'd go running this morning. Remember? I've been looking forward to it."

Although it sounded strange to say that, I had been looking forward to going for a run with him. It was one of the many things we had in common, which was rare for me since I never seemed to date men who did anything I liked.

Gage grinned and slowly ran his finger between the swell of my breasts. "I like a good run as much as anyone else, but you can't say this isn't better than a jog through the park. We can go this afternoon."

I shook my head. "Nope. It's supposed to rain this afternoon. So we need to get out of this bed and get moving."

"I see I'm not going to change your mind, but how about a compromise? We make love once more and then we go for a run," he said as he moved his hands down to my hips.

"Can you remember one time sex with us didn't go for hours?" I asked with a grin, quickly coming around to his idea of what to do with our day.

"No, but that's why we should just forget about the run and stay right here."

His lack of logic made me chuckle. "That makes no sense. I can't even follow that line of reasoning."

Gage pulled me down on top of him and kissed me long and deep until any thought of leaving that spot had faded away. "It's not about reason, Jordan. It's about two people in love enjoying each other."

For a moment, I stared into his eyes, stunned by what he'd just said. Even though we'd been dating for over a month, neither of us had used the L word. But now he'd said it so casually that I wasn't sure I should say anything.

But I had to say something. He'd just told me he loved me.

Quietly, I said, "In love?"

He smiled that sexy Gage grin that never failed to make me go weak and nodded. "Yeah. In love. I love you, and I think you love me, right?"

"I do love you," I said, unsure if admitting that would be the kiss of death to our relationship as it had been to so many other ones I'd had in my dating life.

His blue eyes sparkled. "Good. So about that staying in bed all day..."

Closing my eyes, I tried to convince myself that every moment I spent with him wasn't some of the happiest of my life. That Gage wasn't the only person, other than Nina, that I felt completely and utterly at home with.

But it was no use.

The reality was that I still loved him, no matter what lies I tried to tell myself. I missed his sexy grin and the way he made me smile after a long day at school. I missed how we could just spend hours in each other's arms watching TV. I missed feeling like the happiest woman in the world because of him.

Not that it mattered. I'd said yes to Brock and would marry him in seven months, as we planned. He offered me a life I'd always dreamed of, and whatever romantic dreams I'd had for Gage and me had to be forgotten. I couldn't give up surefire happiness for a past that should stay right where it was.

Grabbing my phone from the other end of the couch, I typed a text to Gage, even though I knew I shouldn't.

> *I'm marrying a wonderful man who loves me. I would have married you if you didn't dump me like I was the least important thing in the world. Your loss.*

I'd hoped saying that would make me feel better, but it didn't. Maybe calling myself the equivalent of garbage wasn't the way to cheer myself up. Normally, I was so much better at dealing with this kind of thing. It must have been the bourbon. I definitely wasn't a happy drunk. That was sure.

My phone vibrated against the couch cushion, and I looked down to see a response from Gage. *Don't.*

Don't? That was his entire answer to me saying I was officially never going to be his again. Don't. Quickly, I typed out another text.

> *That's it? You must really love me, Gage. Nice way to fight for the woman you love.*

I didn't know why I was continuing this conversation. I

didn't want him to fight for me now. It was too late. I had Brock in my life now, so what the hell was I doing? It definitely was the bourbon.

Again, my phone vibrated as Gage's next text came in.

I never stopped loving you. Come to me tonight and I'll protect you.

Ah, now I understood. This whole thing wasn't about any kind of romantic feelings. This was about him keeping me safe from those crazy letter writers. I couldn't do this anymore.

Goodbye, Gage. I don't need a protector now. I have Brock.

He texted back, but I didn't read the message and instead deleted it. There was no point. I was with Brock, and in a few short months I'd become Mrs. Brock Hannon and begin a life only he could offer me.

I SLID INTO BED NEXT to Brock and wrapped my arm around his waist to pull him close to me. He murmured something in his sleep and took hold of my hand as his body melded to mine, kissing my engagement ring. Pressing my lips gently to his bare shoulder, I closed my eyes and loved the sense of security he gave me just being there.

"Hey you. You asleep?" I whispered in his ear.

Brock rolled over and looked at me through bleary eyes. "Everything okay?"

"It is now. I just wanted to tell you I love you and can't

wait to be your wife."

His sleepy face lit up as he smiled. "Good. I love you, Jordan. And I promise I'll never let anyone hurt you."

"Why would you say that?" I asked nervously, praying to God he hadn't heard any of my conversation with Gage in the next room.

"No reason. Just feeling protective of the woman I love tonight. I have a big day tomorrow, so I need to sleep, but I promise after my meetings we can pick up right where we're leaving off tonight, okay?"

As he kissed me on the tip of my nose in that way he loved to do just before he went to sleep each night, I couldn't help but feel loved and cared for.

"Okay. It's a date."

Brock rolled over and fell asleep as I told myself I'd made the right choice. He offered me security, a good life, and love. Those things were important. So maybe we weren't what anyone else would call madly in love. That kind of thing was overrated anyway.

What we were was secure and comfortable, and I liked that. For the first time in my life, I felt cared for, and no matter of great sex or unforgettable romance was better than that.

So I'd marry Brock and make compromises for the greater good. And I'd forget Gage Varo and all the feelings he brought out in me.

Chapter Seven

Gage

For hours, I lay in bed reading over Jordan's texts and wishing she was in my arms instead of miles away in another man's bed. I'd promised myself I'd stay away from her to make sure whoever was after me didn't hurt her, but now that I'd seen her again all those pledges to let her go forever had gone out the window.

I should have never gone to her engagement party. What the hell was I thinking?

Rolling over, I buried my face in the pillow. I knew what I was thinking. I wanted to really see that she had moved on from what we'd had. That she had moved on from loving me.

Well, I guess I got what I wanted. She'd definitely gotten over us. Her future husband wasn't much to speak of, though. Sandy blond hair, weak chin, and beady eyes were his best features, and that wasn't saying much.

Not that it mattered one fucking bit. Whatever romantic dreams I still harbored about getting back together with Jordan someday were just that. Meaningless dreams I had to forget. I couldn't let her get hurt because I was too selfish to stay away from her.

Her life was more important than my missing her, even if missing her felt like someone was ripping my heart out of my chest every night. She didn't deserve to pay for my mistake.

AFTER A FEW HOURS OF restless sleep, I woke up with a new focus. I needed to make sure Brock Hannon was who he claimed he was. If I had to give Jordan up to some guy, I had to know he wasn't part of whoever continued to send me those letters threatening her.

I got to the office and there waiting for me slipped under the front door was a white envelope sent from Texas and addressed to me. Turning it over in my hand, I saw no evidence that it had actually been delivered by the post office, so this was meant as a clear warning since I'd seen Jordan just the night before.

But who had sent it? More and more I began to think the person behind these letters was none other than Jordan's fiancé himself, Brock Hannon. I needed to find out just who the hell this guy was.

Since it was a Sunday, I had the place to myself. An hour's worth of searching online only resulted in the party line on Brock Hannon. Wealthy entrepreneur with an internet startup worth multi-millions, he seemed perfect in every way. No bad press, no former relationships with unhappy ex-girlfriends or spouses. Not even a speeding ticket in one of his dozen or so luxury sports cars.

But nobody was that perfect. I just needed to find the right kind of help to dig up the real goods on Hannon. I only knew of one person who could find out all the dirty details about a person, and all it would take was one phone call to find him.

It had been a while since I saw the guy, but with the right help, he'd get me what I needed. I dialed Tristan's cell and hoped he wouldn't mind me interrupting his Sunday morning in the country.

"Hi, Tristan. I'm hoping you can help me. I need Daryl's number."

He remained silent for a long moment, and then in a quiet voice barely above a whisper, he asked, "Are you going to have him check out Jordan's fiancé?"

"Yeah. Did you already have him do that?"

Another long pause. "Not exactly. I did a basic check of him and found nothing. He seems like a decent guy."

I heard hesitation in Tristan's voice. "But? I hear a but in there somewhere."

"He seems too good to be true, to be honest. I've wondered if I should check deeper, but when I mentioned it to Nina a couple weeks ago, she told me Jordan's happy. Something just seems off about him, if you know what I mean. And last night seemed strange. He and I don't necessarily travel in the same circles socially, but I would have thought I'd know at least a few of his guests. I didn't know anyone."

Tristan's words sent up all sorts of red flags in my mind. "That's why I want to have Daryl dig up whatever there is to dig up on him. I just don't feel like she knows all there is to know about this guy."

He gave me Daryl's cell number and as I thanked him, he

said, "Good luck, Gage. I hope you find what you're looking for."

"Thanks. Say hi to Nina for me."

I keyed in Daryl's number as the thought of finding what I wanted passed through my mind. If I did find out that Brock Hannon wasn't all he claimed to be, Jordan would be heartbroken. Again, I'd be the one to ruin her happiness.

But that was a chance I had to take. I couldn't take the risk that Hannon was involved with whoever was threatening her. She could hate me all she wanted. As long as she was safe, I could live with her hating me.

Daryl answered with his usual relaxed way of making someone feel like he knew exactly what they wanted from him before they said a word. "Hey, Gage. Tristan just texted me that you would be calling me. I assume it has to do with that pretty blonde friend of Nina's you used to date marrying another man?"

I sighed at his succinct assessment of my problem. "I guess I'm thankful Tristan gave you the rundown. At least I won't have to go through the preliminaries for you."

"Tristan didn't tell me a thing, other than saying you wanted to talk to me."

"Then how did you know I needed your help with something involving Jordan?"

With a chuckle, he said, "Because that's my job. I'm supposed to know things, buddy. So what can I do for you?"

So I would have to go through the details. Better to get it over and done with so he could move on to actually finding out about good old Brock.

"I need you to find out everything you can about Brock Hannon. And I mean everything—not just what it says when you Google the bastard."

"Well, I was right then. You do want to know about your girl's fiancé. At least you're smart enough to know you can't believe the bullshit you find when you do a search for him. He's a fucking millionaire. He can afford to keep the dirt hidden and hidden well. I'm sure he has someone like me on his payroll like Tristan does, and it's that guy's job to make sure when people look into his boss's past that nothing but roses come up."

Daryl's mention of Tristan and hidden dirt made my mind wander for a moment as I wondered what he could be hiding and if Nina knew. What exactly was the perfect guy keeping buried?

"Thankfully, I'm better than the guy Brock Hannon has, so whatever he's hiding, I'll find out."

I had to laugh. Daryl was always so confident, even if everything about how he looked inspired anything but confidence with his unkempt bushy mountain man beard and almost troll-like appearance.

"That's big talk. You sure this guy's dirt will be that easy to find?"

"If I didn't know this was for a good cause, I'd hang up on you right now for that insult, Gage. But I'm an incurable romantic, so I'll let that one slip up slide."

"No offense intended, Daryl. Just worried this guy has pretty crafty people on the case and his past might be a hard nut to crack."

"I've never met a nut I couldn't crack, so don't worry. Here's the thing, though. Do you have any idea what you think I'll find?"

I cringed at the thought that this Brock guy might be associated somehow with anyone who wanted to punish me for my past. While I didn't want to discuss the dirt I was hiding, I didn't really have much of a choice.

Clearing my throat, I said quietly, "He might be connected to something that happened with me years ago."

"The girl who got killed on your watch? That something?" he announced casually, as if everyone had the murder of a girl in their past.

"Yeah. That."

"So why would you think he's connected to that? Seems like an odd coincidence, doesn't it?"

I opened my desk drawer and lifted out the stack of letters. "Because a year or so ago I began getting anonymous letters threatening Jordan's life if I didn't leave her. And then she meets this guy out of the blue and he sweeps her off her feet? And now I've begun getting more letters."

Daryl suddenly sounded genuinely interested for the first time in the conversation. "Hmmm, the plot thickens. I think I want to see these letters before I go digging. I'll be at your office in twenty minutes. Make sure there's coffee because I'm no good without caffeine."

"Okay. I'll be here with the coffee."

He arrived in just under a half hour, and after a few gulps of coffee, Daryl focused on the pile of envelopes in front of me on my desk. "Those the poison pen letters?"

I nodded. "Yeah. I started getting them when I was out in LA. When I broke up with Jordan, they stopped, but recently they started up again."

"So what's changed?"

Daryl's question confused me. "Nothing changed. I'm still doing what I do every day. Same shit, different day."

He shook his head, his red hair and shaggy red beard moving with it. "Nope. Something changed. That's the only reason for the letters to start coming again. Tell me exactly what was going on when you began getting them the first time."

"I was watching that kid Tristan helped connect me with out in LA. He was filming a movie and I spent most of my time making sure teenage girls didn't get close enough to touch him. Other than that, I spent all my down time at the hotel at his beck and call and in my room."

"That's it? Sure do know how to live, don't you? You're out in La La Land and you spend your time in your hotel room."

"I was there for a job. Nothing more."

"No extracurriculars with your ex Angela while you were there?"

Surprised to hear Daryl bring up her name, I leveled my stare at him. "How do you know about her?"

He rolled his eyes as I realized of course he'd know about her. Tristan had Daryl check me out before hiring me.

"Oh yeah. Dumb question. Well, the answer is no. I didn't see Angela in all the time I was there."

Daryl pursed his lips and stroked his beard. "Do you remember anything from the day you received the first letter?"

I shook my head. "No. The only thing I remember is being surprised I received any mail at all. Anyone who wanted to communicate with me called or texted me, and my sister handled all my bills while I was there. I had no expectation of receiving any mail."

"Okay. Let me see the first letter."

Handing him the envelope from the top of the stack, I said as a sort of joke, "I hope you're not expecting cut out letters from a magazine. It's nothing that telling. Just some words on a sheet of paper."

He rolled his eyes again and snatched the letter from my grip. "How was your trip back to 1972? This isn't Watergate. You have someone trying to keep you away from that pretty blonde. Simple. But why is the question."

Daryl turned the envelope over to examine the back flap and then flipped it back to the front. "Sent from Dallas, Texas. Wasn't that where that girl and her father lived?"

Nodding, I swallowed hard as I remembered that day I let her get killed. "Yeah."

"Well, that seems pretty obvious that it certainly could be someone from that period of your life fucking around with you. Let me see what the letter actually says."

As he slipped the plain white sheet of paper out of the envelope, I mumbled, "Like I said, not much."

"Hmmm…done on a computer using basic printer paper. Nothing much to see there. *You let Tiffany die, so how do you think it will feel when Jordan is taken from you? Now you'll feel the pain of losing someone you love.* Subtle," Daryl said with a snort.

"Yeah. I didn't really take it seriously because I think I was just in shock that anyone would refer to her death like that. But when the next one came two days after, I knew I had to do something."

Daryl looked up from the letter. "You mean break it off with her?"

I didn't answer his question and instead just handed him the second letter. "This one is blunter. No mistaking the intention with this one."

"*That girlfriend of yours has no idea the debt you owe. Her life for Tiffany's if you don't end it now.*"

Daryl shook his head, and I saw by his expression that he wasn't impressed. "Any chance this could be an ex of Jordan's instead of someone involved in the incident with the girl?"

I thought about that for a minute, but none of Jordan's exes ever sounded like the types who would do anything like this. At least not the way she described them. "I never got the sense that anyone from her past had any interest in coming back after they'd broken up."

"Hmmm…boys will be stupid, won't they? Pretty girl with a good job and they don't come back. Okay, so how many of these have you gotten?"

Picking up the remaining letters, I thumbed through them. "Six total, including the most recent ones that began a few weeks ago and the one I found here under the door this morning."

"Well, you say nothing changed, but we know something did, right?" he asked, his voice full of suspicion. "Let me see the last two you got."

Handing him the envelopes, I repeated myself. "I told you nothing changed. I wouldn't keep anything hidden if it could help figure out who the hell is behind this, especially if it's Brock Hannon."

He slipped a letter out and held it up to the fluorescent light hanging from the ceiling. "This one's different. *She still isn't safe, Gage.*" Looking at me, he grinned. "Short but definitely not sweet. And the one from this morning?"

I pushed it across the desk toward him. "From Texas, as they all have been, and the threat is clear. If I don't stay away, she'll get hurt."

Daryl's eyes lit up as he examined the front of the envelope. "This one wasn't mailed like all the others. So something definitely has changed now. Let's see what it has to say." He held the letter up to the light and grinned. "*This is your last warning. Stay away.* Seems whoever's behind these is getting antsy."

"Antsy? Like what? Scared? Nervous?" I asked, hating how he sat there looking at me like I was hiding something from him, something that might be the key to keeping Jordan safe.

Daryl finished his coffee and leaned back in his chair, folding his arms behind his head. "Best for me to just ask the question. When did you start talking to her again?"

"After they started coming again. I'm telling you I didn't change anything. Whatever changed, it changed with the people behind this, not me. That's why I'm thinking it must have something to do with that guy she's marrying."

"No recurring drive-bys of her place late at night after

you've had too much to drink that someone might have noticed? No being in the same general area as her when you think no one's looking?"

Even though I was guilty of both of his accusations, I shook my head and rolled my eyes. Daryl didn't need to know how lost I was. "If you're asking if I've been stalking her, the answer is no."

"Okay. I just know how your kind works. That's all."

"My kind?"

"Yeah, your kind. The dark and brooding kind. The still waters run deep and dirty kind. You know what I mean. You don't say much, but you're like an iceberg—most of you is below the surface."

"Jesus, Daryl. I never knew you paid that much attention to me."

His profiling hit a little too close to home, but I still had no desire to admit to him just how much I still loved Jordan. Daryl and I weren't exactly confidants.

He nodded, as if he finally believed me. "Okay, then let's attack this from another angle. What changed with Jordan or this Brock guy recently?"

Only one thing had changed with either of them recently that I knew of. The announcement of their engagement. Hanging my head, I said quietly, "They got engaged."

"How long before that did you begin getting the letters again?"

"A week or so."

"Well, they'd have to plan the engagement party months in advance, wouldn't they to get a decent place in the city? So that doesn't sound like it fits."

I lifted my head as something he said clicked. "I don't think so. They haven't known each other very long, so I don't think it was months in the planning."

"Whirlwind romance, huh?" he said with a grin. "Okay, then maybe there's something to the timing of the engagement being announced and these letters coming to you again. But why? If he's behind them, why start up again? You hadn't seen her recently, had you?"

"No. I stayed away because I was afraid if I didn't that she'd get hurt."

Daryl leveled his gaze on me. "That's not entirely true, now is it?"

"What do you mean?" Jesus, I felt like I was being interrogated.

Picking up the letter I'd found under the door that morning, he waved it around. "Hello? I just told you whoever is behind this is getting antsy. They're afraid you're back in the picture, so when did you see her? Right before the party? Probably not after since the happy couple likely left the party to go home for a wonderful night of celebration for the just the two of them."

His description of Jordan with Brock made me cringe, even if I knew what he thought they did the night before wasn't true. Taking a deep breath, I blew it out slowly and admitted the truth. "I saw her at the engagement party. I was working security for a party in the room next to it and stopped over to see her."

He threw his head back and laughed one of his deep belly

laughs. "I knew it! For what it's worth, Gage, you're lucky you didn't have to stand in line behind all those other fools who let her go. She's a beautiful girl. The guy who snags her is a lucky man."

"Yeah, and right now, that's Brock Hannon, but I still think he's no good."

Abruptly, Daryl stood and tapped his knuckles on the top of my desk. "Well, I think I know all I can from you. I'll check out this Brock Hannon. I doubt he's as clean as he comes up in a regular search, but I'm not sure he's going to be connected to the threats against her. By the way, you might want to put one of your guys on her for a while if you aren't already doing it."

"Why?" I asked, terror racing through me at the thought of Jordan getting hurt even after I'd done everything they'd asked.

"Because she's the key here and I'm not sure it's about hurting you so much as it is about hurting her. But maybe it's all nothing but a jealous fiancé trying to keep her ex-boyfriend away. I won't know until I dig up some of his dirt."

"Let me know as soon as you can, okay Daryl?"

"Don't worry, Gage. I'm sure as of right now she'll have the finest protection available. As soon as I know something, I'll call you."

He turned on his heels and headed out the door as I thought about how I'd protect her and still stay far enough away from her so whoever was behind those letters wouldn't see me around her. Daryl was right. Even if it meant my life, I'd make sure she was protected.

Chapter Eight

Jordan

Rolling over, I let my arm fall onto the empty space where Brock had slept next to me as my head began to pound like a freight train was tearing through it. Never much of a hard liquor drinker, I definitely couldn't handle bourbon. I closed my eyes and prayed to God for some relief from my pounding headache while what I'd done settled into my consciousness.

Drunk texting was literally the worst thing a girl could do, and I'd one upped it and gone old school, adding drunk dialing to my repertoire of drunken stupidity. Well, if you're going to do something, you might as well do it all the way. Anything worth doing is worth doing right.

My inner smart ass didn't make my behavior any better. I should have never spoken to Gage in any way, shape, or form. What was the point? I had Brock now and we were ready to set off on a life of our own.

I looked around on the night table to see if my sweet fiancé had left me a little note just to say hi or when he'd be home from the office, but found nothing. Cute things like that weren't exactly his style, but I had hoped he'd leave me something after our engagement party last night. But that was foolish. Most guys didn't do those kinds of things.

Gage did those cute things.

Ugh!

I needed to get that man out of my head before I began to sabotage my wonderful relationship with Brock. So what that he used to leave me little sticky notes telling me how much he couldn't wait to see me again or apologizing for having to leave before I got up? It wasn't as if that made him the perfect man or anything.

Cute was definitely overrated. Brock had many other terrific attributes. He was smart, attractive, wealthy, and successful. So cute wasn't one of his qualities. No matter. He made up for it in so many other ways.

I needed to get out of this bed or I'd waste the entire day away. Maybe Nina and the kids could come into town for a visit to the zoo. Pressing speed dial, I waited as her phone rang and wondered where Brock kept his Advil.

"Hey you! You're up early considering last night's party," Nina said in a chipper voice. "What's up?"

"I was wondering if you and the kiddos would like to hit the zoo today."

"Honey, it's Sunday. Aren't you and Brock spending the day together?"

It was Sunday. I'd lost track of what day it was, likely due to my bourbon hangover. But working weekends wasn't anything strange to my fiancé. He seemed to work every day of the year. A man didn't get to be as successful as he was without a little sacrifice.

"No, he's at the office. You know how those Type A executives are."

Nina chuckled, knowing all too well how those types were since Tristan was the same way. "I hear you. We'd just planned on hanging out today, though, but let me call you back in a minute. Maybe we can leave the burbs for a day."

"Okay. I'll be here."

I placed the phone next to me on the bed and covered my eyes with my forearm, hoping the world's worst hangover would soon just be a distant, awful memory. I knew I really should get up to find something for my head, but Nina would be calling back in a few minutes, so I'd just wait.

A few minutes turned into nearly a half hour, and when my phone rang again, it startled me from a sound sleep. Still in a groggy haze, I answered it and heard Nina's happy voice announce that Tristan was taking the kids to the park and then for a drive, so she and I could have a girls' day out. I didn't have the heart to tell her I may not be able to even extricate myself from Brock's bed at the rate I was going.

"Oh. That sounds great," I croaked out.

"Is everything okay, Jordan? I thought the two of us spending some time together would be fun."

Sitting up, I forced myself to come alive from my funk. "It is. It will be. What time do you want to get together?"

"I'm ready now, but you sound like a bus hit you. Can you be ready in an hour or do you need more time to recover from your celebration hangover?"

Groaning, I mumbled, "I wish it was that." I quickly changed the subject, hoping Nina didn't pick up on what I'd just said. "I can be ready in an hour. Do you want to meet somewhere or will Jensen be coming here?"

"Is here at Brock's?"

"Yeah."

"Okay, let's say an hour down in front of Brock's building. I remember where it is. Then you can fill me in on all the romantic stuff you and he did last night."

"Uh huh. Okay, see you in sixty."

I moved the phone from my ear but heard Nina say something. "Jordan, is something wrong?"

Shaking my head, I said, "No. It's all good. Just have a bit of a headache this morning, but some Advil and girl time with my best friend will chase it right away. See you in a bit."

Now I had to get out of bed. Slogging my way to the bathroom, I looked in the mirror and saw my pounding headache wasn't the only physical manifestation of my hangover. My face looked like someone had been beating me with the ugly stick.

I groaned. "Oh. No wonder Brock left without saying goodbye."

Forty-five minutes later, my hair was washed and dried, my makeup was applied so I didn't look like death warmed over, and I wore a cute t-shirt and cut-off jean shorts look that made me feel much better than I had when I woke up.

I put the finishing touches on my face and grabbed my purse, ready for a girls' day out with Nina. As I rode down in the elevator, I couldn't help but think she was the luckiest woman on earth. Gorgeous husband who also had no problem taking care of their triplets? There weren't too many guys like that in the world.

The elevator doors opened and before me stood Nina dressed in a sunny yellow dress with little blue stars. "I was hoping you'd meet me here. I forgot which floor Brock's apartment is on and didn't look forward to going door to door looking for you."

"You're so silly. He has the penthouse. So what should we do today? Shopping? Eating like pigs at our favorite restaurant? Hang out in the park?"

She screwed up her face like she was thinking about our choices and then flashed me that Nina smile that never failed to brighten my day. "How about we grab something to munch on and a couple coffees, and we can decide what we want to do with the rest of the day while we do that?"

"Okay. Sounds like a plan. Onward to find Jensen and our chariot."

WE SETTLED INTO A BOOTH in a little coffee shop a few blocks away from my apartment with our mugs of coffee and blueberry muffins. I missed doing this with Nina. Two or three times a week when she and I lived together we used to hang out in this place with its red Formica topped tables and paper placemats with ads on them, but since she moved out, I hadn't been to any of our old hangouts. It just wasn't the same without her, and none of my other friends enjoyed strong coffee at dive shops like she did.

"So is it okay to ask how you're doing after Gage showed up at the party last night?"

I took a sip and carefully placed the mug on the table. I didn't know if the caffeine was working incredibly fast this morning or if the mention of his name was the problem, but suddenly my hands began shaking. Hoping Nina hadn't noticed, I slid them under the table and pressed them onto the tops of my thighs.

"I'm fine. It's no big deal."

My hands continued to shake as she leveled her gaze on me, as if she were judging whether or not I'd told the truth. Of course I hadn't. It was a huge deal and as much as I wanted to forget everything about Gage, I didn't seem to be able to.

"Well, that's good," she said, but I knew she didn't believe my nonchalant attitude toward what had happened.

I wanted to change the topic, but my head filled with thoughts of him kissing me in that quiet room as my fiancé and all our guests stood celebrating our engagement just outside the door. How long had I waited to know he cared like I did? Too long. But with just one kiss, he had a way of making me fall back in love with him like nothing had ever happened to tear us apart.

But it had. He broke up with me over the phone and I had to remind myself all the time of how it felt for months afterward. God, if only memories brought back how we really felt when things were happening. Then I wouldn't have been sitting in a coffee shop in Brooklyn lying to my best friend about how much I still cared about a man I should have forgotten a long time ago.

Nina tapped on the table, startling me out of my daydreams. "Jordan, did you hear me?"

"No, sorry. This hangover is kicking my ass. What did

you say?"

"I just said that I'm happy you're not upset over the Gage thing. I'm sure he was just feeling bad because he lost you, but you're happy now, so too bad for him. Right?"

"Yeah, right."

Why I thought I could pull the wool over Nina's eyes I had no idea. She knew me better than anyone else in the world, except for the very man I wished I could forget, and the expression on her face said she knew I was full of it.

"So are you planning to treat me like someone you can talk to about things or are you going to keep up this charade all day?" she asked with a sharpness in her tone I rarely heard from her.

"Is that your mom voice you're using on me?" I asked, trying to avoid the conversation I knew was inevitable. Sometimes the people who knew you best understood better than you did that talking about it was what had to be done.

"No, but I can whip out the mom voice if you want."

Taking a deep breath, I closed my eyes and let the air out of my lungs slowly. "I got drunk last night and drunk dialed Gage. And drunk texted because if you're going to make a mistake, you should make it big, you know?"

"Why did you do that? I thought you said everything you had to say to him at the party."

I opened my eyes and saw Nina looking at me with confusion. "I guess bourbon didn't think so."

"Bourbon? And how about a better question. Where did you find the time to call or text Gage at Brock's on the night of your engagement party?"

Forcing a smile, I took a sip of coffee and mumbled, "He had an early morning at the office today, so he went to bed early."

Nina sat back against the red vinyl booth seat and stared at me, those cornflower blue eyes looking at me like she was figuring out who or what I was. "Jordan, what's going on? I thought you were crazy about Brock."

I rolled my eyes and looked away from her questioning gaze. "Just because we didn't have sex last night doesn't mean I'm not crazy about my fiancé."

"Don't be intentionally obtuse. You're smarter than that. You know I wasn't referring to the sex thing, which I admit I find odd in people who are supposed to be madly in love."

Another deep breath. "Oh, you mean about the drunk dialing and texting. I don't know. I just felt like I needed to tell him I'm over him."

"You don't think him seeing you announce your engagement to another man took care of that?"

She wasn't buying any of my bullshit excuses. Not surprising since I wasn't buying them either. I couldn't explain it, but I needed to speak to him last night. True, the telling him I was over him was just an excuse, but I felt like it had to be done. The problem was it just made me think of him even more.

My mind felt like it was trapped in some horrible emotional hamster wheel. I thought of him more now than I had for months, just at the moment he should be the last thing on my mind. And the more I thought of him, the more I wanted to speak to him.

Humiliated at how ridiculous I felt, I lowered my head and said quietly, "I don't know why, Nina. I just had to tell him I was happy with another man. It's stupid and juvenile, but there it is."

Touching my arm, she said in that sweet voice of hers, "Oh, honey. I get it. I do. What I don't get is why you're marrying someone else when you obviously can't get Gage out of your mind."

I sighed, exhausted from thinking about him. "Because whatever hold he still has on me, it isn't the same as what I have with Brock. My relationship with him is based on a solid ground. Gage can't offer me the life Brock can. It's just that simple."

A frown settled into her features, marring her beautiful face, and she glanced down at my diamond ring before she looked up at me again. "Why is it you never mention love when you talk about why you're marrying Brock? It's always other reasons, far more pragmatic reasons, but not love."

The older woman at the table near us looked over as Nina asked her question, her eyes trained on me like she needed to know the answer too. Lowering my voice, I leaned over the table toward Nina and whispered, "Because that stuff only happens in fairy tales."

Confused, Nina asked, "What stuff? And why are we whispering?"

"Because that lady over there heard you ask why I never talk about love when I talk about Brock and I don't feel like having the whole world know my personal life. And the stuff I'm talking about is that true love nonsense you think I should buy into."

"You used to believe in true love. We both did."

"And you got your Prince Charming while I kissed a pond full of frogs."

Nina frowned again at my defeatist attitude toward true love. "I kissed a lot of frogs before Tristan. You know that's true. You met most of them."

"I know."

"But I never gave up, and I don't like that you are. I know Brock is rich and handsome, but where's the love? Without love, it's more a business transaction than a marriage."

I leaned away and considered her description of what Brock and I were doing. Well, what I was doing. Brock seemed to genuinely love me, at least in his own way. "And what's wrong with that? People do that every day. Marriage isn't always about hearts and flowers, Nina."

Her blue eyes grew wide. "Who does that? And I'm not saying it's all hearts and flowers, but where's the passion? Where's the need to be near that other person so much that you get so distracted you can't think of anything else?"

"What you're describing is the kind of thing that gets your heart broken. No thanks. I'll take what Brock and I have any day over getting hurt again."

She began to defend the fairy tale beliefs she still clung to, but I cut her off. "This is just the way it is, Nina. I need you to accept this. I'm making sure I'm taken care of, so no more talk about hearts and flowers and passion. Okay?"

Hesitating for a moment, she let out a sigh and accepted the reality she couldn't change. "Okay. As long as you're happy, I'm happy."

"Good." I took my last sip of coffee and gobbled up the last morsels of my blueberry muffin. "Now let's go have some fun. I start school in a few weeks, so I think we need to do some serious shopping. You up for it or has living out in the country taken all the power out of your shopping skills?"

We stood from the table, and pointing at me, she narrowed her eyes to slits. "You're on. You don't know who you're messing with, honey. I have an entire wardrobe covered in spit up and baby food stains that needs to be replaced. You should be asking yourself if you're up to it because I'm shopping until I drop today."

It was like old times for us, and I loved it. I knew Nina didn't agree with my outlook on love and marriage, but she loved me enough to not press anymore. And more importantly, she knew to let go of the Gage nonsense.

Now if only I could do the same.

AFTER A DAY OF POWER shopping with Nina, I finally returned to my apartment just before five in the afternoon, my body dragging from the hangover and too much exertion the day after drinking. But our time together had been the most fun I'd had in a long time, so although I felt like a bus had hit me, I was happy we'd had our girls' day out.

Just as I closed my front door behind me, my cell phone rang. Dropping my new clothes and shoes on the living room couch, I dug my phone out of my purse as I prayed to God it wasn't Gage calling. I so didn't need the temptation. But instead of him it was Brock calling, just in time to hopefully offer me a great dinner and a night together.

"Hey you! I just got home from a day of shopping. Did you have a good day at the office?"

"I did. But I had a thought I hope you're okay with. I want us to elope."

Elope? We were planning a wedding with nearly five hundred guests. I had four bridesmaids and a matron of honor who were supposed to begin dress shopping in the next few weeks, and we'd already picked a date, for God's sake!

"What are you talking about elope? Why? When? Why?"

"I know it sounds crazy, but I don't want to wait to marry you. We can have the actual ceremony when we planned it, but I don't think we should wait until then. What do you think?"

His voice verged on excited, which was very much not like him. I liked it, though. The idea of someone so eager to marry me that he didn't want to wait all those months made me feel wanted and loved. Why shouldn't we elope? It could be fun.

"Okay. Let's do it! When?"

"Great! We can go to my place in Hilton Head two Fridays from now. It's before you have to go back to school, so we can get in a brief honeymoon too before you return to work."

"You're going to take a week off of work? Really? That's so not like you, Brock."

He chuckled in a way that told me he was nervous. "I know, but you like that, don't you? I've been working hard for a long time. A week off with you is long overdue."

"Definitely! So what do we have to do before we go?" I asked, suddenly aware that actually eloping took a little bit of planning, in reality.

"Don't worry about a thing. I'll take care of everything. I'm going to have to work some pretty long hours beforehand, though, so you might not see me much for the next two weeks. As much as I want to marry you, I can't let the company slip because of my romantic notions. What do you say we plan for me to pick you up at noon that Friday?"

"Oh, I won't see you until then? Okay. I understand. Friday at noon. I'll be the blushing bride standing on my front steps," I joked.

"Good. I can't wait. I'm so glad you don't want to wait, Jordan. But I don't think we should tell anyone. Let's make this our secret."

"Why? I want to tell my family and friends, especially Nina. She's going to be so thrilled, and it would hurt her feelings if I didn't tell her. It would be like lying to her."

Brock's tone turned serious. "Jordan, I don't want the press to get a hold of this news, so you can't tell anyone. We'll have the formal ceremony when we planned, so it's not like your family and friends won't get to be a part of our big day. It's just that our first big day will be our secret."

I didn't like the idea of keeping the biggest thing in my life a secret, but I saw his point. If the press found out, they'd announce it to the world and then our elopement would be news in all the gossip pages. I had to keep in mind that I wasn't marrying some ordinary man, and when Brock Hannon married someone, it would be news.

"Will we at least talk during that time?"

Brock's voice softened. "Of course. I promise we'll talk all the time in the two weeks we're apart. Okay?"

I didn't like the idea that we couldn't see each other for two weeks and that I'd be basically alone during that time. The temptation to reach out to Gage might become too much.

But he offered me nothing that Brock could, so all I had to do was remember that and those two weeks would fly by.

"Okay. I love you and I can't wait to see you on Friday afternoon."

"I love you too, Jordan. How about I ask Monique if she can come up and visit while I'm busy during that time? Would you like that?"

I knew he was trying to be helpful, but since I'd only met his sister once and for just a few minutes right after Brock and I started dating, I didn't know if I wanted to spend the upcoming two weeks with her. I didn't want to hurt his feelings, though.

"That would be nice, but I don't want to impose on her. She likely has things in her own life she has to take care of instead of hanging out with me, Brock."

"Nonsense. She'll love it. She was so upset she couldn't make it for the engagement party. I'll call her right now and let you know when she's coming."

"Okay. I love you."

"Love you too. Just think. This time two weeks from now we'll be a happily married couple."

"I like that. Talk to you later."

We hung up, and I tried to feel good about two weeks apart from him. Maybe having his sister around to entertain would be good for me. Any distraction to make sure I didn't call Gage was welcome. I just had to make it two weeks and then everything would be fine.

Chapter Nine

Gage

Day after day, I waited to hear from Daryl, but he never called. Watching Jordan became my full time job, so my crew's assignments had to be rearranged to accommodate my being absent from the office and all other Varo Security jobs. Thankfully, I had the best workers in the business and each of them without knowing why I had to be away picked up the slack and helped me keep my company's commitments.

The doorman at Hannon's building proved incredibly helpful once I got him into a conversation about the Mets. Even though Brock was one of his favorite tenants, Dennis had no problem pushing aside professional etiquette and divulging that on his way out Sunday morning he made a point of mentioning that Miss Wright wouldn't be around much for the next two weeks, so any packages that came for him would have to wait until he returned each night. Although Dennis was sure the two were certifiable love birds, he did wonder if Mr. Hannon had something on the side.

As I made my way to watch Jordan's apartment, I had to question why immediately after announcing their engagement they were to be apart for two weeks. Was Hannon seeing another woman? But if he was, why would he publicize his engagement to Jordan?

Daryl may not have thought there was anything shady about this guy, but I was sure from the minute I heard about this separation that something was going on with Brock Hannon.

At least their spending time apart made watching her easy. From a little cigarette shop at the corner of her block, I could keep an eye on her comings and goings. Like she had since she lived out at the Dutchess County house with Nina, Jordan went to the gym every morning, usually before seven a.m. and worked out for at least an hour. After that, since it was summertime and she hadn't returned to work at school yet, she jogged back to her apartment and stayed there until at least noon. Then depending on the weather or the day, she either walked to one of the nearby grocery stores in her Sunset Park neighborhood to buy lunch or caught the subway to head into the city to grab a bite to eat with girlfriends and shop.

I never got too close but always saw who she was speaking to and what she was doing. To be honest, she didn't seem much like the woman I'd dated all those months. I didn't remember her loving shopping so much, but maybe that was because I hated shopping. Her friends were women I'd never met while we were dating, and I wondered if that was because I wasn't like her fiancé.

Powerful. Wealthy.

But at least they seemed like her. I guessed they were fellow teachers since one day they all left a downtown restaurant and headed to the school Jordan taught at.

By the end of the first week, I hadn't seen Brock stop by her apartment even once and every night she stayed in her bedroom. Through the open window that faced the street, I saw her sitting on her bed watching her favorite TV shows until around midnight. Then she'd turn the lights off and go to sleep.

It seemed like a strange life for someone who was preparing to marry a millionaire.

Beginning on the Wednesday after I started to watch her, one woman began visiting Jordan every day. This woman didn't act like Nina or like her work friends did. Haughty and spoiled, she didn't seem like the kind of person Jordan would want to spend time with at all. While Jordan wore khaki shorts and tank tops with her usual flip flops or sandals, this woman never failed to be dressed in far more expensive designer dresses for the heat of the New York summer. She always seemed awkward around the woman, as if she knew deep down inside she didn't belong with her, but day after day they got together and went to lunch or for manicures or spa dates until nighttime when she returned to Brooklyn alone.

The new woman reminded me of those femme fatales in the old black and white films. She appeared a strange companion for Jordan, who was down to earth and sweet. Her light brown hair was cut in a sharp angle to just above her shoulders, and I couldn't tell what her eyes looked like because she wore enormous sunglasses no matter if the sun was out or not. Lean, she had almost a flinty look about her, like she'd seen things Jordan as an elementary school teacher couldn't even imagine.

It didn't take long for me to dislike and distrust her. On Friday afternoon as I followed them to their second spa appointment for the week, I secretly took a picture of her and sent it to Daryl, hoping he could shine some light on who she was and why she suddenly seemed to need to be with Jordan every day. At the very least, I hoped it would spur him on to call me with any information he might have found about Brock Hannon.

As I watched the front of Roget's Day Spa waiting for Jordan and her new friend to emerge after nearly an hour inside, my cell finally rang with a call from Daryl.

"It's about time," I said, frustrated from not knowing who the hell this woman was. "Any news?"

"Well, hello to you too. That picture you took wasn't exactly photographer level. I couldn't find out anything. What do you have on that phone of yours? A two megapixel?"

"Fine. I'll try to grab another one if they ever come out of this damn spa. Anything else you can tell me, maybe about Brock?"

"Nothing yet. I think if you want to know who this mystery woman is you have to let me put my guy on the case. He's much better than you are at taking pictures, and he'll only need one day to get me what I need. You know, he's got the telephoto lens and all that good stuff."

I watched as the door to the spa opened and yet another woman who wasn't Jordan came out. "Yeah, whatever. Any chance he can do it today? I don't like this person being around Jordan. My gut tells me she's no good."

Daryl sighed. "She didn't look too bad in that shitty picture you sent me. Nice body. What's your problem with her?"

"My problem is she came out of nowhere. I've never seen her around Jordan before, not even at the engagement party. If they were that close that they spend every day together, don't you think I would have seen her before this?"

"Sounds likely. How about Nina? Does she know her?"

I hadn't thought of asking Nina, mainly because somewhere in the back of my mind I didn't want her or Tristan to know I was still so hung up on Jordan. Plus, I knew Nina's feelings on having people guard her, and she likely wouldn't be a huge supporter of my watching Jordan day and night.

"I haven't asked her. I'd like to keep this thing with Jordan between you and me."

"I get that, but if anyone would know about Jordan's friends, it's Nina. She is her best friend."

"True," I said, thinking out loud. "But they aren't as close since Nina began living out at the house and married Tristan."

"I can't deny that, but I still think if Jordan is friends with whoever this woman is that Nina would at least know her name and something about her. I say ask her. What's the harm?"

"The harm is she'll find out what I'm doing," I admitted quietly as I watched two women leave the spa's front door. Had Jordan and her friend snuck out a back entrance? What the hell were they doing in there all this time?

Daryl let out a deep chuckle. "Do you think anyone who

knows you two doesn't realize you're still in love with Jordan? Because if you're worried about letting that cat out of the bag, you can put your mind at ease. Everyone knows. You're still crazy about her, and I suspect she's still crazy about you. Call Nina and see what she says. No need to make our job harder, and if this woman is bad news, the sooner we know who she is, the better."

He was right. Whatever fear I had of showing how much I cared for Jordan didn't matter. Nina likely knew I still loved her friend. Crashing the engagement party had probably proved that already.

"You're right. While your guy is doing his paparazzi thing, I'll see what I can find out from Nina about this woman, assuming she and Jordan ever leave this goddamned spa again."

Another chuckle from Daryl only served to make me more irritated about being stuck watching the front door of Roget's for nearly an hour and a half. "I'll call you when I get the pics. Until then, enjoy your day, Gage."

I didn't react to Daryl's busting my ass. As I stood waiting, I thought back to when Jordan and I dated and I couldn't remember her ever even mentioning going to a spa the entire time we were together, other than once when she was a bridesmaid in someone's wedding. The person I knew wore her hair up in a messy ponytail and rarely wore much makeup at all, even when we went out at night. She couldn't be bothered trying to put on airs and pretending to be someone she wasn't.

That's what made her so great, though. It was her genuine

way—her realness—that I loved about her. Even with no makeup, her hair undone, and wearing yoga pants and a t-shirt, Jordan still was more beautiful than any other woman I'd ever met before. It was that ease with who she was that made me fall head over heels in love with her.

But now as I saw her leave Roget's Day Spa with this mystery woman, the two of them pictures of perfection in every way, I felt like I didn't even know her anymore. My sadness as I watched them almost made me forget to take another picture, but I pushed it aside and focused long enough to get the best picture I could of her friend. Hopefully, it would be good enough for Nina to identify who she was.

A HALF HOUR LATER, JORDAN and her friend parted ways at her apartment building, and as much as I knew I needed to watch to make sure she was okay, I wanted to see where the mystery woman went to. Maybe that would help Nina tell me her name and what she knew about her.

So I followed her as her driver made his way across the bridge and back to Manhattan. Before long, I saw where she was going. As I watched, she was let into the same building Brock Hannon lived in. I gave her enough time to get to whatever floor her apartment was on and quickly ran across the street to say hi to my favorite doorman and Mets fan, Dennis.

"Hi Dennis! How are you today? I saw the Mets clobbered the Phillies last night. It's a good time to be a Mets fan!" I said as casually as I could.

"Mr. Jones, how are you? I did enjoy my team's win last

night. I think they're going to go all the way this year."

"Hey Dennis, I wanted to ask you a question about the woman who just went in. My friend and she were at a spa and the lady left one of her shopping bags with her. I have it in the car, but I didn't catch her in time. Does she live here or is she just visiting?"

Dennis opened the front doors for an older couple and wished them a wonderful day before he turned back to me. "Oh, she's here visiting Mr. Hannon. That's his sister. I can make sure the package is delivered to her, if you like."

"My friend was very specific. You know how women are with their shopping. It's like baseball is to us, right?" I said with a smile, not exactly exaggerating.

"So true, Mr. Jones. I can't let you go into the building without permission, though. I do apologize."

Poor Dennis looked downright unhappy about disappointing me, so I chucked him lightly on the shoulder and smiled even broader. "No problem. Let me go get the bag. What name do I put on it—hers or Mr. Hannon's since she's staying in his apartment?"

Happy again, Dennis said, "You can put her name on it. Monique Hannon. A beautiful name for such a beautiful lady, don't you think?"

"Truly. Thank you, Dennis. I'll be right back."

As he opened the doors to the building for a group of people exiting a cab, I jogged back across to my car and took off down the street back toward Brooklyn and Jordan's apartment. Traffic on the FDR going toward Sunset Park was a bear even though it was only mid-afternoon, so as I crept along at a snail's pace, I called Daryl to share the information Dennis had given me.

"Gage, did you finally get to leave the spa? Get yourself a mani/pedi while you were there?" he joked.

"Yeah, yeah. I got something even better. The name of the woman with Jordan is none other than Brock's sister, Monique Hannon."

"Monique," he repeated in a singsong voice. "Sexy. I think I'm liking this mystery woman even more."

Daryl could sometimes be too much with his ass busting. Sick of him for the moment, I said, "Just find out all you can on who the hell she is and why she's here in town while her brother seems to be absent, okay?"

"No problem, Gage. I'm on it. I guess this means you don't have to call Nina and ask, huh?"

"Let me know the minute you find out anything, Daryl," I said before pressing END and tossing the phone on the seat beside me.

Twenty minutes later, I crossed into Brooklyn and found traffic thinned enough so it only took me another ten minutes to get back to Jordan's neighborhood. As always, parking was practically non-existent, but I found a spot to squeeze my Jeep into two blocks from her apartment, and beggars not being able to be choosers, I grabbed it and quickly made my way back to near her building.

By eight o' clock, I was sure it would be another night of Jordan in her bedroom watching TV, but a few minutes after the hour she came out of her building and began walking toward the subway. I followed her, keeping a safe distance, but just before she reached it a car pulled up that I recognized immediately.

I crept as close as I could and watched as Jensen stepped out of the driver's side of the black car and smiled toward Jordan. "Good evening, miss."

As he opened the door for her, Jordan patted him on the shoulder. "Thanks a million, Jensen."

"My pleasure, miss. Mrs. Stone has instructed me to take you wherever you need to go."

"Then it's the upper west side for us tonight. I'll show you where when we get close."

Jensen closed the door and walked around the back of the car before he got back in and drove away. I took off toward my car in the hopes that his usually slow driving would allow me to catch up to them so I could see where she was headed.

I had a guess, though. Brock's apartment was in that part of the west side, but why was she going there tonight? It hadn't been two weeks like Dennis had mentioned, but maybe he'd been wrong.

Jensen lived up to his reputation for being a Sunday driver no matter what the day, and I caught up to them just as they pulled up to Brock's building, as I'd expected. Jordan got out, and Jensen waited, which I found interesting. She clearly didn't plan on staying long.

Parking my car halfway down the block, I watched as she entered the building. What was this visit about if Brock had told Dennis she wouldn't be around much for two weeks? Clearly, Nina knew about what was going on since she'd sent Jensen to drive Jordan. I really didn't want to involve her and

Tristan in whatever this was, but curiosity got the best of me and I called her.

She answered in her usual cheery way. "Gage, what are you doing on a Friday night calling me?"

"I need some information, Nina."

"Oh. Okay. Do you want to speak to Tristan?"

"No, I'd rather to speak to you since I'm sure you were the one who sent Jensen to Jordan tonight."

The phone was silent for a long moment, and then Nina asked, "How would you know about that?"

"I make sure to know things," I said as I kept my eye on the front doors to Brock's building. "What's going on?"

"I can't tell you, Gage. She'd kill me if she found out I told you."

"Well, I know Jensen drove her to Brock's apartment, even though her fiancé told the doorman last weekend that she wouldn't be around for two weeks. I know she's been spending time with Brock's sister too. So I doubt much of what you know is that secret, Nina."

"You've been following her, haven't you? Why?"

"I can't tell you, but you know I would never do anything to hurt her. Just tell me what's going on with Jordan and why she's suddenly going to his apartment after not seeing him for a week."

"She thinks he might be seeing someone else. Please don't let her know I told you, Gage. She'll be furious. I think she's crazy."

"Seeing someone else? Why?"

"She told me he said he needed some time apart to catch

up on work, but she didn't believe him. The guy never takes any time off, so why would he need to catch up? So she asked me if Jensen could drive her a few places tonight. She didn't tell me where. You probably know more about that than I do."

I thought about what the doorman had told me, and I could understand why Jordan might think something was going on with Brock. Right after announcing their engagement was a strange time to suddenly need time apart, even if it was involving work. But if Brock was cheating on her, Dennis didn't know about it, and I had a feeling his opinion of one of his favorite tenants might change if he knew he was being unfaithful.

"Nina, what do you think is going on?"

She sighed, and I heard the sadness in her voice. "I don't know. I've always thought there was something wrong with Brock, but I can't put my finger on it. I intentionally didn't have Tristan get Daryl to check him out because I wanted to believe she could have found a great guy who could give her everything after you two broke up. But it's weird that the day after they announce their engagement he suddenly has to work more, like spending time with his fiancée is something he wants to avoid."

"I'm worried he's not who he says he is."

Nina audibly gasped at my statement. "Why? What do you know?"

"Nothing yet. Daryl thinks it's just me being jealous, but I'm worried."

"Gage, is there something you're not telling me?"

"Yes, but I don't want you to worry. I watch her every day and night to make sure she's okay. I would never let anything happen to her, Nina. I promise you that."

"Is it that he doesn't love her? If that's it, why did he ask her to marry him and then have that big engagement party?"

"I don't know what's going on yet, but I won't let her get hurt."

Just then, Jordan walked out of Brock's apartment building and got into the car. Putting my car into drive, I followed them.

"Nina, I have to go. Just believe me that she's going to be okay."

"I trust you, Gage. I don't know why you broke up with her, but I know you still love her. Just let Tristan and me know if you need anything."

"I will."

Jensen drove directly back to Jordan's apartment, and once she was safely inside, drove away. Parked down the street, I watched her bedroom window to see her watch TV as she had done every night until midnight when she turned out the lights and went to sleep. I had no idea what that night's visit to Brock had been about, but if her expression when she came out of his building was any indication, my gut told me something was wrong.

Very wrong.

CHAPTER TEN

JORDAN

STRETCHING MY LIMBS, I OPENED my eyes and looked around my bedroom as the bright morning sun streamed in through my windows. The DJ on my clock radio said the weatherman was calling for temperatures to soar into the nineties by mid-afternoon. Although many New Yorkers bemoaned the heat, especially when it got up toward triple digits, I loved it. To me, it was just another beautiful day in the greatest city in the world.

Summer was my favorite time of year in New York. True, it often got hot enough that heat waves rippled off the pavement and your feet felt they were melting to the sidewalk. And riding the subway in the scorching summer heat was always an adventure for anyone with a working olfactory sense. But these things didn't matter. The city was still the best place in the world.

I heard children playing outside, and for a moment a feeling of loss passed through me. When Brock and I married, he planned for us to leave and move down south. After all these years here, for the first time I wouldn't have my students to return to once fall came around. I might be able to convince him to stay for this school year, but he had his heart set on leaving New York and there was no way I'd be able to dissuade him from that.

Maybe his sister could, though. Monique seemed to adore the city. Well, at least one part of it. Every day since she arrived in town, she'd dragged me to store after store on Fifth Avenue. The woman could shop, no doubt. I wondered if she had some kind of addiction to spending money because despite my suggestions to visit museums, walk through the park, and check out tourist attractions like the Statue of Liberty and the Empire State Building, all she wanted to do was buy more things.

I cringed at the thought of today being yet another day of shopping til I dropped. One or even two days was all well and good, but every day?

Grabbing my cell off the night table, I looked for a text or missed call from Brock, but there were none. Not that this surprised me. My fiancé wasn't exactly the type of guy who liked to leave cute messages. Brock liked to show his feelings in person more than thoughtful words left on a phone.

I saw a text Nina had sent earlier. *Did everything work out okay last night? Please call me. I worry about you.*

That was quintessential Nina. The opposite of Brock, she loved letting me know she cared. I hadn't wanted to ask her to have Jensen drive me last night, but my suspicious mind got the best of me.

Sometimes I could be so foolish.

I'd gotten it into my head that something fishy was going on with Brock, and being the best friend she always was, Nina jumped at the chance to help me get to the bottom of it all. I didn't know what I'd do without her. Thankfully, Jensen drove me to Brock's apartment, and I saw everything was on the up and up.

How could I have thought there was something going on between Brock and Monique?

For the second time that morning, I cringed, but this time at my own behavior. I should have known better than to suspect Brock would ever cheat on me. He may not have been the type to send cute texts for me to read when I woke up in the morning and he may never be the type of guy who sent flowers often, but he was true.

It's just that Monique had been acting so strange about him that I began to think the most bizarre thoughts. Whenever she talked about him, she got a look in her eyes that I'd only seen before in women when they talked about the man they loved. It was like they began to sparkle when she said his name.

But that was crazy. Sure they weren't full brother and sister, instead becoming family when her mother and his father married when they were only ten. But even that was creepy of me to think. Monique no more loved Brock in that way than Nina did. I knew that deep down inside, but still after nearly a week of her gushing over every part of him—his looks, his intelligence, his success, and his wealth—I'd let myself think that maybe she did feel something more for him than just sisterly love.

God, I really could be an idiot sometimes.

I'd seen that firsthand when I went over to Brock's

apartment and found the two of them working on business. Spreadsheets and graphs laid out across his dining room table and the two of them hovered over them told me all I needed to know.

I didn't dare give a clue as to the real reason I was there, so I quickly made up a lie about thinking Monique and I were supposed to meet at a club and I'd become worried when she didn't show up. Brock and I weren't the type of couple to be as sentimental to act like we missed each other in front of anyone else, so I couldn't say that, even though I did miss him during the week. But thankfully, they believed my fib and I got out of there before I made a fool of myself in front of my future husband and sister-in-law.

I dialed Nina's number and hoped she'd be able to talk because I desperately needed to at that moment. By the fourth ring, my disappointment began to set in, and I waited for her voicemail to send her happy voice into my ear. Not that I should be surprised. Being the mother to three children all under the age of two was like a full-time and a half job. I didn't know how she did it some days.

But then just as I expected to hear her message, she answered, her voice barely recognizable between the heavy breaths.

"Jordan, can you hang on a second? I've got to catch Ethan before he…" Her sentence trailed off, and then she yelled, "Ethan! Honey, don't touch that!"

"Sweetie, this sounds like a bad time. I can call back later."

"No, no. It's fine. Just give me a second and I'll be all

yours, at least for a few minutes."

I listened as Nina explained to her son that eating cater-pillars wasn't good for him or them. Ethan giggled at her reprimand, but in just a few more seconds, he quietly told his mother he was sorry and through the phone I heard her give him a kiss.

"Okay, that drama is over. Talk to me, Jordan. Tell me something involving adults in the next ten seconds or I might lose my mind."

"I was just calling to let you know what went on last night, but it's not really anything," I said, suddenly feeling foolish for spending any time on my silliness. What Nina did day and night was real. The trials and tribulations of my life felt like nonsense in comparison.

Nina chuckled. "Right now, it's everything to me. I'm literally hanging on by a thread to my sanity this morning, so talking about anything other than eating bugs and who's touching who or who's stealing whose toys is just what I need. Spill the details, woman, and save your friend's sanity."

"If you're sure…"

"I hoped you'd call this morning, so give me the details. I'm all ears."

I sat up in bed and got my thoughts together. "Okay. I had Jensen take me to Brock's last night, but I didn't tell you the truth about why I wanted him to take me there."

"Really? Why?" A twinge of hurt colored her words now.

"Because I was embarrassed. I thought Brock was seeing someone else."

Nina remained silent for a long moment and then finally

said, "You're not kidding, are you? But you just announced your engagement. What would make you think he was cheating on you?"

"I'm humiliated to say what it is."

"Well, now you have to, no matter how bad it is."

"I thought he was doing something with Monique."

"His sister?" Nina's amazement at what I'd said couldn't have been clearer. "You thought he was cheating on you with his sister?"

"Step-sister," I said in my defense, knowing it was still a pretty lame reason to not believe someone was faithful. "They aren't related by blood."

"What are we talking about here? Like Cesare and Lucrezia Borgia, for God's sake?"

"They were actual blood relatives, Nina."

"I know that. Whatever. What were you thinking?"

"I don't know. She just seemed so lovey dovey about him every time she mentioned him. I just had a vibe."

"A vibe? Like a gut feeling?"

"Yeah. I can be so stupid sometimes, Nina. I know. But it's okay now. I went over there and saw that everything was on the up and up. It's all good now."

"Jordan, you had a gut feeling about something. I don't think that should be ignored. Remember what we've always said?"

"Yes. 'Go with the gut. It never does you wrong.' Well, this time my gut was wrong."

"Has your gut ever been wrong before?"

I thought back and silently had to admit no gut feeling

had ever led me astray before. But I couldn't be right about this. Related or not, Brock cheating on me now with Monique was preposterous now that I'd seen them together last night.

"No, but it was wrong this time. I saw how they acted together, Nina. It was all in my head, probably because I'd just been missing him."

"Jordan, that's weird in and of itself. You two announce your engagement and then he needs to put his nose to the grindstone for two weeks and can't see you during that time? Who does that?"

I couldn't tell her the truth of why Brock couldn't spend time with me for those two weeks, but I wanted to. I didn't like keeping secrets from the one friend who knew me better than anyone else in this world, but I wanted to stay loyal to my future husband too.

"He's just a busy man, Nina. You know how it is. Tristan works long hours too, and there have been times when he wasn't around much. It's the same thing."

"I guess. I don't think about those times anymore because Tristan's always around these days. That's what having three children does to a man. I swear I fully expect him to come home one night and tell me we don't have any money anymore because he's been taking so many weekends off."

Swinging my legs off the bed, I stood up and stretched. "Like that could ever happen. You guys are jillionaires," I joked.

"You're going to be soon too, Mrs. Brock Hannon to-be."

"Maybe, but my husband won't be getting three kids

from me anytime soon. He's going to be lucky to get one."

"No big family for you guys?" Nina asked in a tone full of disappointment. "I was hoping all your kids could play with all of mine."

"I'm not like you, honey. I have a feeling I might not even be a good mother."

"Another gut feeling? Well, I can tell you that one is definitely wrong. You'd be a great mom. You're fantastic with my kids. I think you might be Ethan's first crush. Every time I mention your name, his eyes glaze over with that 'He's dreamy, Marcia' look."

Chuckling, I walked out to my kitchen to brew some coffee. "You know I love that little guy, don't you? I love all three of your munchkins, but that Ethan is just such a cutie. Give him a kiss from me when you tell them all I said hi, okay? I've got to get this day going or I'll be late to meet Monique for today's real life episode of Shop Til You Drop."

"Will do. But you seem to be spending a lot of time shopping with Monique. Maybe today she might want to do something other than that."

I scooped the coffee into the filter and started the coffeemaker. "Yeah. She'll want to go out to eat. That woman has a two-track mind. Shop and then eat. Rinse and repeat."

"Well, call me later and let me know how your day was. I get lonely for adult conversation out here when Tristan is gone to work. I might just chew Cara's ear off, and we wouldn't want that."

"God no!" I teased. "I'll give you a call later and give you the details of my exciting shopping binge for the fifth day."

"Okay, honey. I'll talk to you later. Love you!"

"Love you too!"

As I sipped my coffee, I couldn't help but think about what Nina had said about my gut. It never had been wrong. Not once in my life. How could I have been so off the mark this time? Replaying the entire scene from last night, I tried to think of anything that would make my gut feeling right. Brock and Monique had been casual and relaxed, like a brother and sister would be. Their jokes didn't seem forced or strange. They hadn't touched one another in any suspicious way.

God, what was I thinking? To suggest that they would ever touch each other in any way other than the way two family members would was just insane. That was it. Not only was my gut instinct on the fritz, but I was batshit insane.

"I need to forget this nonsense and get ready for another day of shopping," I mumbled as I finished my mug of coffee. "Because God knows there are at least a few stores Monique hasn't visited yet."

Trudging off to the shower, I worked on forcing myself to remain chipper. Brock's sister was a perfectly nice person, as far as future sister-in-laws went, and if she found some kind of joy from shopping in New York, who was I to blame her?

An hour later, I stood waiting for her on my front steps in a red form fitting dress she'd insisted I buy on one of our trips down Fifth Avenue. A little too tight for my style, I'd planned on returning it as soon as she left town, but when she called and said she couldn't wait to see me in it today, I didn't have a choice.

Even if I felt like at any moment someone was going to stop in the street and ask me what the going rate was.

Monique's driver pulled her car up next to another car, and she rolled down the window. "Come on! Javier is double parked, and I don't want to hang out not one more minute in this neighborhood when there are stores just waiting for us!"

Her sandy brown hair and makeup looked perfect, even in the sweltering heat and humidity that had settled in after a very brief rain shower overnight. Seeing her looking so great instantly made me self-conscious about my hair pulled up in a ponytail and the barely there makeup look I was sporting.

I tugged on the ends of my hair and headed down the stairs to join her in the back of her Town Car. She practically pulled me in next to her as she ordered her driver to head back to civilization, as she liked to refer to Manhattan.

Maybe I should have been insulted about her jabs at Brooklyn and the location of my apartment, but I couldn't deny that being out in the boroughs wasn't everyone's idea of the best place to live. Anyway, I'd be leaving this place as soon as Brock and I married, so it didn't matter much what she thought of it.

"You look so good today, Jordan," she said with a huge smile as she pushed the stray hairs from my ponytail back off my face. "I love how you always look so beautiful with so little makeup and such a casual hairstyle. I'm jealous!"

I forced a smile as I silently wished I'd taken more time to make myself up. "That's me—no makeup and totally casual."

She looked me up and down and threw her arms around me. "And you wore the dress! It's so gorgeous on you. Just remind me when we go to MAC that you need a little more color on those cheeks to pull this off. But you look great!"

As she hugged me tightly to her, I felt less and less great by the second. Clearly, my no makeup look wasn't enough for the dress she'd picked out. For a moment, I felt a little put out, but I reminded myself that this was Brock's sister and it meant a lot to him that the two of us got along. So I sucked up my hurt feelings and hugged her in return.

"Thanks! You do too, but that's nothing new. I love how put together you always look."

She backed away from me and pretended to be flattered, but I had the feeling that was what she expected to hear from people.

"So are you ready to have some fun today? I thought we'd do some shopping and then get a late lunch before I have to get back to Brock's. There's this wonderful little place he took me to a few nights ago and I think you'd love it."

There it was again. That way she had of talking about her brother like he was her boyfriend. She sounded like Nina did when she spoke about some place Tristan had taken her.

"Oh, okay. I'm sure it will be nice. What's the name of the restaurant? Brock and I may have already gone there. We were on quite a fine dining kick for a while."

Monique smiled in a way that looked more like a smirk and waved off my idea. "Oh, I don't think so. We just went there the other night, and I'm sure it was the first time he'd been there. But don't worry. At least it was just with his sister."

She continued talking about our big day out and how

much fun we were going to have, but my gut told me something wasn't right. It was impossible what I was thinking, though.

Wasn't it?

CHAPTER ELEVEN

GAGE

AS I WAITED FOR DARYL'S call to find out about who this mystery woman with the shopping addiction really was, I spent yet another day ducking in and out of doorways watching Jordan and her new friend as they visited store after store. A quick text to my sister Lily with the names of a few of the stores filled me in on their objective for the day.

Makeup.

That struck me as strange since Jordan rarely wore much makeup, preferring a natural look over a lot of garbage on her face. As I stood across the street from the third store of the day, I wondered what was happening to the woman I knew. Was it Brock who wanted her to become someone else? His sister certainly wore a lot of makeup. Even from a distance, I saw there wasn't a natural thing about her. Collagen lips, all the signs of Botox, and from where I was standing, those breasts were at least two times the size nature had given her.

Definitely not sexy at all. Not like Jordan.

I watched them walk out of the MAC store and my mouth dropped open. Was today dress up like a clown day? When they'd walked in, Jordan had looked herself. Well, herself in a red dress that she tugged at like it was a straitjacket. Now an hour later, she looked like she'd been jumped by a car full of clowns with the single goal of making her look like she belonged in the big top.

She knew she looked ridiculous too. I could tell by the way she kept her head down as they headed up the street. Something inside me screamed to go yank her away from whoever this madwoman was intent on changing her and whisk her back to her apartment in Brooklyn so she could wash all that crap off her face and return to who she really was.

Pulling my baseball cap down until the brim hit the top of my sunglasses, I blended in with the crowds and followed them as they made their way toward yet another store. I'd guarded movie stars and musicians and none of them ever spent money like these two women. Brock's sister must have been either well-married or independently wealthy because she dropped cash like a champ.

Jordan and she turned into yet another makeup store, this one dedicated to brushes or something, as I wondered how either woman could possibly put more on their faces. Less than five minutes later, Jordan exited the store without Brock's sister. A tiny part of my brain rejoiced, and I hoped that her time with her had finally ended. Any more days shopping with Monique and Jordan might be unrecognizable.

She made her way toward Saks without her friend, so I took the opportunity to get a closer look. I got to within ten yards of her and saw even under all that makeup that the Jordan I knew and loved was still there. As she walked, she adjusted her dress, and I couldn't help but notice how nice it made her ass and legs look. The dress made her look more like Monique than herself, but the body beneath it was still as fantastic as it always had been.

I wanted to come up behind her and pull her away from this street with its painted up women in designer dresses and shoes. She didn't need all of that to be beautiful, and with every minute I watched her, I hated this Brock guy for making her think she had to.

At an intersection, she looked around, probably for her friend, but turned her head back as she crossed the street. Lost in watching her move, I heard someone yelling her name behind me. Quickly, I lowered my head and ducked behind a group of tourists hovered in a circle around a city map as Monique hustled by to catch up with her.

"Why did you leave? I had the perfect brush set I wanted you to get," she said in syrupy tone that set my teeth on edge.

Forcing a smile, Jordan said, "I just needed some fresh air. I guess I didn't realize how far I'd walked."

Monique tugged on her arm to force her back toward where they'd come from. "Well, you have to come back. I want you to see the brushes."

"Another time. I'm feeling hungry now, so I think I'm going to grab a bite to eat. I don't mind waiting for you as you shop, though."

There was the Jordan I remembered. The hint of sharpness in her voice as she told someone she had no intention of doing what they wanted her to do. The forced smile that masked how irritated she truly was. I was happy to see some fire still existed inside her.

Monique had no plans to give in so easily, though. Still pulling Jordan toward where she wanted her to go, she said in a voice almost a whine, "But I don't want to shop alone. Brock would be so disappointed if we didn't have fun together."

For a moment, I saw indecision in Jordan's eyes. Clearly, Monique knew what buttons to push to manipulate her, but that fire I was so thrilled to see still existed in her didn't want to be controlled by Brock or his sister. I waited, not realizing I was holding my breath until I saw her shake her head.

Slowly, I let the air out of my lungs, relieved part of the woman I loved was still in there somewhere.

She hadn't caved.

"I'm just going to get something to eat, Monique. I'm sure Brock wouldn't begrudge his fiancée some food, would he?"

I couldn't help but be proud of Jordan. Monique wasn't the only one who knew how to manipulate.

Brock's sister frowned, obviously unhappy about not getting her way, and I wondered if she'd be able to tear herself away from her gluttonous need to buy things in favor of spending time with her future sister-in-law. I secretly hoped she wouldn't, but something told me she needed to keep close tabs on Jordan.

What I didn't know was if it was for herself or for her brother. And why.

"Well, I'll come with then, but after we eat lunch, I want to go back to the brush store."

Jesus, this woman didn't know how to take no for an answer.

For her part, Jordan seemed to be happy with her win over her friend's demands. Likely, if I knew her like I thought I did, she'd find a way to get out of returning to that store Monique so desperately wanted to go to.

The two of them headed off to lunch, giving me a reprieve from their constant shopping. I'd thought I needed to keep a watchful eye on Jordan to keep her safe from the people behind the threatening letters, but it had turned out that afternoon she was in danger from no one and nothing, except for emptying her bank account with repeated splurges on Fifth Avenue.

When Daryl called just after one, I eagerly answered, desperate to talk to anyone who had nothing to do with shopping or makeup.

"Hey, Daryl. Just the man I hoped to hear from. What did you find out?"

"My guy got me the pictures this morning, so I haven't gotten anything definite yet. Something strange popped in my early search a little while ago, though. There's no record anywhere of Brock Hannon having a sister."

I paid the hot dog vendor for my lunch and took a bite, tasting only bun. "Monique isn't his sister. She's his half-sister. I told you that already."

"Right. But there's no record anywhere of him having a half-sister either. No sister anywhere of any type."

"Are you sure?" I asked, fear suddenly settling into my brain.

Who was this woman?

"I can't find anything yet. But don't jump to any crazy conclusions just yet. I'm still looking. All I'm saying is that Brock Hannon's sister doesn't seem to exist, as far as I can tell."

"Why would someone be pretending to be his sister? All the woman seems to do is shop and force Jordan to shop with her. I haven't seen her do anything nefarious in the entire time I've been watching them."

"I don't know, but I'm thinking what you were worried about might be right. What was the name of the man you guarded who was the father of that girl?"

"Gregory Michaels." Even saying his name made me feel like someone had just set thousand pound weights on my shoulders.

Daryl repeated the name and mumbled a question about what that would have to do with Brock and Monique and whatever they were up to. "Gage, I'm just not sure these things are connected, but it would be too much of a coincidence if either Brock or his sister had any acquaintance with Michaels. Don't you think?"

Racking my brain for any connection between them, I said, "Michaels is wealthy. That's really the only thing they have in common, as far as I can see."

"Do you still talk to him? I mean, after the incident with his daughter, are you two on speaking terms?" Daryl asked with an uncharacteristic awkwardness to his voice.

Gregory Michaels had every reason in the world to hate me for the rest of his days, but he didn't. He never blamed me for his daughter's death, even if I blamed myself. After her funeral, he sat me down and in his sadness found a way to express to me that he believed everything happened for a reason. That neither of us wanted to accept that about Tiffany's death didn't change the fact she was gone. She had been killed by someone wanting him dead, and he'd have to live with that for the rest of life, like I would have to live with the reality that in choosing to do my job and protecting him, I had unwittingly made it easier for the assassin to still fulfill at least part of his objective. He killed the wrong person, but in some way, he killed Gregory Michaels that day too.

"We haven't spoken in years," I choked out, hating the memories of that moment in time that flooded my mind. "But he never blamed me for her death."

"Good. Good. We may need to contact him if we run into a dead end, and the fact that he's still willing to speak to you might help."

I said nothing in response to the idea that I might have to call Gregory after all this time. It never mattered that he didn't blame me. I blamed me, and all those sleepless nights staring up at the ceiling in my bedroom as I tried to forget that day had done nothing to change that. If I hadn't been so focused on him, Tiffany may be alive today.

And if forgetting was difficult, then forgiving myself was impossible.

"Let me know," I said quietly as I watched down the street for Jordan.

"Will do. In the meantime, keep your eyes on that pretty lady and make sure nothing happens to her. I can't say why, especially since I wasn't convinced when you first told me, but my instincts tell me something's going on with this fiancé of hers and his sister. I'd hate to see something happen to Jordan."

I balled up the foil wrapper and my half-eaten hotdog inside my napkin and tossed it in a trash can. "Yeah, me too."

"Keep your phone nearby. I'll call you when I find something out."

"Thanks, Daryl."

"It's my pleasure. We have to make sure that little lady isn't being used in some horrible way, and if she is, we have to make sure you get to her in time to stop it."

Stuffing my phone in my jeans pocket, I wiped the sweat from my forehead on my arm and pulled my hat back down over my eyes. The temperature had climbed into the low nineties, and even standing felt like an effort in the heat. For the next hour, I watched the front door of the restaurant, at times wondering if I'd somehow lost track of them and they'd slipped by me, but then I remembered Monique's comment about wanting to return to the brush store. At the very least, I would have seen her pass by.

Then I saw them come back out and begin to head directly toward me. Jordan looked different, and as I ducked into a store doorway behind a few shoppers I saw she'd wiped off some of the makeup she'd had on earlier, bringing her face back to its more natural and far more beautiful state. Monique looked irritated, likely because for the first time since they'd begun to spend time together she didn't seem to be having the success she wanted in manipulating her.

As they walked by me, I heard her grumble, "Well, at least come with me to buy a new pair of shoes. These New York sidewalks have all but ruined my Jimmy Choos. We can find some at Saks. Come on. Let's go."

I followed behind them to listen to their conversation and realized the Jordan I had hoped was still inside her somewhere had come back even more, thankfully.

"I'm pretty worn out from this heat, Monique. I think I'm just going to head home."

Clearly, lunch hadn't been all Brock's sister had hoped it would be. And if anyone knew how hard it was to change Jordan's mind once she dug her heels in, it was me. Monique could try, but if Jordan didn't want to do something, it wasn't going to happen. That stubbornness had damn near driven me out of my mind more than once when we were together, but now I prayed for it to return with a vengeance.

Her deep red stained lips drooping into a pout, Monique practically whined like a child. "But we just spent all that time in the air conditioning at the restaurant. Surely, you can't be tired from the heat already." When Jordan didn't budge, her voice changed to its usual scheming tone. "Just one more store. We can go see my brother after Saks, if you want. That would be nice, wouldn't it? I'm sure you'd love to see Brock today."

As I walked behind them, I listened carefully and waited to see if Jordan would take the bait. Monique obviously felt like she was losing control if she trotted out the offer to see Brock, but since he'd even told the doorman he wouldn't be seeing Jordan for two weeks, why would Monique now be wanting to take her to him and in the middle of a work day, no less?

But Jordan didn't bite. "I'm really not up to seeing him right now. Maybe after a shower and a change of clothes into something a little less hot, but for now, I'll just have to settle for his call later tonight."

Whatever Brock's devious sister was up to, Jordan had jammed a monkey wrench into her plans for the day. Maybe Monique was just lonely and wanted a shopping buddy, but I doubted it. She was up to something.

"Well, if that's the way it has to be, I'll get the driver to take you back to Brooklyn."

Jordan smiled and shook her head. "No, that's okay. I can take the subway. I don't want you to have to go all the way out there and then back here. Go shopping. Enjoy yourself!"

I couldn't tell if her words were genuine, but her happiness at leaving Monique certainly looked real. Leaning in to give her an air kiss, Jordan said her goodbyes and turned to head toward the subway, even as her future sister-in-law tried to convince her that taking that way home would be even worse than shopping in the heat.

The woman sure didn't know how to take a hint.

Monique stomped away in her Jimmy Choos and I considered following her to see exactly what she really planned to do, but I had a sense it was nothing more exciting than buying shoes at Saks, just as she'd said. Whatever she was up to, her main concern at the moment seemed to be spending more money on herself.

But whose money was it? Hers or Brock's?

Choosing to stick close to Jordan, I left the puzzle of Monique and her spending for another time and headed toward the subway for the ride out to Brooklyn. But just as she crossed the street to descend down into the tunnel, a black Town Car pulled up, one I recognized immediately.

The window rolled down and Nina stuck her head out, her smile stretching from ear to ear. "Excuse me, ma'am. Did you call for an emergency escape?"

"Thank God! I thought I'd have to sweat it out for real on the D Train."

"Get in. We've got air conditioning and two children dying to see you."

As Jordan got into the back of the car, she asked, "Why only two? Where's the third munchkin?"

I didn't hear where Tristan and Nina's third child was, but it didn't matter as much as knowing that at least for the time being, Jordan was safe. Jensen would take her back home to her apartment in Brooklyn, so I'd have time to get to my car and get out there to begin the night watch.

CHAPTER TWELVE

JORDAN

NINA, DIANA, AND TRESSA FOLLOWED me into my apartment and I quickly excused myself to change out of my ridiculous red dress before I traumatized the kids and their first real memory of their Aunt Jordan was me looking like some high paid call girl. In less than five minutes and after a quick scrub of my face, I was back to my usual casual self in khaki shorts and a white tank top.

The kids played with their wooden blocks on my living floor as Nina lounged out on my couch and looked so at home there it was like she'd never left.

Grinning as I walked into the room, she said, "Glad to see you looking like yourself again. I was beginning to wonder for a few moments there."

"I'm just not cut out for high fashion, I guess. Monique is all about the designer dresses and makeovers."

"You don't need a makeover, unless it's with this apartment and getting some air conditioning. I have to tell you I don't miss the heat in this place during the summer," she said as she fanned herself with a bridal magazine.

Knotting my ponytail on the top of my head, I nodded in

total agreement. "I feel you on that. I think one of the few demands I'm going to make in the new place will be air conditioning."

Nina wiped the sweat from her hairline and pulled her hair up off her neck. "I'm sure Brock's apartment has air conditioning already."

"I mean the new place when we move," I said and immediately realized I hadn't told her about moving away.

She sat bolt upright and stared up at me with a look of hurt in her eyes. "Move? Where are you moving? When? Why didn't you tell me?"

"It just slipped my mind, I guess. Brock wants to move to Dallas after we're married."

"Dallas? As in Texas?"

"Yeah. Do you want a drink? What can the girls have?" I asked as I turned toward the kitchen, eager to escape our conversation and the hint of betrayal that had settled into her expression.

Nina followed me, unwilling to let me off the hook with such a vague answer. Leaning against the doorway between the two rooms so she could watch the kids and still grill me, she said, "I can't believe you didn't tell me this. Dallas is so far away. Why does Brock want to move? His business is right here in New York."

I lifted the pitcher of iced tea from the refrigerator door and silently offered it to her. She nodded and I explained, "I didn't intentionally not tell you, Nina. It's just been so busy. I know Dallas is far, but he's got business interests down there and wants to move out of the city. Can the girls have cranberry juice?"

She nodded and sighed, like my news had taken all the air out of her. I tried to ignore how sad she looked as I poured us all drinks, but I had to admit I felt a little like that every time I thought about moving away.

Nina handed me the girls' sippy cups and as I filled them, I said, "It's not like we can't see each other whenever we want. You can fly down to see me on your plane since you're uber rich and own a plane."

My attempt at humor was met with an even deeper frown. "It's not the same. I had hoped when you married you'd move out to the burbs with me so we could be soccer moms together."

I walked past her and gave Diana and Tressa their drinks. Watching them take turns digging more toys out of their diaper bag and sipping on their juice, I knew I'd miss them when I left.

Nina followed and as we sat down on the couch, it was my turn to frown. "I'm not a burbs girl, honey. And you don't live in the burbs. Scarsdale is the burbs. You live out in the country. But that's just not me. I like living in the city."

"Then why are you leaving?"

"Dallas is a city too. I'm sure it will be great. I hear it's a great place to live."

"It's not this city. There's this one and all the rest. If you love living in the city, you should stay here."

"And what about Brock? Are you saying if Tristan didn't want to live out where you guys are now that you wouldn't at least consider moving?"

Nina took a drink of her iced tea and shook her head. "It's not the same. Tristan never wanted to move a million miles away from everyone I was close to."

I couldn't help but chuckle. Nina could be so pouty when she didn't like things. "It's not a million miles away. It's a couple hour plane ride from JFK. Maybe less if you're in your own plane."

"Stop saying that like it changes things. It's more a company plane anyway. And it doesn't change the fact that I'm going to miss you something awful. And who's going to drive into Dallas to pick you up when that awful Monique woman wants to shop the day away and you just want to kick back and put your feet up? See, you can't leave. Jensen can't drive that far."

I squeezed her hand and smiled at her sly attempt at convincing me to stay. "It'll be okay, Nina. Maybe Brock will want to move back here after a while."

"Why does he get to say where you two live?" she asked. "What if you told him you didn't want to move?"

"I do plan to tell him I want to stay until the end of the school year, so it isn't happening right away. This is what happens when you get married. You know that. It's all about give and take and compromise, right?"

"I guess. I just hate the idea of you being down there without any of your friends or family around you."

"It's going to be fine, Nina." Turning toward the girls, I smiled and said, "But for now, I want to see my two most favorite girls in the world. And their names are Diana and Tressa!"

The two girls leaped up from their toys and ran over to me for hugs, but I saw out of the corner of my eye that their mother wasn't able to move past the news that for the first time since we were in college we wouldn't live within a short drive from one another.

As I tickled Diana and then Tressa, eliciting giggles from both of them, I thought about that reality and secretly wished something would happen to make it not come true. Maybe this could be the one thing Brock compromised on.

ALONE ONCE NINA AND THE girls left, I plopped back down on the couch and let the air from the fan in the window blow over me. Mostly just warm and humid, it felt good for about a minute before I began to sweat again, making the fan nothing more than just a noisy box that spread the heat and drowned out the sound of the television.

I wouldn't miss the summertime temperatures in this apartment, but I would miss this place. Filled with memories of all those times Nina and I stayed up late and talked about our jobs, the men in our lives, and every other topic under the sun, it had truly been home for all these years and now I'd be leaving it behind.

My eyes filled with tears at the mere thought of not living there. Leaving felt wrong for some reason. I wiped my eyes and pushed that out of my mind. It wasn't wrong to leave a place for something better. Brock offered me a wonderful life with him, and I was always going to be leaving this apartment, one way or another, whether we moved to Dallas or not.

Leaving had to happen sooner or later. It was for the better anyway since in addition to all those memories I'd made with Nina there were all those memories I'd made with men in my life. I'd dated some winners in my single days, and this couch had seen some wild times. I couldn't help but chuckle at those memories. Sometimes being a single girl in New York had been incredibly fun.

But any thoughts of the past here brought up memories of Gage, and whatever good there had been was always eclipsed by how he'd ended it. This same couch that had seen all those fun times was the spot I cried for days until there were no more tears after he broke up with me. Curled up with a blanket, I sobbed until my body ached at the thought that all we'd had was gone in one phone call.

"No. I can't keep thinking about him," I said in defiance of whatever my heart thought it was up to.

I wanted a drink, but of course in times like this, I had not even a shot of something left in the cabinet. Slipping on my flip flops, I grabbed some money and my driver's license and headed down to the market two blocks away for a six pack. It wasn't exactly high class, but it would do. Nothing like an ice cold beer on a hot summer night.

Living in Brooklyn all these years had taught me to always pay attention to my surroundings, and as I walked back to my apartment with my refreshments for the night, I had the surest sense that even though there were people all around and no one gave me the feeling that I was in danger, someone was following me. Every few feet I'd turn around and look, but I saw no one who looked like they were doing anything more than hanging out with their friends or going out for the night.

I hit my front stairs and just before I put my key into the lock, I turned around one last time to check if my gut feeling was right. Nope. Nothing. Shrugging, I opened the door and walked up the stairs to my apartment to enjoy a cool one.

My gut was clearly on the fritz.

Settling in on my comfy couch, I turned on the television and enjoyed the first refreshing taste of the wheat beer the local market had on stock. Brock and Monique could have their bourbon and champagne. I'd take a beer any day of the week over those drinks.

I'd finished my second beer and something made me go to the window. Maybe it was wishful thinking, but I had a feeling Brock may have come by to surprise me. He hadn't called yet tonight, so it could happen. Looking out down at the street below, I scanned the sidewalk for any sign of him since it was likely he wouldn't find parking anywhere close tonight.

Nope. No sign of him. Just the usual people in my neighborhood out on their front steps having a good time on a summer night. Then out of the corner of my eye I saw someone familiar. Turning my head to look down toward the corner of my block, I saw him.

Gage.

There he was standing against the side of a building like he belonged anywhere near my street or for that matter Brooklyn at all. I knew he saw me too because I watched him slink back toward the shadows, but it was too late. I'd seen him spying on me and after two beers, I was ready to give him a piece of my mind.

I stormed down the stairs and made a beeline to where he stood, surprised he didn't even try to leave. Probably no point in doing that since I'd caught him red-handed anyway. He stood there against the building with his arms crossed like he was Joe Cool or something and had done nothing wrong by lurking in the shadows and watching me like some crazy stalker guy.

"What the fuck are you doing here, Gage?" I asked as I pointed my finger up toward his surprised and all-too-attractive face. "And don't give me some bullshit story because I'm not those dumb Hollywood starlets you hang out with."

With one of his incredibly sexy crooked smiles, he answered, "I don't hang out with starlets, Jordan. I never have."

"Don't smile like that. And don't try to change the subject. I asked what the hell you're doing here in my neighborhood where you know nobody but me."

"You don't know that. I might be waiting here for someone to come out of the store."

His dark blue eyes sparkled as he stared down at me with a look that told me he was enjoying himself. Why I had no idea.

"Well, are you?" I asked as I looked around him for any sign he was with someone.

Quietly, he admitted the truth. Or at least a tiny part of it. "No. I'm not with anyone."

The man was infuriating! "Then the question stands as asked, Gage. Why are you here?"

He took a step toward me and lowered his voice. "I wanted to make sure you were safe."

"What? Why?"

"I can't say right now, but I'm worried you might be in danger."

"In danger of what? Are you still sticking to that crazy ass story about the letters?" I asked, my exasperation quickly rising to a point where I felt like the top of my head was about to blow off.

Gage gently took hold of my arm and moved to guide me across the street. "Why don't we talk about this somewhere more private?"

Why he thought we should talk about anything escaped me. I jerked my arm from his hold and threw my hands up in the air, finished with his madness. "That's it! First you come to my engagement party uninvited to tell me some bullshit story about you still caring for me, and now you're here lurking about spying on me. I'm done with you and your crazy nonsense, Gage."

"Come on, Jordan. Just give me a chance to explain as best as I can and you'll see it's not nonsense."

"You don't get it. The only danger I ever was in was with you. You're the only man who ever really put me in danger, Gage. No one else."

He stepped back, a look of confusion settling into his face. Was there hurt there too? "Me? How can you say that? I would never let anyone hurt you, Jordan."

Suddenly, the effect of the two beers coupled with my feelings of frustration with him and all his craziness rushed through me and I felt like everything around me began to whirl. I opened my mouth to tell him that the only person who ever really hurt me was him, but it was no use. My legs gave out beneath me and I felt myself falling to the ground.

But just as everything began to go dark, I felt Gage's strong arms around me catching me before I fell.

And then he swept me up off my feet and as my head flopped around on my shoulders, he carried me across the street to my building. I wanted to demand he put me down that instant, but somehow the words in my head didn't make it to my mouth.

"I need your key to get us in," he said, his lips way too close to mine.

I didn't know how I did it since my brain felt like it was on overload, but I mumbled, "Right pocket." He gently slid his hand into my shorts and got my key as I tried not to like being in his arms again.

My wits returned to me slowly, so by the time we reached my living room I at least could speak full sentences. He gently lowered me to the couch and smiled, like there was anything to be happy about, but I didn't want to see him smiling at me.

"Don't think this changes anything. It doesn't. I don't know what happened back there, but whatever it was came from having to deal with you and your craziness."

"How are you feeling? Do you want me to get you some water?" he asked and then proceeded to walk toward the kitchen before I had a chance to tell him no.

Sitting up, I yelled in to him, "No, I don't want a drink of water. Why ask if you didn't even care to know my answer?"

Gage reappeared in the doorway of the kitchen with the glass full of water in his hand and that same ridiculous smile he'd worn a few seconds ago. "I think some water would help you. You might be dehydrated from the heat. I'm not surprised considering how you are. All day out in the heat will do that to a person."

He walked over to the couch and handed me the glass as his words sunk in. All day out in the heat? Had he been stalking me all day?

I put the glass down on the coffee table in front of me and watched him as he got comfortable in the chair across from me. "Don't sit. You aren't staying. I have no intention of having a night in with my stalker."

A look of hurt settled into his eyes, but if my words had stung, it didn't show in that smile of his. I tried not to focus on it since I'd always loved that smile. No matter what else he had going for him, Gage could charm the birds out of the trees with that sexy smile. Ever so slightly crooked, it made him look so confident that I'd never been able to deny him anything once he flashed it.

"Take a drink. You look flushed," he said leaning toward me.

"Whatever I am, it's none of your business. And why do I have the sneaking suspicion that you've been watching me all day? That's how you know I was out in the heat, isn't it?"

A slight chuckle escaped his lips. "I know you well, Jordan. You're not the type to sit inside on a beautiful day."

I couldn't have stopped my eyes from rolling if I wanted

to, which I didn't. I knew bullshit when I heard it. "Smooth. I didn't realize you were such a bullshitter, Gage. So that's how this is going to play out? You're going to try to play slippery with me and I'm what? Supposed to pretend to be a dumb blonde? Fall at your feet and tell you how much I appreciate you saving me?"

He leaned back in the chair and arched one eyebrow. "I think what you did out there could be considered swooning. That's close to falling at my feet."

"Don't try to smooth talk me, Gage Varo. It won't work. I'm not one of those Hollywood bimbettes you spend your time with."

My sharp reply made his smile fade a little. "How is it that you can be so intelligent with me but with other men you're practically a Stepford Wife?"

"By other men you mean my fiancé, I assume? This jealous ex-boyfriend act you have going on isn't flattering."

A look of concern came over his face and for the first time that night, he was serious. "Jordan, what do you know about him really?"

"I'm not doing this with you, Gage, and you need to just accept my marriage to Brock is happening."

"I'm worried about you. I think there's something strange about him and his sister. He won't see you since last week, and she's all over you like white on rice. Why?"

"Oh my God! You've been following me for days. How do you know Brock doesn't want to see me? He's busy at work and we're planning on—"

I stopped explaining myself just before I let it slip that we were eloping in just days. That's all I needed was to let that cat out of the bag and have Gage go all Sherlock Holmes on me with his theories that Brock was up to no good.

"Planning on what?" he asked. God, he was like a dog with a bone. He wasn't going to let this go.

"Our wedding? Christ, Gage. I'm getting married to the man. We need to plan. A big wedding doesn't come together in a few days or even a few weeks. He's an important businessman. His wedding needs to reflect that."

That same look of hurt flashed in his eyes again, and this time the effect of my words settled into the rest of his face. The time for smiling had clearly ended.

"Ahhh, the wedding," he said in a low tone, his voice catching on the word wedding.

"I think you need to go."

I stood from the couch and began making my way to the door. The sooner Gage left, the sooner I'd stop noticing how hurt he looked at the thought of my marrying Brock. And how sexy that smile of his still was. And how when he took me in his arms just a few minutes ago my body reacted like it had never done with my future husband.

He grabbed my wrist and stopped me before I made it very far. I turned around as a flash of excitement skittered up my forearm from where his fingers touched my skin and looked up into those blue eyes of his, always so intense.

"Don't. Just don't, Gage."

For a long moment, he just stood there looking at me like I was the most important thing in the world to him. Then, in a voice barely above a whisper, he spoke and every inch of my body came alive.

Chapter Thirteen

Gage

"I missed you."

The words came out so quietly I wasn't even sure I'd said them loud enough for anyone but me to hear them. Jordan's eyes filled with something I hadn't seen in so long I wasn't sure I'd ever get the chance to see it again.

Love.

"I don't want to go."

Hanging her head, she said in a whisper, "Please don't say that. I've had too much to drink. I might do something stupid."

"You had two beers, Jordan. Whatever you're thinking of doing has nothing to do with them."

She sighed and let her shoulders droop, like all of this was too much for her. "Then I'm just stupid. Whichever it is, please go."

"You don't want me to go. Just say it."

Her deep green eyes filled with tears, and she shook her head back and forth. "Please, Gage. Just go. If we did anything, it would be a mistake. We're over. For good or for bad, that's the way it is. You made that happen, so own it."

I moved my hands up to cradle her face, but she caught me by my wrists. She may have been afraid of what would happen between us, but I wasn't. Leaning in close to her, I said, "Jordan, I never wanted to leave you. I love you. I've loved you since the first time I kissed you right there in that kitchen. And I don't believe we're over."

"I'm marrying another man. I think that's pretty much a sure sign we're over."

Her blond hair fell over the side of her face, so I tucked it back behind her ear and watched her shiver at my touch. No matter what she was saying, the feelings were still there for her too.

"You never say you love him, Jordan. Why?"

"I say I love him all the time. I love him. I love him." She stopped for a moment and cleared her throat. "I love Brock. There. I said it. Now please go."

I hated hearing her say those words. She couldn't love him. Not the way she loved me. She just couldn't, and I couldn't bear the thought of her not loving me anymore. Desperate to feel her kiss me again, I leaned forward that last inch that had separated us and pressed my lips to hers in a kiss full of how much I missed her.

As much as I knew she'd likely pull away, or even worse push me away, I couldn't stop myself. I'd missed feeling her lips on mine every night we'd been apart, and at this moment in her apartment where we'd spent all those hours together happier than either one of us had ever been before, I couldn't let the chance go by without kissing her again.

But she didn't pull away and she didn't push me away.

Instead she kissed me back, and for a long moment it was like all those months apart had never happened and we were happy again.

I felt her let go of my wrists to slide her arms around my neck, and with each second that ticked by her kiss deepened. My body came alive for the first time since I kissed her at her engagement party, and I wanted everything she possessed that had been missing from my life since that night I said goodbye.

Her beautiful smile that lit up every room she entered. The sweetness that hid beneath her strong-willed façade. That sexy look she gave me when she wanted me as much as I wanted her.

I pulled away just far enough that our lips didn't touch anymore and whispered, "I know you missed that as much as I missed it. I don't know why you're marrying him, but I feel in your kiss that you don't love him like you love me."

Jordan wiped her mouth on the back of her hand and hung her head. "I don't love you anymore."

"Yes, you do." I gently lifted her chin to make her face me. "You still love me like I love you."

Shaking her head, she frowned. "No. I don't. I don't love you. I love Brock. See? I said it again. I love Brock. I love Brock. I love Brock!"

Those words made something snap inside me, and I pulled her roughly into my arms. Now my kiss wasn't gentle and full of reminiscing but demanding. I wanted her to admit whatever she felt for him wasn't what she felt for me. I wanted her to be mine again.

Burying my hands in her hair, I tugged her head back and

I kissed her and slid my tongue past her lips to tease hers, but playtime was over. I was sick of only seeing her from a distance and living without her touch. I needed to show her what we were still burned as hot as it ever did, and we could get past what I'd done.

"Jordan, I don't care how many times you say it, it won't change the fact that you love me and not him."

"Why won't you just stay in the past where you belong? It wasn't bad enough that you broke my heart, Gage? Now you want to do it again?"

I kissed her and pressed my forehead to hers. "I never meant to hurt you, Jordan. Please know that."

"I have a chance at a great life with Brock. Don't mess that up for me," she pleaded quietly. "Please just go and leave me be."

"I can't do that. I left you because I thought it was the only way to ensure your safety, but now I realize that whoever it is sending me those letters isn't going to give up whether I see you or not. And if that's the case, I want to be around so I can protect you."

She pushed against my chest to force me back away from her and snapped, "This again? Why do you insist on lying to me about why you dumped me? Why not just tell the truth?"

"It is the truth. I would have never left you if it wasn't for those threats I began getting."

Jordan stormed off toward her room. "I'm done with this conversation. What you say makes no sense. People threatening me to you so you break up with me." Turning around to face me, she asked, "Who does that? Nobody. That's who. All of this is some kind of story to fix the fact that you dumped me for some Hollywood bimbo. Probably your ex-girlfriend Angela."

I followed Jordan to her room, pushing the door open when she attempted to slam it in my face. "I didn't break up with you for anyone and I haven't seen Angela for years. Why can't you believe me?"

She folded her arms and turned away. Quietly, she mumbled, "Because if you loved me, you wouldn't have let anyone chase you away, threats or no threats. Therefore, you didn't love me."

"I did love you. I still do. It's never changed for me."

Spinning around, she stared at me with a look like she was trying to figure out if I was telling the truth and finally said, "If only you'd told me that months ago."

"Why?"

"Because then maybe I wouldn't be marrying another man."

I knew she'd just admitted she still loved me too, but I needed to hear her say it. "How can you marry someone you don't love? You love me. Just admit it."

"What I feel for you is inconsequential. Brock and I are getting married, and that's it."

I took a step toward her and shook my head. "Admit it. You love me like I love you."

"No, and you shouldn't be in my bedroom. Leave."

"Admit it," I repeated as I took two more steps toward her.

"Go. Now," she said trying to deny what she knew was

real.

Raising my voice, I took one last step to stand in front of her and said loudly, "Admit it, Jordan! Goddamnit, admit it!"

"Fine! I admit it, all right? I love you! I always have. You broke my fucking heart into a million pieces and still being next to you makes all of that disappear because I still love you!"

Her words reverberated off the walls of her bedroom she yelled so loud, and for a moment, we stood there staring at each other in shock. Her for actually admitting she still loved me even though she was getting ready to marry someone else, and me for finally getting to hear that the woman I'd missed for so long still loved me like I loved her.

And then the entire world ceased to matter because she was back in my arms.

She kissed me like she did that first night—soft and sensual with an uncertainty that only made her more beautiful to me. I reveled in the feel of her with me, giving herself to me again. I'd dreamed of this moment every night for months and now it was happening and I didn't want to forget a single thing.

Cradling her face, I returned her kiss as she pulled me to her, any reluctance fading away with each moment that passed. When she finally broke the connection, she looked away and whispered, "Why can't I figure out how to let you go?"

"Because you still love me."

Jordan sat down on her bed and hung her head. "Why couldn't you just stay away? I was okay when I didn't see you.

Sad and missing you, but okay." She looked up at me and frowned. "But now I'm not."

"Why? Because you have to admit you love me still? Why is that so bad?"

"I have a chance at a nice life with Brock. So it's not the kind of love we have. That doesn't make it wrong. He's just different than you."

I sat down next to her and stared into those beautiful green eyes so full of emotion. "He's not the man you should be spending the rest of your life with, Jordan."

She chuckled. "You always were such an old-fashioned romantic, Gage Varo. The rest of my life with? I'm not sure I've ever thought I'd spend the rest of my life with anyone. Why should Brock be so different?"

"You thought that about me."

Tears welled in her eyes. "And where did that get me?"

"How many times do I have to tell you? I didn't leave you because of you or anything between us. I left because I thought I was protecting you."

"Gage, could we at least be honest here? We're sitting in my bedroom for the first time since you broke up with me over the phone as I sat right over there on the edge of my bed. I listened to you coldly tell me you didn't think we were working out. In no way did you sound like a man who was torn up about not seeing me anymore. So if you're going to continue with this craziness about someone threatening me in letters to you, at least remember how it all went down, okay?"

That night replayed in my mind every night as I lay in bed alone thinking about her. I couldn't forget that moment if I wanted to. It existed as the equal only to the memory of Tiffany dying because of me.

"I remember. I remember waiting for you to call and dreading what I knew I had to say. I remember hearing your voice so full of happiness to talk to me, like you always were, and thinking I couldn't do it. I couldn't tell you goodbye. But I also remember getting another letter that day and holding it in my hand as we spoke that night and knowing no matter how much it hurt either of us, I had to do it."

She forced a smile and nodded. "Well, I guess I should thank you. I'm still here, so if these threatening letters are real, your breaking up with me did the job. Thanks."

I heard the sadness in her voice and hated that I had done that. "It tore me apart to do that, Jordan. Every night for months I looked at my phone and thought about calling you. I wished you would text me at least, even though I knew I couldn't answer back, but you'd still be with me if you did. But you never sent even one or called even once."

"Of course I didn't. You know me. No matter how devastated I was at losing you, I couldn't let you see that. I cried my eyes out to Nina, ate about twenty gallons of moose tracks ice cream, and listened to every sad song on my playlists over and over. And then after a while, it wasn't so bad until one day when I thought of you I didn't want to cry anymore."

"I never stopped thinking of you, Jordan."

She cleared her throat and stood from the bed. "Well, that was the past and there's nothing we can do about it. You stopped getting letters and I met someone else. I hope that you can meet someone too."

Before I could say anything, she walked out of the room. I found her in the kitchen pouring a glass of iced tea for herself, her back to me as I stopped in the doorway.

"Is that really what you hope?"

Without turning around, she said flatly, "I wish you no ill will, Gage."

"That's not what I asked. Do you really hope I meet someone and move on?"

She stayed silent for nearly a minute as she stood there drinking her iced tea. Then she took a deep breath and nodded. "Yep. You deserve to be happy."

I heard the trembling in her voice and understood why she wouldn't turn around. She didn't want me to see her cry as she said the words that hurt her as much as they hurt me to hear them. I walked up behind her and put my arms around her shoulders to gently turn her around, and I saw the tears in her eyes.

She didn't want me to move on and be happy with someone else as much as I didn't want her to.

"I don't think you want me to meet another woman any more than I want you to marry Brock Hannon. Why won't you admit that?"

"Because it gets us nowhere."

"A few minutes ago you admitted you still love me. How can you say you want me to move on to someone else?"

Looking up at me, she asked me, "Do you remember when we were together and I used to tell you all I wanted was you to be happy?"

"Yeah. And I used to tell you all the time I was happier

with you than I'd ever been with anyone else before."

"Well, that's all I ever wanted for you. I'm marrying Brock, and I want you to be happy like you were when you and I were together, Gage."

"And what about you? You aren't happy with him like you were with me. You know it."

She nodded. "I know, but life is about compromise a lot of times. I thought I had it all with you, and then you left me and I swore I would never let myself get so lost in someone that I would feel like I had nothing left if he ever broke up with me. Being with Brock means I don't feel a lot of the things I felt with you, but then again, I don't have the risk either."

"What risk?"

"The risk of having my heart broken again."

"And in return what do you get instead of real love?"

"Security. Pretty ironic that it was the one thing I couldn't find with you, huh?"

Her words made me feel defeated, and I took a step back from her. "I guess that's my cue to leave."

"I'm sorry, Gage. I didn't mean to be hurtful there."

I shook my head and swallowed hard to push my hurt down inside me. "No need to be sorry. Have a good night."

She didn't try to stop me as I left, and as much as I didn't want to admit it, she was right. I could protect Tristan's Upper West Side cronies and the wealthy benefactors he sent to me, but for her, the only way I could make sure she was safe was to stay away. As long as I'd stayed away, I'd stopped getting the letters and she'd been okay.

I walked away from her building, but I couldn't bring myself to leave. No matter what she thought about Brock, I still wasn't sure he and his sister weren't up to something, and until Daryl and I found out what that was, I'd still watch Jordan day and night.

I had no choice. I loved her.

CHAPTER FOURTEEN

JORDAN

ADMITTING TO GAGE THAT I still loved him left me reeling, even if I'd been successful in hiding how it truly made me feel from him. He'd barely gotten out the door before Brock called to see how I was doing and to remind me that it would be just a few days more until our secret elopement. The excitement in his voice made me happy, but to be honest, seeing Gage had made me question if I'd made the wrong decision when I said yes to Brock about running off together.

I tossed and turned all night thinking about all the things we said to one another, just like when we were dating. He had that effect on me still after all the time apart.

Right before eight, my phone woke me up, and answering it I found Monique planning my day once again. Barely awake, I already knew I didn't want to be a part of another one of her shop 'til you drop marathons. The sun was shining, the birds were chirping, and I wanted to spend the day like I usually did during the summer.

Having fun.

"Sorry, Monique, but I can't today. I've got plans already. Maybe tomorrow."

The shock in her voice was unmistakable. "What do you mean you can't? I was so looking forward to spending this week with you getting ready for your big weekend coming up. I know Brock will be disappointed we aren't spending the day together."

I stretched the few hours of sleep from my body and rolled out of bed. "I'll be sure to tell him it was all my fault when I talk to him tonight, but I have to go now. I have about an hour to go before my friend gets here. Talk to you later!"

Before she had the chance to try her hand at talking me into something I didn't want to do, I clicked END and immediately called Nina. For the first time in months, I felt like I wanted to enjoy life, and there was no one better to do that with than my best friend.

"Jordan, you're up early. What's up?"

"What do you say to a day at the zoo with those kidlets of yours? Sun, animals, and more fun than we know what to do with."

"Sure! The kids will love it. Do you mind if Cara comes? Three on three puts the adults on equal footing, so to speak. These type of outings usually go better when there are three of us around."

I made my way into the bathroom to look at myself in the mirror. Scrubbing the night from my face, I said, "Sure! Bring her along. The more the merrier! I'm in love with life today, so bring anyone you like. Maybe Tristan would enjoy a day at the zoo. You know, get him out of that downtown office building and into the wild!"

Nina laughed. "You sound like that zebra from that movie the kids love. The wild! I'm not sure Tristan can go since he's in the middle of that villa deal in the south of France, but the rest of us are good to go. What time should we pick you up?"

"I can be ready in an hour. All I need to do is shower, put my hair in a ponytail, and throw on my clothes and sneakers and I'll be ready for the wild."

"Then I'll get the kids ready and inform Cara that we're going to the zoo. See you in a little bit!"

Nearly ninety minutes later, I watched as Jensen pulled a brand new black Chevy Suburban up to in front of my building and Nina poked her head out of one of the back windows. Her hair pulled up in a ponytail like mine, she looked like she used to when we went to classes together.

Bounding down the stairs, I joked, "New wheels? What happened to riding in luxury?"

"Get in and see what kind of luxury this baby has," she said with a grin.

I climbed in the other side and saw the three kids in their car seats in the last row behind us and Cara sitting up in the front seat with Jensen. Loaded with all the bells and whistles, the new Stone family vehicle was definitely luxury.

"Hi guys!" Reaching back, I tapped on each child's knee. "Tressa, Diana, and Ethan. The three musketeers. How are my favorite kiddos?"

All three giggled and said my name as best they could with Ethan saying it clearest. As Jensen pulled away from the curb, I turned to face Nina. "This is nice. What made you guys get an SUV?"

"The last time Cara and I took the kids out it became perfectly clear that with all their stuff and the three car seats that we needed something more than the Town Car. So we got this the other day. Pretty nice, huh?"

"I'd say so. You Stones know how to travel. But I thought maybe this was a sign you were adding to your family."

Nina reacted to my bombshell of a question by opening her eyes wide, like I'd just announced I had met a Martian. "Uh, no. For now, three's enough. We're quite happy with the kids we have."

We continued to joke around and play with the kids as we rode toward the Staten Island Zoo, a much closer attraction than the Bronx Zoo, where we took the kids last time we visited the wild. A quick trip of about a half hour and we were there, ready to see the animals and have a fun day out.

After unloading all three kids and their diaper bags with all the essentials and getting them into their strollers, we were off. It didn't take long for Nina to bring up Monique, who I was trying to forget about for a day, and as we watched the foxes play in their attraction, she asked, "How did you escape spending the day with your future sister-in-law today?"

"I lied. I'm not above that if it means I get to spend time with you guys."

"From what you told me in the car yesterday, she's a real piece of work. Will you be living near her when you move to Dallas?"

That was a good question. I hadn't thought about it, and Brock hadn't mentioned if we'd be living close enough to her for us to have the chance to spend time together. I hoped not.

My brain couldn't withstand much more of her one track mind focused on shopping.

But I didn't want Nina to know I didn't exactly like Brock's sister, so I smiled and shook my head. "No, she lives far enough away that we won't be spending a lot of time together."

Bending down to give Ethan his sippy cup, Nina winked at me. "Good. I was about to get jealous thinking she was going to take my place."

"Are you crazy? She could never take your place. No one can. You're my best friend, Nina."

We walked toward the leopard habitat, and I thought about how I'd just lied to her about Monique. I didn't like lying, but especially not to her. She was my best friend, and unlike virtually everyone else in the world, I could trust Nina.

Desperately wanting to share my news about eloping in only a few days, I leaned over as I kids ooohhed and ahhhed over the leopards and whispered, "Brock and I are eloping this weekend. I promised him I wouldn't tell anyone, but I can't hold it in any longer. But promise me you won't tell anyone, other than Tristan, of course."

Nina's mouth fell open and for a few moments she couldn't speak. Finally, she said, "What? This weekend? But we have an appointment to get fitted for my matron of honor dress next month. Why are you two in such a rush? Are you pregnant? You just said yesterday that you aren't really the motherly type, so what's going on?"

I gently touched her shoulder, hoping to calm her down before everyone around us started staring. "No, it's nothing like that. Brock came up with the idea, actually. He doesn't want to wait, so I said yes and we're going down to his place in Hilton Head this weekend. You're still going to be my matron of honor at the big wedding ceremony just as we planned. Nothing's changed."

"Nothing's changed? How can you say that? I'm not going to be there for your real wedding day! What about your parents and your brother and sister? What about your grandmother? Jordan, she's going to have a coronary if she finds out you got married months before the day she gets to see you walk down the aisle!"

"It's not that big a deal. I thought you'd understand of all people, Nina. You're all about the romance, and what's more romantic than running off and eloping with the man you love?"

That what I was doing didn't involve the man I loved in the way I was making it sound was another lie, but at least it calmed her down. God, I seemed to be all about the lying lately. What was I turning into?

Cara wisely began to guide the children toward the next area as Nina and I followed. For her part, she was the best friend I probably didn't deserve at that moment, and after a minute or so, she gave me that classic Nina smile that told me everything was okay between us.

"I get it. I just wish I could be there. Why does everything with Brock have to be so far away all the time?"

"I'm happy you're good with this, Nina. And don't worry. The big day will still be great. I'll make sure of it."

"Of course it will be. I didn't mean to say it wouldn't be

anything less than incredible. Just promise me you won't become like Monique, okay? Promise me you'll always be down-to-earth Jordan and you won't let anyone change you."

"I promise. No one's changing me, so you're stuck with this girl."

"Good."

✧   ✧   ✧

HOURS AFTER NINA AND THE kids dropped me off, Brock called like he did every night. Happy to hear from him, I began to tell him about my day but he cut me off.

"I'm sending my driver to pick you up. I want to see you."

Thrilled that he'd decided to change his mind about us not being together before Friday when we eloped, I said, "I can't wait! I've missed you, Brock."

"I'll see you in a little while. My car should be there in a few minutes."

His statement confused me. "You sent it already? How did you know I'd be home?"

"Where else should you be?"

A nervous laugh escaped my lips. Should be? Why should I be anywhere? We hadn't made plans for tonight. Why would he expect me to be home just waiting for him?

The driver arrived less than five minutes later and just under an hour later I was standing in Brock's living room happy to see him but unsure by the cold expression he wore if he was as happy to see me.

Folding his arms, he cleared his throat and frowned. "Jordan, why didn't you go with my sister today? She was offended by your choosing to go with your friend instead. I thought we talked about you having to let go of your friends when we got married."

His unhappiness with my wish to spend time with Nina stung, and I instantly became defensive. "We're not married yet, Brock, and I've spent every day with Monique since she arrived in New York. One day with my friend isn't a crime."

"Don't you care about how you made her feel? She's going to be family, Jordan. It's not okay to brush her off like that."

"I wasn't trying to brush her off. I'm sorry if she and you felt like that's what I was doing, but I wanted to enjoy a summer day and shopping isn't what I call fun. We always do what she wants to do. If I thought she'd want to go enjoy a day at the zoo or the park, I would have asked her."

Brock remained silent, his face completely placid, but I knew by the look in his eyes that he was displeased. Finally, he said, "Jordan, my sister feels slighted. I think you owe her an apology."

Something in his voice told me that this wasn't a request. I didn't want to fight with him about this, though. Monique was going to be my sister-in-law, not my ruler. All I could hope was that she wouldn't be around much once we were married.

"I'll be sure to say I'm sorry when we hang out tomorrow."

"She's already left to return home."

I walked toward him and slipped my arms around his waist. Looking up into his hazel eyes, I smiled. "I'm sorry, Brock. I'm used to spending my summer days outside, and I missed that. I never meant to offend her."

My apology made his expression soften, and he kissed me lightly on the tip of my nose. "What am I going to do with you? We're so different. Sometimes I forget who you really are."

"I'm just an average American girl. Perfectly average."

He gently pushed my hair off my face and pressed a kiss onto my forehead. "You're anything but average, Jordan. Someday soon you'll see that."

I slid my hands down the front of his shirt and began tugging it out of his pants, wanting more than just vague compliments after being apart for so long. Thinner than I usually liked the men I dated to be, he still had an attractive body and at that moment I wanted to feel it against me without clothes between us.

But he held my hands still to stop me. "Not now. I have a lot of work to do before Friday."

I looked up at him, hurt by his rejection. "We don't have to go for a marathon. Just a little to take the edge off our loneliness. I know you have to be as lonely as I am, aren't you?"

Brock took a step back from me and tucked his shirt back into his pants. "I wish I could, Jordan. I really do. But I have to keep my focus on work—my eyes on the prize, so to speak. It's okay, though. Once we're married, there will be all the time in the world for us to be together."

I didn't understand how that could be true since his job would still require him to work all the time, but even if I wanted to ask him about it, I couldn't since he already had begun guiding me toward the front door.

"Do you have to get back to work so soon? I was hoping we could spend some time together."

With a smile, he shook his head. "I wish I could, sweetheart, but I still have one more project to complete before we can run off and get married."

"Have you taken care of all the necessities? We're going to need a marriage license, two witnesses, and rings. We haven't done anything together about any of those."

Brock kissed the top of my head and hugged me to him. "Not to worry. We can get the license on Friday, and I've taken care of the rings. As for witnesses, I'm sure we'll be able to find two people to stand for us there. Just remember to bring your birth certificate."

Feeling like I was getting the bum's rush, I pushed down my bruised feelings and just smiled, reminding myself that the man I was marrying was busy running a multinational business and I'd have to get used to life being like this. For all I was receiving in return, this compromise surely wasn't that bad.

Even if it felt that way at the moment.

"Okay. I can't wait until Friday, Brock. I've missed you."

I slid my arms around his neck and pulled him to me. Kissing him with all the desire I hoped we'd share soon, for one of the first times I felt him truly return that desire to me. Brock had never been the kind of man I'd call a passionate lover, but now as he kissed me goodbye, I felt something different in him.

He quickly pulled away and his demeanor returned to that far cooler person he usually was, though. "I'll see you at your apartment at noon on Friday."

I wanted to say I loved him, but the coolness in his expression made me stop before the words came out. So I just nodded. "Friday. See you then."

BROCK'S DRIVER TOOK ME BACK to my apartment, and as I sat in my living room watching TV, I couldn't help but feel more alone than I ever had, even though I'd finally gotten to see my fiancé and it was just days until we ran away to become husband and wife. I couldn't put my finger on why, but I felt lonely.

I thought about calling Nina or one of my friends from school, but all of them were married women happily spending time with their husbands and children. I should have been used to it. I'd been the only single girl in my circle of friends for a while, but on beautiful summer nights like tonight when all I could think of was how nice it would be to share a drink with someone as we talked and laughed about old times, the solitude of my life pressed down on me like a weight on my chest.

When life gets you down, sometimes the best person to talk to is your mother, so I called her since I had to get my birth certificate from her anyway. She answered immediately, and just hearing her voice made me feel better.

"Hi Mom."

"Hi honey. I'm surprised to hear from you tonight. I thought you'd be with that fiancé of yours."

"No, he's working," I said, trying unsuccessfully to sound happy about being alone again.

"Well, what's going on? You sound down."

"Nothing. Just tired. I called because I need my birth certificate."

For a long moment, the phone fell silent. When she finally spoke, my mother sounded distinctly distant. "Birth certificate? Hmmm…I'm not sure where it is. I'd have to look. When do you need it for?"

As had become my habit, I lied to yet another person I cared for. "I need it this week for something at school."

Another long pause and then my mother said, "I'll look for it in the morning. I can just send a copy of it to whoever needs it like I did when you first needed it for your job. The lady at the education office said they were fine with that."

Great. Now I had to lie again. "Oh, I think they need to see me with it this time, Mom. I was thinking I could take the train out tomorrow to get it. We can have dinner together."

Quickly, she answered, "No, no. We won't be home tomorrow. We're leaving early and won't be back until late."

"But you just said you were going to look for it tomorrow. I really need it as soon as possible and it's probably a good idea that I have things like that with me now."

"We're having the carpets treated tomorrow, so that won't work. I have to go, honey. Your father is calling for me, so let me go. I'll look for it and let you know when I find it, okay?"

"Is everything okay, Mom? I know you didn't want to

give me my birth certificate before because you were afraid I'd lose it, but you know I've gotten much better with keeping things organized since I left school."

"I promise I'll look for it. I'll talk to you later."

Damn, this was the second time that night someone had given me the bum's rush. I was beginning to get a complex.

"Maybe I'll just go out to the Hartford County courthouse and get it myself. I don't want to bother you every time I need my birth certificate. You can keep the original one safe with you just in case. Sound good?"

In a panicked voice, she said, "No! I mean, you don't have to do that. I'll make sure I find it. Your father is still calling for me, Jordan, and you know how he is when he finds something he wants me to see on TV. I'll call you in the morning, okay?"

"Mom, is everything okay? Is Dad all right?"

She sighed into the phone. "Everything's fine, Jordan. I just don't want to see you making the trip all the way up to Hartford if you don't have to."

In truth, I didn't relish the idea of spending four hours of my day trekking up there and back just to get my birth certificate, but I had no choice. If I didn't get it from my mother, I had to get it from the state or I wouldn't be able to marry Brock when we eloped in just a few days.

"Okay, Mom. It's all good. Call me tomorrow and let me know when I can come up for it."

"Okay, honey. I'll talk to you then. Love you."

She ended the call before I could tell her I loved her too.

Talking to my mother had alleviated my loneliness for a

few minutes, albeit replacing it with concern about my parents. Something was definitely wrong with my mother. The woman organized things like no one else. Martha Stewart could take lessons on organizing from my mother. The idea of her not knowing exactly where my birth certificate was, which she'd protected all my life like it was the Rosetta Stone, was ludicrous.

I'd just have to make the trip out to Hartford the next day and get it there. The problem was I didn't want to. And there was the truth of it. I didn't want to make the effort to get the one thing needed for me to be able to marry Brock.

I sipped on one of the beers I'd bought the night before and hoped it would help me forget how much I wished I had someone there with me. As much as I didn't want to admit it, the truth was it wasn't Brock who I wished sat next to me on the couch in my tiny living room. My attempt to seduce him at his apartment had been more an expression of just wanting to feel something with him instead of a true desire to be with him in particular.

I knew why I was feeling like this. Damn Gage! It was because of him that I couldn't even convince myself that the compromises I had been so prepared to accept to end my loneliness weren't okay anymore.

Why couldn't he had just stayed away and let me live my life, no matter how lacking it was?

Standing, I walked over to my front window and looked out to see if he was nearby watching over me. People stood out on the sidewalks on both sides of the streets talking and laughing, but there was no sign of him.

When I wanted to see Gage, he was never close. When I didn't want to see him and wished to just pretend I didn't love him anymore, he was all around me. It was the story of us.

But I didn't want it to be that anymore.

I slipped my engagement ring off my finger and placed it in a drawer in the table near the window. Grabbing my phone, I texted him and hoped wherever he was that he'd understand.

Do you remember that July night we sat in Sunset Park and looked out at the city?

It was the first time we talked about a future together. I'd never forget that night. The sun had gone down and the sky still had tinges of orange and purple left over from the sunset. It looked like someone had painted a picture just for us, and as we stared up at it, my head on his shoulder, he bent down and kissed me on the top of my head.

"I can't imagine life without you, you know that?"

We'd never talked about anything but the present, making no plans and keeping everything light and fun. We'd just said the L word earlier that day, and his mention of a future together unnerved me. I had no idea how to react, but as Gage gently ran his fingers through my hair, something came over me and for the first time ever, I didn't feel scared at the idea of letting a man know I didn't want to imagine life without him either.

And when the words came out they sounded more right than anything else I'd ever said before in my life.

"I don't want to imagine life without you, Gage. I love what we are."

He kissed the top of my head again and whispered, "Then I guess you're stuck with me because I'm not going anywhere."

If only that had been the truth.

I closed my eyes and tried to remember how wonderful it had felt to feel his arms around me as we sat there in silence, the two of us finally able to express the love we'd felt for so long. I missed that.

I missed him. I missed how he made me feel like no man had ever been able to before.

My phone vibrated against my leg, and I looked down to see a text from him responding to mine.

Look out the window again.

I did as he said and saw him standing in the shadows right where he'd been the night before. Then another text made my phone vibrate and my heart skipped a beat.

Open the door.

CHAPTER FIFTEEN

JORDAN

GAGE WALKED PAST ME AS I held my front door open and stopped when he reached the kitchen doorway. Smiling, he said, "I'd love one of those beers, if you haven't drank them all."

"Drank them all? What am I, some kind of alcoholic?"

His blue eyes sparkled and he laughed. "You had two last night. I figured you might have had a few more to make you text me tonight."

Shaking my head, I walked to the refrigerator, grazing his muscular chest with my shoulder as I passed. Grabbing a beer, I handed it to him. "Nope. Just one. No drunk texting for this girl tonight."

"That's good to know. Very good to know."

We stood there staring at each in silence, and I wondered what I was doing. What did he have that made me incapable of forgetting him?

"I was happy to see your text."

Gage's voice was low and deep, like always, but it felt like silk sliding over my skin now. I tried to contain my excitement at having him so close, but it was hard.

"I was just thinking about that night. You know, nothing in particular. The sunset. I guess tonight just reminded me of then."

He took a gulp of his beer and I watched his Adam's apple bob as he swallowed. The action had a raw masculinity to it that touched me deep inside and made my breath catch in my chest.

"I remember that night. Actually do you know what I remember most about that night?"

Wanting so badly to know the answer, I squeaked out, "No." I cleared my throat and asked, "What is it?"

He walked toward me and stopped just inches away. Looking down at me, he slid his tongue over his gorgeous lower lip and grinned. "How your hair smelled. Like vanilla. Warm and sexy, like you."

I closed my eyes to hide from his inexorable gaze that felt like he was staring right into the deepest, darkest depths of me. "Don't say things like that...when you're close like this it's no good."

His thumb brushed my cheek as he tucked a lock of hair behind my ear. "All I said was the truth. Warm and sexy is exactly who you are, Jordan."

Shivering from his touch even as a bead of sweat trickled down my neck, I squeezed my eyes shut, sure I shouldn't be doing this. "Gage...I...maybe you should go."

"Is that what you really want?" he asked as his fingertip lightly traced the path the bead of sweat had taken down between my breasts. "You didn't text me just to send me away, Jordan. Open your eyes and look at me if you plan on telling me to leave."

I did as he commanded and saw him looking at me like he used to. There was always something so sensual in his eyes when we were alone back when we were together, and as my eyes met his, there it was again, making me want him even more than I already did.

"So you were about to tell me to leave?" he asked with sex lacing every word.

"No," I heard myself say as I struggled not to slide my hands up under his t-shirt to feel the taut muscles I knew were hidden just underneath the blue cotton fabric.

"Good."

"It's not good, Gage. You make it hard to think straight. I shouldn't be doing this with you."

He angled his hips slightly forward and I felt the gun he always carried press against my lower ribs. Our bodies barely touched, but it was enough to send a shot of electricity straight to my core. I wanted him to kiss me so much.

"Doing what, Jordan? We're just talking here."

Trying to change the subject and regain some control, I looked down at his hip and said, "Still with the gun, huh? Is that necessary?"

"If it means I can protect you better, then yes, it's necessary."

"It makes me nervous."

He grinned at me like he always did when I made a big deal about his gun. "I've been around guns since the day I was born, Jordan. You know this. I come from Wyoming. Everyone grows up around guns there. You have no reason to be nervous."

I didn't want to admit it to him, but I'd never really been uncomfortable because of the gun. Bringing it up was just a way of putting off the inevitable, no matter how much I wanted it.

"Now getting back to us doing something here. I've got some ideas about what we could be doing instead of wasting time with words."

"Never did think much of talking, did you?"

He ran the pad of his thumb against my bottom lip and shook his head. "I'm a bigger fan of actions. You can trust them more."

"Typical Gage," I said as he leaned in just an inch away from me.

"Stop talking, Jordan. There are so many better things you could be doing with that beautiful mouth of yours."

I felt like I couldn't breathe as memories of my mouth on him filled my head, but I croaked out one word to stave off what I knew was just seconds away from happening. "Like?"

He didn't bother to answer, and when he pressed his mouth to mine in a kiss as incredible as any he'd ever given me, my legs felt like they might give out. His lips were so soft, yet he kissed me like I was his to do with as he wished.

And what he wished to do with me I wanted so badly.

My head swam from the feeling of him being everywhere around me as he took me into his arms and pulled me to his body so hard and strong. He buried his right hand in my hair, sending chills down my back in the nearly ninety degree heat that continued to cling to the city, and placed his other hand on the small of my back to hold me to him.

His cock, already hard as a rock, pressed against the front of my shorts through his jeans, thrilling me with a sense of what was to come. This was quintessential Gage—raw, earthy, and commanding our lovemaking from beginning to end.

I'd missed this so fucking much.

He slid his lips down my neck to the hollow at the base of my throat and moaned, "You feel so good. It's been too long."

"Yes," I murmured, unable to think of anything but that single word for what he brought out in me. I wanted to be that sensual being he fostered in me again. For so long, I'd been closed off and fearful, and with Brock those hadn't been changed by his timid, yet perfectly acceptable lovemaking.

I wanted more, though. I wanted this. I wanted what Gage offered.

But as he dragged his tongue over the sweat-damp skin of my neck, a thought sprung up in my mind. I'd become closed off because of him and what he'd done. Pushing his head away, I looked into his eyes full of need for me.

"You made me afraid of love. You know that? When you broke up with me, you tore me in half."

Knitting his brows, he frowned at my mention of that night and the phone call that changed me. "I know. I can never erase what I did, but I want to start making up for it right now. Let me make up for it, Jordan, so you can see you can trust me."

"I'm not that same person anymore, Gage."

His hands moved up to my cheeks, and cradling my face, he shook his head. "Don't say that. You're still the woman I fell crazy in love with. Don't let my stupid mistake change what's so beautiful about you—that unshakable belief that love is worth it, no matter what."

I wanted to say that I'd only really felt that with him, but before I could form the words, he kissed me again and any thoughts of anything but how much I wanted to feel him inside me vanished in a haze of desire and need.

Playfully flicking the tip of his tongue against mine, he teased my mouth as his strong hands slid under my t-shirt to cup my breasts I'd thankfully chosen not to hide beneath a bra. With every caress of my skin with his hard hands, my body yearned for him more and more.

But I had to know something first before I surrendered my heart and body to him again. Leaning back, I savored the taste of beer he'd left on my tongue and pressed my fingertip to his lips.

"I need to know who you've been with since we broke up. How many women since me?"

His face grew serious, and I waited to hear his answer, afraid to find out that he'd tried to forget me through a series of meaningless fucks or even worse, a relationship with someone. Either would hurt, but Gage being who he was with someone day in and day out would crush me.

His eyes narrowed like he was in pain from what he had to say, and in a low voice he said, "None."

"Don't lie to me. That's not what we were all about, so don't start lying now because you want to sleep with me."

Wincing, he repeated his answer. "None. I didn't want anyone else, and it wouldn't have been fair to another woman.

I was still in love with you."

"Was?"

"Was. Am. Will forever be."

"Jesus, Gage. When you say things like that, I can't think straight."

"Good. No more talking or thinking. Just doing," he said, the serious expression gone now and replaced by that sexy as all hell look he always wore when we made love.

Scooping me up in his arms, he turned around and carried me to the bedroom with a sense of purpose I couldn't help but love. No other man in the world knew how to handle me like Gage did.

He lay me down on the bed and as I watched him strip his shirt over his head, I couldn't help but be turned on. His body hadn't changed at all. God, he was still as built as ever. My gaze traveled over the muscular peaks and valleys of his torso down to his ruggedly cut abs settled in between hipbones and creating a delicious V that seemed to point directly to his hard cock.

"You just going to lay there staring at my body or are you waiting for me to undress you?"

"The first one. I'd forgotten how much I love looking at you without clothes on."

Tossing his t-shirt at me, he said, "Oh yeah? The second half of the show begins now, so settle in."

I threw his shirt on the chair in the corner and watched in rapt attention as he removed his gun from its holster at his waist and slowly walked around to the opposite side of the bed to place it on the nightstand. Returning to stand in front of me, he slid his jeans and boxer briefs down his legs to reveal his cock settled against his stomach, hard and ready to go. Without missing a beat, he hooked his fingers in the waist of my shorts and tugged them and my panties off my body, throwing them on the chair to join his shirt.

As I slipped my tank top over my head, Gage teased the inside of my thighs with his tongue, sending my body into overdrive. Christ, he had a magical tongue! His touch was always perfect—not too light and never too heavy, he knew exactly how to make every inch he reached come alive. My eyes rolled back into my head with each inch he moved toward my needy pussy.

"Don't look away, Jordan," he groaned from between my legs. "I want you to see me worship you like no other man has."

Oh God, when he said things like that I didn't want to be with anyone else. I didn't want to settle for someone who could give me security. I only wanted to spend the rest of my life with him, the only man who'd ever made me truly believe in love.

His warm breath drifted over my skin, sending shockwaves deep inside me. I wanted to feel his gorgeous mouth with its perfect lips on me, giving me pleasure like only he could, so I lifted my hips off the bed and watched him stare up at me with a devilish look in his eyes.

"I knew that woman I loved was still inside you," he whispered as he kissed his way closer and closer to my core, all the time keeping his gaze locked on mine.

"You're driving me crazy, Gage."

Licking his lips, he grinned. "Good. You should be crazy when a man is about to lick your pussy."

My eyes rolled back in my head at the mere mention of what he was about to do, and then I felt the tip of his tongue touch my needy clit and the world ceased to exist except for him and me and the sensations tearing through me with every second his mouth was on my body.

I had no idea how much time passed as he worshipped me and I reveled in how much I loved the attention he lavished over me. I'd missed this so much. No other man I'd ever met made love like Gage Varo.

Slow. Like he had the rest of time to kiss and adore every inch of me.

Intense. Like his entire focus was on pleasing me.

Raw. Like he knew no boundaries and possessed no defenses when it came to sex.

And I loved every second of it.

My orgasm began to uncoil deep inside me as Gage's tongue flicked against my swollen clit. Stuffing my hands into his hair, I tugged hard to keep him right there as my release overwhelmed me. His hands gripped tightly on my hips as his mouth rode me through every shudder and tremor until finally I released his head and he sat back with a look of satisfaction on his face.

"God, you taste so fucking good."

"You always say that."

He licked his lips and grinned. "You always taste good."

I knew what he wanted now and I wanted to give it to him. Sliding off the bed, I kneeled down in front of him and smiled, knowing how much he loved this. Before Gage, I'd never known how erotic going down on a man could be, mainly because it was always so much work but also because no man before him had made it feel sexy. Mostly it had just felt like a chore.

But Gage was different. His raw sensuality made the act more than just his cock sliding in and out of my mouth. And even though it terrified me to be so under a man's control, I loved it.

All the time apart hadn't made me forget how particular he was with this part of sex. Almost ritual with his tastes, he always stood and I always kneeled in front of him. It was as much about power and control for him as it was wanting to please him for me. While with other men I would have balked at the idea of getting on my knees like this, for Gage it only made the act better.

Like he always had, he stared down at me, his sensual gaze focused on my mouth, and then wrapping his hand around his cock, he slowly fed it into my mouth. Never in my life had anything felt more erotic than when I felt the tip of his cock touch my lips and saw the expression of pure pleasure wash over his face.

Unlike in every porn movie I'd ever seen, I was not to use my hands. I was also forbidden from bobbing up and down on him, as I had always done with other men. What he loved was being in total control until the very end, and what I loved was giving him that.

He set the pace, slow at first as he inched his thick cock in and out of my mouth, his hips barely thrusting forward and his hands buried in my hair gently tugging my head down on him, and then faster as he moved toward coming. It was freeing in one sense and entirely submitting in another. While I did none of what I'd always thought of as the work, I was his to completely do as he liked.

And what he liked was watching me take his cock inside me as fucked my mouth. There was no other way to describe it.

Hands clasped behind my back, I watched as he gradually moved from slowly easing in and out of me to genuinely fucking me that way, perfectly enraptured by how masculine he looked above me. When his movements became shorter and rougher, his cock jabbing in and out of my mouth, his fingers caressed my jaw like a sign he loved what I gave him and wanted to show how much it meant to him.

Never much for words, he spoke little as I knelt before him sucking his cock. Sometimes he'd close his eyes and moan low and deep as I'd flick my tongue around the base. Other times he remained silent, his eyes telling me how much pleasure I was giving him.

He was never more raw than at that moment when he cupped my chin and slid his palm down to tenderly squeeze the front of my throat. He could have roughly thrust his cock to the back of my mouth and I would be powerless to do anything with his hand holding me, but he never did. Always in control of himself and me, Gage knew how hard and fast to fuck me without going too far.

As he inched closer to his release, he groaned and spoke for the first time. "I'm getting close. Just a few more times…"

His words trailed off as I wrapped my hand around the base of his cock, touching him for the first time. Each time he gave me that tiny bit of control, and it meant so much to know that even as he had all the power, he could share some with me and still be more powerful than any man I'd ever been with.

Gage tightened his hands in my hair as he came, the purely masculine taste of him on my tongue as I took everything he had. His face twisted into a look of pain followed by a look of satisfaction, and then he smiled. In the quiet moment when he slid his cock out of my mouth, he gently ran his fingers along my jawline and the outline of my mouth, sensually visiting the place that had given him so much pleasure.

"Come here," he said as he pulled me up off my knees and kissed me full on the lips.

No other man had ever done that after I'd gone down on them, but that was Gage. Every part of sex between us was shared without limits or boundaries. Of all the things about him, I adored that the most. He gave everything of himself to me when we made love, and I wanted to be that kind of woman for him.

"I missed that," he whispered against my lips. "The feel of your mouth on my cock is like nothing else in the world."

"For a man who doesn't like to talk much, you say the sexiest things," I teased.

Gage groaned and pushed his hips forward so his still hard cock slid through my wet pussy. "Enough talking. We have better things to do."

He slid his hands down over my breasts to my hips and

then to my ass, cupping it as he lifted me off the ground. His cock waited for me, and I wrapped my legs around his waist as he slowly eased into my body, filling me completely.

My fingernails dug into his muscular shoulders, and I moaned in his ear as his cock grazed that perfect deep inside me, "Oh God, Gage…Faster…fuck me faster. Please…"

Kissing me hard, he squeezed my ass in his strong hands and pushed into me over and over, grunting with each thrust. His hard body pressed against mine, crushing me, but I loved it. I wanted everything about him.

His hardness. His silence. His rawness. It intoxicated me and made me need him more than I ever thought possible.

Our bodies were covered in sweat from the temperature of my apartment and the heat between us as he fucked me like a man never had before. Every inch of my body pulsated with the pleasure he gave me.

I dug my heels into his back to keep him inside me as I felt the first twinge of my orgasm begin. I wanted every inch of him filling me when I came. With one last hard plunge into my pussy, his cock sent me tumbling over that sweet edge and my body surrendered to him once again.

I was his, completely and without regret, and I knew I'd never be able to pretend not to love him again.

Falling against him, I struggled to find the strength to keep up as he continued to push into me. Wanting to give him what he'd given me, I kissed him long and deep and then clutching his neck, said in his ear, "I love you. Don't ever leave me again."

Gage tugged my hair and kissed me as his cock twitched

the first of his release. "Never again. I promise. Never again."

Sated, we fell back onto the bed and I couldn't help but smile. He may not have ever had much to say, but sometimes when he did speak, he said all the right things.

Chapter Sixteen

Gage

THE NOISE OUTSIDE FROM THE street below woke me, and I opened my eyes to see Jordan's head on my shoulder, her long blond hair covering her face. Lifting my right arm, I looked at my watch to see it was already almost ten a.m. Ordinarily, I'd jump out of bed and race to get a shower if I overslept this late, but this morning I didn't want to move from my place next to her.

The place I was meant to be.

I lightly ran my hand over her shoulder, loving the feel of her soft blond hair against my rough palm. It felt like silken strands teasing my skin.

Lost in how happy I was to be lying there next to her, I didn't notice her wake up and look at me. In a sleepy voice, she said, "Good morning. How long have you been up?"

"Not long. Just a few minutes."

"Do you have to leave? I imagine it's pretty late, right?"

"No," I said with a smile. "I was thinking I'd stay right here with you."

Jordan rewarded me with a huge smile. "Oh yeah? I like that. I know you have a business to run."

I kissed her to stop her talking and then pulled her close to me. "My business is my work and I have very competent people to help me with that so I can be in the arms of the woman I adore when I'm lucky enough to get the chance."

Pursing her lips, she planted a light kiss on my mouth. "Well, when you say it that way... And when did you become so good with the words, Mr. Varo?"

"Sometimes I'm good with them."

Jordan rolled me onto my back and threw her leg over my hips. Resting her chin on my chest, she looked up at me and asked, "So what should we do today? It's a gorgeous Thursday and you've decided to take the day off, so we should do something."

"I thought staying right here all day might be good," I said with a smile. "Maybe get up to grab something to eat and then come right back here?"

She looked up toward the ceiling as if she was thinking about my idea and shook her head. "We need to get out and enjoy life, Gage Varo. No more walking up and down Fifth Avenue with some obsessive shopper for me. I want to throw a Frisbee, take a run—do something that makes me feel alive."

Nuzzling her neck, I groaned, "Only if we promise one another that we'll be back in this spot tonight in each other's arms."

Jordan pushed my head back and ran her hands through my hair. Looking deeply into my eyes, she nodded. "I promise. Every night from now on we can be here together."

As she finished speaking, her expression grew darker and

she turned away from me. I didn't know what I'd said or done, but she was different all of a sudden.

"What is it? What's wrong?"

She sighed and said quietly, "I have something I have to do before I can do anything with you out in public."

"Oh." That something tore me up inside. She had to see another man.

Sitting up next to me, she took my hands in hers and brought them to her lips in a kiss. "It's only right, Gage. Brock's never been awful or mean to me. He doesn't deserve to see the evidence that I'm leaving him on the street as he's going out to lunch or traveling to a meeting. He's not a bad man. He's just not someone I want to marry."

"I get it."

I didn't like it, but I got it. Jordan wanted to treat him with respect, and I understood. It was who she was, and I loved her for it. My jealous side didn't give a fuck about how he found out she was leaving him, though.

She caressed my cheek and gave me one of those Jordan smiles that never failed to make me give in. "It won't take long. He's not the type to fight it."

"Then he's fucking crazy because he should be fighting to keep you. Any man who doesn't see that doesn't deserve you. But don't do it today. Let's have today be about us."

"Okay. Tomorrow will work. So I guess you get your wish to stay in today."

I wrapped my arms around her and pulled her down on top of me. "Good. I say we stay in bed until we get hungry and then and only then do we get up. And once we eat, we get right back here."

"I like the way you think, Gage Varo."

BY FOUR O'CLOCK IN THE afternoon, we'd gotten up only once to snack on some potato chips for a few minutes before we headed back to bed. It was like old times between us when we'd lay in bed all day on a Sunday and watch movies on TV. Hours would go by without a word spoken from either one of us, but we never needed to fill our time with constant talking. It was one of the greatest things about being with her.

"Want to watch one of the X-Men movies? Between HBO and Starz, I think we have our choice between like three of them."

"Always a woman after my own heart. You pick your favorite."

As she scrolled through the choices, finally picking X-Men First Class, I leaned back against the headboard and watched her, still in disbelief that I was there again in her bed spending the day with her. I'd dreamed of this very place and the two of us together virtually every day since we'd broken up.

Sometimes when I thought about being with her again I couldn't believe it would ever happen. When those doubts crept in, all I could do was tell myself that I had nothing to lose by never giving up. Life without her wasn't much of a life at all. It was more going through the motions than anything else.

An existence but not much more.

"Did you hear me?" she asked as she pushed on my

shoulder, shaking me from my daydreaming.

"Sorry. What did you say?"

"You looked like you were a million miles away. I just asked if you wanted me to make an iced tea run before the movie begins."

"How far do you have to go?" I asked, twirling the ends of her hair around my finger and not wanting her to leave for long.

"Just to the kitchen. I'll be back before you can say Magneto."

"Okay. If you're going for a drink, grab me one. Hanging out in bed all day makes a man build up a thirst."

She stood from the bed and slipped my t-shirt over her head. "I can see that," she said with a giggle. Bending over to kiss me, she joked, "All that lying there and everything."

I tugged the bottom of my shirt and pulled her close to kiss her again. "Actually, I'm planning ahead for later."

"Later, huh? Well, I better hurry then. I don't want to miss what you have planned."

"You won't. It can't happen without you."

Jordan trotted out to the kitchen, leaving me naked in bed as the first scenes of the movie began to play. I loved how comfortable we were able to be with one another again. No other woman had ever made me want to be playful like she could. The lightness in her seeped into me after all those months of being without her, and I felt myself changing even after only less than a day together. The darkness that had made me think I'd lost her for good slowly began to subside, leaving me hopeful that this time we'd make it.

The ice cubes clanking against the glasses in her hands brought me back to the present. She placed them on the nightstand and sat down next to me, snuggling against my chest.

"What did I miss?" she asked as she slipped her arms around me.

I squeezed her to me and whispered in her ear, "I know you've seen this no less than five times. How could you miss anything?"

Turning in my hold, she smiled back at me. "Five times? Multiply that by five, at least."

"Then I'm thinking we should focus on something else."

"Got anything in mind?"

"Yep. I've got a few things in mind, once I get that shirt off you."

Her eyebrows shot up as she pretended to be surprised. "Oh yeah? Well, let me help you out with that so you and I can get going on what you have in mind."

She wriggled out of my t-shirt and straddled me. Instinctively, I slid my hands down her sides and lifted my hips off the bed. My cock, already hard, slid through her wet pussy, grazing her clit, and I gave her nipple a swipe with my tongue.

"Figure out what I have in mind yet?" I asked as she closed her eyes and a tiny moan escaped her lips.

Biting her lip, she moaned again, this time louder. "By the time we're done, I'm not going to be able to walk, Gage."

"Do you want me to stop?"

Her eyes flew open, and she tugged my hair hard so I returned to giving her nipple attention. "Don't stop. Please. I want to feel you inside me again."

I squeezed her hips tightly and lifted her off me to slide my cock into her. One long, slow thrust and I was seated completely in her snug cunt. Jordan arched her back as I leaned forward and dragged my tongue slowly over her skin, tasting the saltiness from the sweat between her gorgeous breasts.

Opening her eyes, she stared down at me with need filling her moss green eyes. "That feels so fucking good. I missed this."

"We just made love like two hours ago," I said with a grin, knowing what she meant.

"I missed this all that time we were apart, silly."

I slowly pressed her open with my fingers and touched the pad of my thumb against her clit, rubbing it in tiny circles. "No more talking about that. I want to see you ride my cock."

She rolled her hips and kissed me long and deep. "We're going to miss the movie, you know that, right?"

"I'm sure those X-Men won't begrudge me great sex. I'm sure they get their own fair share."

Jordan rose up and slid down on my cock. "I love this, Gage. I've missed this with you."

I knew what she meant. The sweetness and fun as we lay there joined together in the most intimate way two people could were things I'd never found with anyone else.

"Me too. It's not every woman in the world who would be okay with me making X-Men jokes while I'm balls deep inside her."

She wrapped her arms around my neck and began fucking

me in earnest. I watched her ride my cock and loved how she held nothing back. There was nothing sexier than a confident woman who knew how to fuck a man. Too many women worried about how they looked or if they were doing something right, but Jordan approached sex like she did everything else in life.

Without fear and with an enthusiasm that only made it better.

But someone so incredible deserved more than to do all the work, even if it was enjoyable for me, so I rolled her over onto her back and moaned, "Enough of that. Time to get yours."

Wrapping her legs around my waist, she dug her heels into my lower back and pulled me into her as she whimpered, "Come back. I need to feel you."

I reared back and buried myself completely inside her as she ran her fingernails across my chest, sending wisps of pain over my skin and making me want her more than I thought possible. Each plunge into her warm, wet cunt felt like heaven on earth. Every inch of my body felt the ecstasy she gave me, and as I inched her closer to coming, I felt my own release begin to build inside me.

"God, I missed you so much."

Looking down at her, I saw that sensuality I'd never found in any other woman that made me want her more than I'd ever wanted anyone. Or anything. She made me believe in good again after years of self-imposed penance that had been nothing more than loneliness. I'd closed myself off thinking I didn't deserve goodness or love, and then one day there she was looking up at me with those green eyes that never failed to enchant me and that smile of hers that could light up a room.

That smile that made me want to see her every morning when I opened my eyes and every night as she fell asleep in my arms.

And now that I had another chance, I wasn't going to let that go for anyone or anything.

Jordan gently sunk her teeth into my shoulder as her orgasm wound through her, and I held her to me, loving the feel of her giving herself to me again. When she finally stopped shuddering, I rolled onto my back and pulled her close.

Breathless, she looked up at me and asked, "Why did you stop? You didn't come yet that time."

I smoothed the blond wisps from her face and kissed her. "I know. I just felt like I wanted to lay here like this."

"Staring up at my ceiling so desperately in need of paint?" she joked.

"No. With you."

"What's the smile about?"

I hadn't even realized I was smiling until she said something about it. Being with her made me so happy I couldn't help but smile.

"Just love being here with you."

Jordan laid her head on my chest and whispered against my skin, "Promise me no matter what we'll always remember this is who we are."

She looked up at me as she waited for my answer. I wanted to believe we could remember. When life got too much and both of us found ourselves stressed out from work and the demands the world put on us, she wanted me to promise that I'd be someone who would shelter her from all that.

Gazing down into her eyes full of love, I pledged to be that man for her. "I promise. No matter what happens."

"You know I never thought we'd ever be together like this again, Gage. It seemed impossible."

I leaned forward and kissed her softly. "I know and I'm sorry about that."

Shaking her head, she smiled. "It wasn't you and what happened that made it feel impossible, though. It was me. I wasn't lying when I said I'd changed. I did. I became closed off after you left. I didn't want to feel good again because I was afraid it would just end up bad. So I just closed myself off."

"I hate hearing that. I hate knowing you changed one of the best parts of you because of what I did."

She shimmied up next to me and pressed her lips to mine in a kiss full of love. "I never thought I'd feel like that again— like my heart was open and willing to love. But then you walked through my door and everything I felt for you came rushing back and for the first time in so long, I was happy. Truly happy."

"I missed this with you. Just lying together talking. The fact that you make me smile just by being next to me."

Tracing my lips, she kissed me again. "I love it when you smile. It's ever so slightly crooked and way too damn sexy."

"I do promise to remember this is who we are, Jordan. I

don't want to forget that, no matter what happens."

She sighed and nodded. "It'll be okay tomorrow. He and I were never like we are."

Every time I thought of him with her, I felt like someone had my heart in their fist and was squeezing. I hated the idea of Jordan lying in his arms like she was with me and sharing those little things between two people that made up so much of who they were.

"I just want him out of the picture so you and I can be together again," I said as I looked away. I didn't want her to see how much I hated what she had to do in just a few hours.

But she knew me too well. Pulling my face back toward her, she gave me one of her smiles that never failed to make me love her more. "I never loved him like I loved you, Gage."

"I did this to us. I know. I just hate this whole thing with him."

"I know, but I have to do this tomorrow. I need to know you understand."

Cradling her face in my hands, I nodded, even as my heart felt like that fist was at it again tightening its hold. "I do. I hate it, but I understand it. I don't want to think about that or anyone else tonight, though. Tonight's about you and me."

"You and me then," she said sweetly.

As we made love again, I told her the words I'd never thought I'd get a chance to say again. To tell her I never stopped loving her and no matter what happened, I wasn't going to make the mistake I made before.

When she fell asleep in my arms, I silently swore to finally do what I should have done all those months ago and ask her to marry me. When you found the woman who made your life complete like she did, you married her.

And that's what I intended to do as soon as I could.

CHAPTER SEVENTEEN

JORDAN

GAGE'S ARMS HELD ME CLOSE to him as I stared out my bedroom window and thought about how I'd break the news to Brock that we wouldn't be getting married. No use in putting it off. It wasn't fair of me to drag it out because I didn't want to tell him. He deserved to know, and even though I'd delayed a day to spend it with Gage, I couldn't wait anymore.

Rolling over, I gently tapped him on the nose and smiled as he opened his eyes. He looked at me still groggy from sleep and said, "I can't think of a better thing to wake up to than your smile."

"Such a smooth talker when you want to be."

He smiled and stretched his arms behind me. "I told you I'm good with words sometimes. What are you doing up so early?"

I sighed. "I have to go to see him. We can't be together while that hangs over my head."

Gage frowned slightly and nodded, even though I knew he hated letting me go. "I know. I don't like it, but I know it has to be done."

"He's not going to cause any trouble. He's not that type of person. But even if he isn't someone who'd die for me, he deserves to be told the truth."

"What time are you going?"

"I'm going to get up now and get ready. The sooner I get it over with, the better."

He pulled me close in a hug and held me to him. "Not yet. Give me a few more minutes here with you before you go running off to another man."

I wanted to say putting it off only made it worse, but I didn't. Instead, I just lay there in Gage's arms as he pressed his lips to the top of my head and kissed me. No man wanted the woman he loved to go see another man she'd been with. I got that. But no matter how much in love with each other we were, that didn't change the fact that I couldn't intentionally hurt someone. Brock may not have been the man I wanted to marry, but he was a man who had been good to me and that counted for something more than an impersonal phone call to break it off.

"Why does it always seem like one of us is leaving?" Gage quietly asked.

Leaning back, I looked up into his eyes and saw fear. "I'm not leaving. I'm not going anywhere. I'm just doing what any decent person would do for someone they cared about. It'll be a short meeting because I doubt he'll want to spend time with a woman who just broke up with him, and then I'll be back with you."

Gage forced a smile. "I know. Just doing the decent thing. It wouldn't be right to break it off with someone without telling them why."

"I didn't mean it that way, Gage."

"I know. I just can't help but see the difference between you and me."

I kissed him lightly on the lips and cradled his face. "You believed you were doing the right thing. I can't blame you for that."

The fear that had filled his eyes morphed into sadness. "Yeah. I can, though."

"I have to go. There's no use in putting this off any longer."

He said nothing but opened his arms so I could get out of bed. I didn't want to talk about this with him. All I wanted to do was go to Brock and tell him the truth so I didn't have to feel guilty about being in love with Gage anymore.

As I walked toward the bathroom, he said in a low voice, "I'm going to head to my place. I'll have my phone with me if you need anything. Call me when you're finished and I'll meet you."

Turning around, I watched him slip his clothes back on in a way so different from when he'd stripped out of them two nights before. Then he'd been playful and sexy. Now he just looked sad.

I stopped him as he moved to walk past me. "Hey, it's okay, right? You understand, don't you?"

He hung his head and nodded. "I do. I just can't help thinking that all of this never needed to happen. If only I'd done things differently."

"Everything happens for a reason, Gage. You thought you

were protecting me. I thought I could move on after losing you, but that wasn't true. Maybe I should have never gotten involved with Brock in the first place since I still loved you. We did what we thought was right. We can't change the past, but I can do the right thing by him now and be truthful. So don't blame yourself."

"I'll be waiting to hear from you, okay? Don't make me wait too long or I might have to come charging in on my white horse because I think I have to save you."

White horse. As I kissed him goodbye and promised to call him the minute I left Brock's, I thought about what I'd said to Nina about a knight in shining armor on a white horse and how she'd found that in Tristan while I'd never found that in any man. Maybe I was wrong.

It seemed like I'd been wrong about a lot of things.

"YOU DID WHAT?" NINA EXCLAIMED into my ear.

"I slept with Gage. Now I'm going to Brock's place to tell him I can't marry him."

Nina was silent for so long I pulled the phone away from my ear to see if the call had been dropped. No, the call was still live. I waited another few moments and said, "I thought you'd be happy."

"I'm stunned. I'm thrilled. I can't believe you did it, though. Oh my God! Jordan, is everything going to be okay?"

I began pacing back and forth across the floor in my bedroom. "It will be fine. Just fine. You were the one who told me I shouldn't marry a man if I loved someone else. You said it wasn't fair to Brock. That's all I'm doing now. Being fair to

Brock."

"I know. I know. And I don't blame you. I'm just stunned about this turnaround. I didn't think you'd ever give Gage another chance, much less call off your wedding to Brock, which I don't think is a bad thing at all. He deserves a wife who loves him, not another man."

I took a deep breath and stopped pacing for a moment. "Thanks, Nina. I needed to tell someone other than Gage, who I know doesn't want to hear about me worrying about Brock's feelings."

"How are you going to do it? What are you going to say to him?"

Pacing again, I passed by my dresser mirror and looked at the woman staring back at me. When did my life become so complicated? I had no idea how I was going to tell Brock the truth. I just knew I had to.

"I don't know. How do you tell someone you're not going to marry them because you're in love with someone else?"

"I can't imagine what I'd say, Jordan. Just remember you're telling someone something they aren't expecting. And just be kind. I think that's all you can do."

Sitting down on the edge of my bed, I took a deep breath. "I've never been on this side of the breakup. I always thought it would be easier, you know? It's not. It's just as difficult, only in a different way," I said as I looked around at the place where Gage and I had made love just hours before.

"You just have to keep reminding yourself that as much as it's important to watch out for Brock's feelings, yours have to be your first priority. He's going to be hurt, but the truth is always better than a lie. I want you to remember that, Jordan."

I listened and knew she was right, even if I felt like the bad guy. "I know. It's just hard."

"Oh sweetie, I know. But it's for the best. You know it. I think you've known it for a while. You just didn't want to admit it."

What I didn't want to admit was something far worse that I couldn't even tell my best friend. I'd been so seduced by the idea that I'd have a life like hers, complete with gorgeous homes, cars, and clothes and the chance to live a life I'd only dreamed of, that I'd intentionally ignored how little there was keeping Brock and me together. I'd let myself believe that things were more important than anything else and forgotten that love was what really mattered.

"I better go, Nina. I have to get over to Brock's and get this over with. I can't put it off any more."

"Okay. I'm only a phone call away, and don't forget that I can have Jensen there for you in no time."

"Thanks. I'll call you after it's all over. At least I won't have to explain to my grandmother that I ran off and eloped instead of getting married in front of her and my whole family."

Nina chuckled. "I know your grandmother. She wouldn't have taken that explanation lightly. She may be in her seventies, but Grandma Mary is a feisty one."

"Thanks for helping me through this. I don't know what I'd do without you," I admitted, truly thankful for having Nina to talk to.

"You don't have to thank me, Jordan. I'm always here for you. I'm just happy you're finally following your heart instead of your head. Remember, good things happen to good people. You said that to me so many times, so now it's my turn to say that to you. Getting back with Gage is a good thing."

I promised again to tell Nina everything about how my meeting with Brock went and ended the call with a feeling that things were going to be okay. Telling him goodbye would be hard, but it was best for both of us.

✧   ✧   ✧

THE DOORMAN AT BROCK'S BUILDING smiled at me like he always did when I passed by him to enter the lobby, but this time I felt like a fraud when I smiled back at him. As I rode up in the elevator to the penthouse, my palms began to grow sweaty and my stomach knotted up like it did whenever I dreaded something. I hadn't felt this nervous since I had to take my teacher exams in my last year of college.

I took a deep breath to settle my nerves, and as the elevator doors opened, my heart sank at the sight of Brock standing there waiting for me with a bouquet of pink roses in his hand. I hadn't told him anything other than that I needed to see him, and he'd mistakenly believed he was meeting with his loving fiancé, not the woman who intended to drop a bomb on him.

"Jordan, I'm so happy to see you. I got your favorite flowers. I know it's been hard these past two weeks, but it's all for the best. I hope you know that."

He handed me the bouquet, and I lifted them to my nose to inhale the sweet fragrance. "Thank you, Brock. This is very nice of you."

"What did you want to talk about, or is it just that you missed me like I missed you?"

Oh, God, this was going to be much harder than I thought.

I placed the roses on the side table in his entryway and took his hand in mine. "About that. We need to talk."

"I know it's been hard, Jordan. I know and I apologize. It's just that my company is relatively new and we're at a critical point in its growth. But that doesn't mean that I haven't been thinking of you all the time in the past two weeks because I have."

We walked toward the living room as he spoke, and with each step I tried to figure out the words to say. I didn't want to be hurtful or cruel. I just wanted to tell the truth and hoped it wouldn't be as bad as I feared.

"I know, Brock. It's just that…"

All of a sudden my brain turned to mush and every thought in my head disappeared. Brock stared at me with a look that told me I was making a complete mess of this. Confused by my inability to even complete a simple sentence, he simply smiled, likely hoping to allay my discomfort.

If he only knew.

He held my hand and gently stroked my arm. "Jordan, is everything okay? You don't look well."

I didn't feel well. My stomach felt like I was about to throw up at any moment, and my head throbbed with a headache that seemed to come out of nowhere. But I had to do this, so I inhaled deeply and slowly let the air out of my lungs before I began to speak again.

"Brock, we need to talk."

The look of concern that had settled into his face instantly morphed into something closer to panic or anger. Which it was I didn't know, but this was already going off the rails quickly.

"Talk about what? We're leaving tomorrow afternoon to elope and I've handled everything for that, so I don't know what you want to talk about."

"About that. I don't think we should elope."

Brock's eyebrows knitted, and he frowned as if he were in pain. "What are you saying?"

I looked away, unable to face him as I said the words. "I can't marry you, Brock. I'm sorry."

Out of the corner of my eye, I saw the shock settle into his features. I felt his stare burn the side of my face and worried I'd never be able to look him in the eyes again. I'd never been the one to break up with someone, and all those times boyfriends had broken up with me it had all looked so easy for them.

Maybe it was, but not for me.

I may not have loved Brock like I should have to marry him, but I didn't want to be like all those guys who'd made this look like a piece of cake.

"What are you talking about, Jordan? Are you joking? I know you have a different sense of humor from mine, but I don't think this is funny."

Slowly, I turned to face him and shook my head as I

slipped the engagement ring he'd given me from my finger. "This isn't a joke. I can't marry you. I'm so sorry. You're a wonderful man and you deserve to be happy. I'm not the right woman for you, though."

The look in his eyes pleaded for me to stop saying these words. "Of course you are. You're Jordan Wright, so you must be the right woman for me."

He tried to smile at his tepid joke, but it wasn't working and he knew it. His shoulders sagged beneath his dark grey suit jacket, and his body hunched like I'd just slugged him in the gut. I recognized that look. It's the same one I'd worn every time some guy had told me I wasn't the one for him.

"I'm sorry, Brock."

Christ, my apology sounded so lacking.

"Jordan, listen to me. I love you. I know it's been hard for the last couple weeks, and I know we're polar opposites like night and day, but we can make this work. I just need you to trust me."

I saw the hope in his hazel eyes and couldn't help but feel like the world's worst person. I wanted to say the truth—that even though I'd honestly and faithfully agreed to marry him, my heart belonged to another man and always had. I hadn't known it or maybe I never wanted to admit it, but my feelings for Gage had never really gone away.

But Brock didn't deserve to hear about all that. Telling him I loved another man would only hurt him, so I told a white lie and hoped it would help him feel better about us.

"You're right, Brock. We're too different, and all that time I spent with Monique showed me that. I'm not the right woman for you. You deserve someone more like you. Like her."

He shook his head quickly. "No, no. I don't want someone like me or Monique. I love how wonderfully different you are from me. I'm so serious all the time, but you're so full of life. I want that in my life."

A noise in the bedroom made me turn my head to look at the door and whoever was in there. "I thought you were alone."

He gently took hold of my chin and turned my face back toward him. "Listen to me. We can make this work. Nothing is ever perfectly smooth sailing for any couple, right? There's too much to lose for us to break up now."

I took his hands in mine, placing the ring in his palm, and brought them to my lips in a kiss. "You have everything a woman can want, Brock. Money, status, great looks, and you're a terrific guy. You won't be alone for long, and you won't be losing much if you don't marry me."

"If I have everything a woman can want, why don't you want to marry me?" he asked with an edge to his voice that told me I hadn't succeeded in hurting him.

"I'm just not the one you want. I know you'll find the right woman and live happily ever after. You deserve that."

Brock stood and walked over toward the bar in the corner of the room. With his back to me, he said in a low, sad voice, "I can't let you go, Jordan. I just can't."

"Please know that this wasn't easy for me," I said as I walked up behind him and touched his shoulder. "I never meant to hurt you. Please know that."

He turned around to face me and handed me a glass of water as he took a sip from his own glass. "I never meant to hurt you either. I honestly didn't."

Cotton mouth had taken me over, so I was glad for the drink of cool water. I took a big gulp and said, "You never hurt me, Brock. You're a good guy."

His gaze shifted behind me as he said in a solemn voice, "I wish that were true."

I opened my mouth to reassure him that my breaking things off between us didn't mean he'd done anything wrong or that he wasn't a good man, but just then my arms and legs began to feel like dead weights and everything grew fuzzy. His lips continued to move, but I didn't understand what he was saying anymore.

Barely able to keep my eyes open, I turned to see Monique standing by my side glaring at me. She said something about me ruining everything, and then the room felt like it was spinning around me.

And then everything went dark.

CHAPTER EIGHTEEN

GAGE

THE VARO SECURITY OFFICE EMPTIED out as my employees all left for their assignments, so I took the time to lean back in my chair and relax for a moment. Not that I expected to have much success at that. I hated that Jordan was at Brock's apartment telling him goodbye. I knew why she had to do it, but that didn't mean I had to like her going there.

My mind raced with what might be happening at that moment. Was he going to try to convince her to stay with him? She wouldn't, but would he try? I imagined him turning on the waterworks right there in his living room as she explained how she wouldn't be marrying him. The mental picture of him crying and begging her to stay made me dislike him even more.

What was he doing home in the middle of the day, though?

No matter. Jordan would tell him she didn't want to marry him and that would be the end of that. Then he'd fade into the past as a distant memory as we began our life together. This time I wouldn't let anyone take me away from her.

Maybe we'd take a trip out to Wyoming to see my family

before she returned to school in a couple weeks. I could trust Casey to keep my crew in line, and some time away from the city out in the open spaces of my hometown would be great. No shopping or crowds. Just fresh air and nature.

As I thought about all the fun we'd have, my body began to relax for the first time since I left Jordan's place in Brooklyn. I hadn't realized how keyed up I'd been until this moment as I felt my shoulders retreat from their place up near my ears. Suddenly, my neck and back felt like the weight of the world had been removed from them at the mere thought of heading west.

"Hey, Gage, I don't mean to interrupt—"

I opened my eyes to see Casey standing in the doorway to my office. Wearing her usual smile, she folded her arms across her chest and leaned against the wall as I collected my thoughts.

"What's up, Case?"

"You looked more relaxed than I've seen you in ages, boss. I feel bad that I had to break up whatever you had going on there."

Chuckling, I sat up straight in my chair and moved back toward my desk. "I wasn't meditating or anything like that, so you don't have to worry about interrupting me. Just taking a few moments to get my head together after the last few days."

She nodded her head like she understood. "I'm glad. You looked a little rough at the Truman party that night. It's good to see you back to your old self."

As much as I liked talking about how healthy I was looking, I had a feeling Casey hadn't come to see me to tell me that. "So what's up, Case? You're handling Nestor today, aren't you?"

Casey stepped into my office and braced her hands on the back of the chair in front of my desk. "Yep. His wife told me they were running late this morning, so I don't have to be out there until after one."

"What's on tap for them today?" I asked knowing that providing security for Nestor Ambers and his wife Renee meant being more babysitter than anything else. Obscenely wealthy and friends of Tristan's parents from years ago, they were my first customers when I opened the doors to this business, even though I doubted they truly needed security from much of anything. Everyone loved the Ambers, so I couldn't imagine much danger existed for them.

"It's a beautiful August day, so I believe Mrs. Ambers mentioned something about a stroll through Central Park and then a nice drive out to the Hamptons where they'll be relaxing until Monday."

I clapped my hands and laughed. "So you're heading out to the vacation spot of the rich and powerful? You must be looking forward to that."

She shook her head so her brown hair bounced around the sides of her head. "You know me, Gage. I'd rather a cookout on the beach or a day at the ballpark, but the work is good and I can't say anything bad about the Ambers. They're nice people."

"That they are. You don't find that in people with money a lot of times, you know?"

"I've learned that in this job, I can tell you that. For every

Nestor and Renee Amber, there's someone who acts like we're their personal slaves. But I wouldn't have it any other way. We do good work here, Gage. I know sometimes we all think that the people we're guarding are a pain in the ass, but we do our job well."

I began to speak, but Daryl's ruddy face appearing in my doorway stopped me and Casey quickly excused herself so we could speak. He looked flustered, like he'd run the last few blocks, and any relaxed feelings I'd enjoyed just a few minutes ago disappeared.

He took a seat in front of me worked to catch his breath. "What's up, Daryl? You look like shit."

Tugging on his long red beard, he contorted his face into an expression of pain. "Think you're funny? Just wait till I tell you what I found out. You won't be Mr. Funny Comedian anymore."

"It's okay, Daryl. Jordan and I are back together and she's with Brock right now telling him she won't be marrying him. So whatever you have to tell me is no reason to get that scraggly ass beard of yours all pulled out of shape."

He stopped tugging on his wiry facial hair and leaned back in his chair, instead stroking it gently as if to calm it or himself. "You don't say. Well, I wasn't expecting to hear that when I came here."

I clasped my hands behind my head and leaned back in my chair. "Yep, so you see, whatever you have to tell me about Brock Hannon isn't important anymore."

"What is this, the pose of the victorious?" Daryl joked. "You look downright gloating. Well, I guess you have every right. The guy had everything going for him. Looks. Money. A ring on her finger. But you're a sly one, Gage Varo. I can admit that."

"No gloating. Just happy. I gave her up once, and now that I have her back, I won't make that mistake again. Brock will just have to go find himself another woman because Jordan's mine and I plan to make that a permanent thing."

Daryl's eyebrows shot up and his eyes opened wide in surprise. "Holy fuck! I stay away looking into things and you two are already racing down the aisle. You work fast, my friend."

"We're not racing anywhere. I haven't even mentioned it to her yet, but I plan to. Nothing big. Just a few close friends and family like Tristan and Nina had. Maybe we'll even do it out in Wyoming."

"Jordan isn't exactly the wide open spaces kind of girl, Gage," Daryl said with a chuckle. "I have a hard time believing she's going to be all about the rolling hills of Wyoming. She's a city girl, my friend. You can't change that. We city people are a breed to ourselves."

"Nonsense. She'll love it. Jordan's the type of woman who can go anywhere and be happy."

Shrugging, he said, "Okay, believe what you want. But I highly doubt when you mention getting married in the mountains that she's going to be thrilled. I see her more on a yacht somewhere than hiking with you out west."

I couldn't help but laugh at Daryl's ignorance. "You really are a city guy, aren't you? I don't think you know one damn thing about Wyoming. Jordan will be fine wherever we are as long as it's together."

"I won't argue with that. Seeing as you're Mr. Love today, I'll let you have your delusions."

"I thought I was Mr. Funny Comedian."

Snorting his disgust with me, he rolled his eyes. "Hysterical. So do you want to hear what I found out or not, smart ass?"

"Sure. Hit me with all the dirt on Brock Hannon," I said as I sat up and readied myself to listen.

Daryl whipped out his tiny notebook and began flipping through the pages. "Him I still have little on, other than some family details. What I found out was about his sister, the lovely Monique."

"Monique with the shopping addiction that's going to land her on an episode of Hoarders someday?" I joked.

Shaking his head, he grinned. "Oh no. She's so much more than a crazy shopper. Just wait until you hear what I found out."

"I'm all ears. Shoot."

"She isn't who she says she is. His mother and father lived happily ever after until their deaths two years ago in a car accident out near Waco, Texas. They were the parents of two children—Brock Jonathan Hannon and Monique Elizabeth Hannon."

I leaned forward and stared across the desk at Daryl. "I thought they were half-brother and sister from when their parents married."

He shook his head slowly and frowned. "Nope."

"I don't understand. Monique isn't his sister, but he does

have a sister Monique? What am I missing?"

Flipping a page in his notebook, he said, "Remember that car crash a couple years ago that killed his mother and father? Seems she suddenly became a fixture in his life right after that."

"So who the fuck is she?"

Daryl leaned back and smiled broadly, pulling on his beard again. "Oh, Monique, whose real name is Hailey Sanders, is the kind of woman all wealthy men fear. Born in a small town outside Lubbock, Texas to Nicole Sanders, an unwed teenage mother who had no idea who'd gotten her pregnant, little Hailey grew up around her mother's various lowlife boyfriends who came and went like the tides. Our girl must have learned something from that experience because by the time she was eighteen, she'd snagged herself a local businessman named Jasper Coltrane. Playing the innocent victim of some attack near his plumbing business, she worked her charms on the aging and widowed Mr. Coltrane and got herself a nice life. At least for a while."

"She's a con woman?" I asked, still reeling from the little he'd told me about Monique or Hailey.

"Yeah. She conned Coltrane out of something like fifty grand, but with the way that lady shops, she probably blew through that in no time."

"So how did she end up with Brock Hannon?"

Daryl held up his hand to stop me. "Patience. The story's just beginning. After Coltrane, little Hailey moved on to the big leagues. She and her boyfriend at the time, Kenny Summers, bilked her next mark out of nearly half a million. A wealthy man named Peter Simpson. He owned a luxury car business. You know the kind, import and export stuff. Well, Summers pretended to be the guy's pool boy while Hailey cozied up to him and got him to take her on trips around the world. While he was busy falling for the con, Summers robbed him blind of as many cars as he could steal while she had him in her clutches for a month on some remote island in the South Pacific. By the time the guy got back to civilization, Summers and the cars were gone. A short time later, so was dear Hailey."

"What happened to Summers?"

"Doing fifteen years."

I worked to process all this information about Monique, but it made no sense. "Are you saying she's playing Brock now? I don't get it. Wouldn't Brock know she isn't his sister?"

"This is where things get really interesting. You'd ordinarily think he would know what his own sister looked like, but from all I've been able to find out about Brock Hannon, he was a wealthy recluse estranged from everyone in his family for nearly a decade when they died."

"Where's the real Monique?"

"Dead. That's the really sad part of this story. She got into drugs after Brock left home and disappeared. She was living on the streets of LA, a strung out junkie, and then the all-too-common end for girls like her came just like it usually does when drugs are involved."

"So this Monique Hannon shows up on his doorstep after the accident to mourn the death of their dearly departed parents. This Hailey's a piece of work."

"Exactly. She looks close enough to Monique Hannon and he likely bought into it."

"She wouldn't be happy once Jordan entered the picture, though. Brock planning a life with someone means she'd be entitled to his money. Little Hailey would be cut out of a lot of the money," I said, thinking out loud.

Daryl nodded. "I think that might be what she was doing here in New York, and that would explain why Brock would be away from Jordan for all this time right after their engagement."

"So what was her plan?"

"I have to be honest here, Gage. I haven't figured that out yet. From what I've put together, it seems she glommed on to Hannon after his parents died and just in time for his business to hit the stratosphere. I'm guessing she had her eye on his money, but then he met Jordan and everything she planned was all of a sudden in jeopardy."

I'd never felt any guilt about getting in between Jordan and Brock, but at that moment as I thought about her involved with people like him and Hailey, I couldn't help but be happy that she was walking away from him today. The sooner she got away from people like that the better.

"Then it's good that Jordan's telling him she won't marry him."

Daryl nodded his agreement. "Your lady shouldn't be anywhere near Monique or Hailey or whoever she is. That woman is dangerous, and Jordan was putting all her plans at risk. Now with her gone, Brock can shower all his money on Hailey, just like I bet she wanted."

"I think I feel bad for him now that I know all of this. He's losing Jordan and stuck with the duplicitous bitch who's pretending to be his dead sister and who plans to rob him blind."

Standing, Daryl pushed back his chair and chuckled. "I wouldn't feel too bad for him. He was your rival until a day or so ago. I'm sure he'll figure out Hailey's game. It's just a matter of when and if it's before she takes him for all he's worth."

I stood to shake his hand and thank him for checking things out for me. "You're the best, Daryl. Thanks again for this."

"My pleasure. Want me to keep looking into Brock Hannon too?"

"Nah. No need now. Jordan will be back soon from telling him, and that will be the end of him in our lives. Anything that comes up I'm sure I can handle."

Daryl's eyes lit up suddenly. "Oh, I forgot to mention this interesting tidbit. Hannon isn't the only guy rolling in the dough involved in his companies. Somehow, and I haven't figured out how yet, an even bigger fish is behind him."

"Bigger fish? Like who?"

"My guy found the name Dalton Spear. You know, one of the richest men in America Dalton Spear."

Dalton Spear wasn't just someone with money. The heir to the Spear chemical empire, he consistently ranked as one of the top twenty wealthiest men in America.

"That's some money there."

Daryl puffed his cheeks and blew the air out slowly.

"There's money, and then there's Spear level money. I'm just wondering what he's doing with Hannon. Still think I should back off checking him out?"

I shook my head, now more than ever wanting to know what Brock Hannon was all about. "No. It may be just for curiosity, but I think we need to find out about our buddy Brock."

"Got it. Will do." Daryl stood to leave and tugged on the bottom of his beard. "By the way, any more letters? We still never figured that out."

I shrugged. "Maybe it was Monique. She seems like the type to do something like that. Whoever it was, I should have never given in to their demands. Nobody can protect Jordan better than I can, so let them try to separate us again."

"That was probably it," he said as he turned toward the door. He took a few steps and looked back at me. "But that doesn't make sense. If Monique wanted Jordan gone, she wouldn't have driven you two apart."

"Yeah, I guess. No matter. She and I will deal with who-ever it was if and when they send any more letters, but their bullshit attempts to break us up won't work anymore."

"Good to hear. Remember, I'm just a call away if you need anything. In the meantime, I'm going to keep working to get to the bottom of this Spear and Hannon business. My gut tells me there's more to this than just a wealthy investor."

"Thanks, Daryl. I appreciate it. Right now, I'm just wait-ing for Jordan to call me so I can meet her for lunch and forget all of this ever happened."

In a tone of disdain, he grumbled, "Lovebirds. Well, you

kids have fun. I'm off to dig up the dirt on a few other people Tristan has me checking into before I get back to your problem. I'll let you know what I find out about your lady's ex."

Daryl left me waiting for Jordan to call and happy to be done with everything associated with Brock and his sister. From now on, we'd live the simple life we'd started back when it was just the two of us, before I made the stupid mistake of leaving the only woman who'd ever truly made me happy.

Never one for daydreaming, I found myself thinking about how great it would be when I got her out to the open country of Wyoming. True she was a city girl, to be sure, but she was so much more than that. The woman I knew would love the fresh air and freedom back home offered.

A FEW MINUTES LATER, MY phone vibrated in my pocket, and I pulled it out eagerly looking for a text from her telling me everything was done and she was fine. Swiping the screen, I saw the text was from her. Slowly, I read the words and suddenly my tiny office felt like the walls were closing in on me.

> I can't go through with it. I've changed my mind. I'm marrying Brock. Don't try to change my mind. I love him.

My hands shook so much my phone nearly slipped out of my grip. Over and over, I read the words she'd texted, but I couldn't believe them. She didn't love him. She loved me and wanted to be with me. How could she have spent all yesterday and last night with me making love for hours and then changed her mind?

I quickly typed out a text to her, confused and feeling betrayed.

What are you saying? Don't do this. Just tell me where to meet you and we can figure this out.

For nearly five minutes, I waited for an answer to my message but got none. After feeling so great about us all morning, I now felt like my world was crashing in around me and I didn't know how to stop it. Was she still at Brock's apartment? And what had happened to make her change her mind?

Unsure if I should race over to Brock's place, I called the one person I was sure would know what was going on. Her phone rang four times and with each ring, I worried that even Nina was avoiding me now because Jordan had truly decided to turn her back on us to be with Brock. I knew Nina wouldn't want to hurt my feelings, so of course, she wouldn't want to talk to me.

But she finally answered and when I heard her usual cheery voice, I hoped I'd been wrong about Jordan.

"Hey Gage! What are you calling me for on this beautiful day when I would think you and Jordan would be celebrating?"

"Nina, do you know where Jordan is?"

"Yeah. She told me everything and that she had to go tell Brock it was over. She's probably still there. No need to worry. She just wanted to do right by him. That's all."

I looked down at my phone as I put her on speakerphone and read the message aloud. "I just got this text from her a few minutes ago. *I can't go through with it. I've changed my mind. I'm marrying Brock. Don't try to change my mind. I love him.*"

My chest ached as I read the words.

"What are you talking about, Gage? Jordan doesn't love Brock. I've known for weeks she didn't love him enough to marry him."

I grabbed my wallet and gun out of my desk drawer and started walking toward the door. "She sent me that from her phone just a few minutes ago. I don't know what to think, to be honest."

Nina's voice turned frantic. "Something's wrong. She wouldn't send you that. That doesn't even sound like her. She's crazy about you. We just talked about you and her getting back together and how happy she was about it. Why would she send a message like that? What could have happened?"

Tearing out of my office, I ran up the street not even knowing where to go. "Nina, something's wrong. I have to go find her. Call me if you hear anything."

"I will. I promise. Find her, Gage. Find her and get her away from that guy. He's no good. I just know it."

"Don't worry. I'll find her," I said in between panting breaths as I broke into a sprint at the thought that at that very moment Brock and his scheming con artist sister were doing some horrible thing to Jordan. I had no idea why they would as none of it made sense, but it didn't matter.

Nothing mattered but Jordan and making sure she was safe.

CHAPTER NINETEEN

JORDAN

SLOWLY, I OPENED MY EYES but everything around me appeared cloudy and hazy. My eyes couldn't focus on anything, but studying the blurry shapes in front of me, I had the surest sense I wasn't in Brock's apartment anymore. I heard voices nearby, but all the words were garbled as they hit my ears.

What had happened? I tried to replay the events of the day as best as I could remember them. Gage and I had made love first thing this morning. Definitely not a bad memory to start with. I'd told him I had to tell Brock in person that I couldn't marry him. I'd told Brock the truth and then...

The memory of Monique standing next to me as everything faded away made terror race through my veins. What had they given me? I racked my brain to think of how they could have done it and remembered the glass of water.

Brock had drugged me by slipping something into my drink.

I looked down at my body, but my eyes still wouldn't focus and all I saw was a blurry version of my tan arm and pink t-shirt. Jesus, I felt like a bus had hit me!

I had no idea what they'd drugged me up with, but whatever it was, it had done a real number on me. It must have been some pretty heavy duty stuff if the way I felt was any indication.

Opening my eyes as wide as they'd go, I tried to figure out where I was. All I knew was I was on a couch somewhere. The room around me didn't look familiar, even seeing it through blurry eyes. It was cold, though. Air conditioned cold, like when you're in a restaurant and they have the temperature so cold that you need a sweater in the middle of summer. I curled up in a ball to get warm as I continued to try to figure out where the hell I was and what the hell was going on.

I was still dressed, which was a good thing and likely meant I hadn't been attacked. Jesus! What was I thinking? Who would attack me?

Working to calm myself, I reminded myself that Brock still saw himself as my fiancé and had never been anything but decent to me. His sister, on the other hand, was an entirely different story. Whatever had happened, I was sure of one thing.

She was behind it.

Since my vision wasn't improving much, I closed my eyes to listen to what the voices I heard were saying. I had the sense they weren't too far away—maybe in a room nearby. But who was speaking?

One person, likely a male, spoke in a low voice. Was it Brock? I concentrated and couldn't figure out if it was his voice. But if it wasn't him, who was the male?

I opened my eyes again but still everything remained blurry. What the fuck had she given me? Anger bubbled inside me. When I got my sight back, that bitch was in for a rude awakening.

One that I'd give her with my hand across her face. Nice Jordan had officially left the building.

I knew I should have listened to my gut when it came to Monique. The woman made me uneasy from the minute I met her.

None of that mattered anymore. Now I had to focus and figure out who was keeping me wherever here was and how to get away. I was smarter than Monique for sure, and while Brock might be incredible at business, he wasn't much for street smarts. That's where I beat both their pampered selves. This chick wasn't merely the smiling third grade teacher I usually portrayed myself to be.

Focusing once again, I listened to the female voice and knew exactly whose it was. No one in the world had a voice like Monique. Whining and insistent all at the same time, it was a voice that made you want to run away, but not before you made her suffer at least a little.

So at least I knew that. Monique and possibly Brock or some other male had brought me to this place. Why, though? Why bring me here or anywhere? And why drug me, for God's sake! Who did that kind of thing?

Shitty people who were likely criminals did that. The problem was Brock had never struck me as a bad man, and even his awful half-sister had never been more than a pain in the ass.

I opened my eyes and slowly waited for things to come into focus, hoping it didn't take too long and Monique found me awake because she'd likely just drug me again. As I waited, my head began to throb like someone had a sledgehammer inside my brain and was swinging it wildly toward the sides of my skull. This was why I didn't do drugs. My head just couldn't handle them.

Gradually, my eyes began to work again and I saw what looked like a living room around me. Someone's living room with seashells and starfish. The room was painted in a pale yellow, and the furniture was wicker and the color blue like every picture of the Mediterranean I'd ever seen.

Was I at the beach?

The pictures on the walls were all seascapes, so figuring out who owned this place by them wasn't going to happen. Nothing else in the room gave me any clues as to who might be behind all of this.

I needed to get out of there and fast.

Then all at once I thought of Gage. He was likely waiting for me to call him like I said I would after I told Brock I couldn't marry him. I felt my shorts for my phone, but it was gone. Suddenly, I became frantic. I didn't know where I was or why Monique and whoever she was with was holding me, and Gage had no idea where I was.

Which meant he couldn't help me. And Nina couldn't either.

I was all alone.

It didn't matter. I was a blond, but I wasn't dumb. I'd skipped out on rotten dates through tiny bathroom windows and escaped unharmed and with all my money from no less than three muggers since I'd moved to Brooklyn. Monique and Brock weren't going to kidnap me and keep me hostage. No fucking way.

I swung my feet off the couch and stood up, too quickly, unfortunately. Not ready to stand quite yet, I fell back onto the couch, too dizzy to try again.

Well, if standing wasn't an option, then I'd crawl. Whatever way I had to, I was getting the hell out of wherever I was.

Carefully, I rolled over and lowered myself to the ground on my hands and knees. The carpet felt like needles jabbing into my legs, but I started to move toward what looked like a door to the outside. It had a window, so at least I hoped it led outside and not into the very room where Monique and the mystery man were still talking.

I hadn't figured out what they were saying yet, and as I moved along the painful carpeting, I tried to decipher the words that floated into the room. She was talking about something concerning a plan. What plan? Was this whole thing planned all along? Why would they plan to kidnap me when Brock just asked me to marry him nearly two weeks ago?

Sure my hearing hadn't returned as well as my vision had, I continued to move toward the door and listened to what they were saying. As I heard the man speak, I began to realize it was Brock in that room with her. My own fiancé had been a part of drugging and kidnapping me!

My knees burned from the pain of rubbing against the scratchy carpet, but I was almost to the door. I prayed to God by the time I reached it I would be able to stand without falling flat on my ass.

And then from behind me I heard Monique snap, "Don't let her get out! Grab her!"

Before I could stand and make a break for it, Brock's hands covered my shoulders to stop my movement forward. I fought him as best I could in my condition, but I was no match for him. Picking me up, he carried me by the waist back to the couch as I kicked and screamed.

"Get your hands off me! You fucking drugged me and brought me to this place! Don't touch me!"

Brock tried to calm me down, but it was no use. No matter what he said, I kicked and screamed and flailed my arms in a pathetic attempt to get away.

Crouching next to me, he said in a plaintive voice, "Jordan, please, I don't want you to hurt yourself. Just calm down. Everything's going to all right."

My blurry vision had all but cleared up, so I looked him in the eyes to see if he could possibly be serious. Everything was going to be all right? How the hell could he think that?

"Where am I? Why did you let her do this to me?" I demanded to know.

His hazel eyes filled with sadness as he shook his head. "I didn't know what she had planned. Please believe me. I love you. I would never hurt you. As soon as I realized what she was doing, I made sure you were safe and in no danger."

"You put something in my drink and filled me with drugs that made me black out. How was that safe?"

His expression sagged into a frown. "I'm sorry, Jordan. I

didn't have a choice."

I opened my mouth to say it didn't matter, but Monique barked, "Don't bother coddling her. We did what had to be done. And don't tell her you didn't know what I had planned."

Brock looked past me toward her and narrowed his eyes in anger. "She doesn't deserve to be treated like this. It doesn't hurt anyone or anything you have planned for me to be nice. And I had no idea the stuff you gave me would do that to her, for God's sake."

Monique grumbled and walked into the other room as Brock returned his attention to me. "I really am sorry. I never meant for any of this to happen this way."

Exhausted after only being awake for less than fifteen minutes, I let my shoulders fall in defeat. "What's going on, Brock? Why did you do this to me?"

"I never wanted you to get hurt, Jordan. I hope you can believe that. I just couldn't let you go."

"So that's it? You kidnapped me to bring me here and force me to marry you?" I asked in horror as my mind frantically sought any other reason why I'd be drugged and brought wherever I was.

"We love each other, don't we? It's not that bad, after all. Right?"

I shook my head in disbelief. "I don't love you enough to marry you, Brock. I told you that."

Brock lifted his hands to cradle my face and looked deep into my eyes. "I think you loved me enough to marry me at some point, didn't you?"

Opening my mouth to explain that I loved Gage and not him, I was interrupted by Monique snapping at Brock, "Stop it with this lovesick puppy bullshit already!"

"You won't get away with this," I said with all the bravado I could muster.

Monique's left hip shot out and her hand landed on it to punctuate her disgust at what I'd said. "We're hours away from the city, sweetheart, so yes, we will get away with this. It's a simple thing, really. When you came to Brock's today to tell him you couldn't marry him, we had to do something. You have to marry him and it has to be today. So we did what was necessary."

I looked at Brock in the hopes that at least he hadn't lost his mind like his sister clearly had. "Don't let her do this. Whatever's going on, it can stop right now and nothing bad will happen to you. You need to stop this."

Brock's face filled with regret, and I knew he couldn't or wouldn't help me. Looking up at Monique behind him, I said, "People are looking for me right now, I'm sure. My friends will miss me when I don't show up at my apartment."

A sinister smile spread across her red stained lips. She reached into her jacket and held out my phone for me to see. "You're right, actually. Someone is looking for you. That's probably because of the text I sent him as we were leaving the city. *I can't go through with it. I've changed my mind. I'm marrying Brock. Don't try to change my mind. I love him.*"

Barely able to hold back the tears at the thought that Gage had received that horrible text from who he thought was me, I lunged forward to grab my phone from her grip, but she just pushed me hard back onto the couch.

"You have him as V in your contact list, but his name is Gage, right? He certainly seems to care about you, if his text he sent you is any indication. *What are you saying? Don't do this. Just tell me where to meet you and we can figure this out.* He sounds so distraught, don't you think? Not that it matters. He won't find you in time."

Tears rolled down my cheeks as she read Gage's desperate text to me. He thought I betrayed him and still begged me to come back to him. Oh, God!

"Why are you doing this?"

"You know, you have terrible luck with men," Monique said in a mocking voice as she scrolled back through my texts. "I mean, you obviously were fooled this time, and your ex killed a girl, for God's sake. I take it your last name is ironic? Miss Wright? I don't think so."

Looking at Brock again, I pleaded, "Don't let this happen. I'm sorry I didn't want to marry you. Please just let me go."

"I never wanted things to go like this. Honest. But I fell in love with you, even though that wasn't the plan."

"What is this plan you two keep talking about? What plan?"

Brock continued to talk but didn't answer my question. "I mean, I tried to do what I was supposed to. It was no use, though. You really are a sweet person, Jordan. If things weren't like they were, I think we could have been happy with each other."

"Enough! You're like two idiotic teenagers," Monique yelled.

I grabbed Brock's hand, hoping to make him focus on helping me. Whispering so Monique couldn't hear, I said, "It doesn't matter now. It's okay. In a different time and place we might have been happy. I get that. What I don't get is why you have to keep me here. Help me escape. If you truly love me, you can do that."

All he did was shake his head and frown. If I was going to get out of there, he wasn't going to help. A chill ran up my spine at the thought of what this plan they kept talking about could be. Were they going to kill me? That made no sense, though. Why whisk me out of New York to do that?

I looked over at Monique who stood reading my text messages from Gage. A ridiculous smile spread across her evil face as she scrolled through them, as if reading our personal intimations gave her some kind of jollies.

"What is this plan of yours?" I asked, almost afraid of what her answer would be.

She looked up from my phone and chuckled. "You haven't figured it out yet? See, I told this one here you weren't very bright. Clearly brains don't run in the genes. Didn't you find it odd that I suddenly showed up after your engagement party, even after I didn't bother coming to the big celebration?"

"Truthfully, I was happy. You were never someone I wanted to spend any real time with, so when Brock told me you wouldn't be there, I was relieved."

She scowled at my answer and shot Brock a nasty look. He cowered and slinked away to sit on the chair across from me as she continued explaining herself.

"Brock here never did seem to get the full gist of the plan, did you? I showed up because he had actually developed feelings for you and that whole engagement thing was real for him. Well, I couldn't abide by that."

"Abide by what? Him being in love with me? Wasn't that what he was supposed to be? We were getting engaged."

"He was never supposed to fall in love with you!" she shouted so loud my ears rang. "All he had to do was get you to the altar. That was it. But even that was too difficult for this fuck up."

Brock stood to defend himself but she pointed her finger at him to stop him from speaking. "Don't say a word or you'll see none of the money. Do you understand me or do I need to use smaller words with less fucking syllables?"

I sat stunned at all of this, not understanding why Brock wouldn't or couldn't stand up to her. What money was she talking about? He was a multi-millionaire. Why would he care about her money, and for that matter, when did she get so wealthy that she had any money to give him?

Monique turned her attention back to me. "So today the plan finally comes to fruition, so wipe the mascara from under your eyes and look presentable."

"For what?"

"Your wedding day, of course. You and Brock are about to become the happiest couple in the world. You won't be wearing white, but that's not exactly the color someone like you should be wearing anyway. You're not exactly pure, especially since you spent last night fucking your ex-boyfriend."

Stunned, I mumbled, "My wedding day?"

Brock nodded and hung his head, as if he wasn't just as guilty as Monique for kidnapping me and now forcing me to marry a man I didn't love.

"How can this be legal? Where the fuck did you bring me to that would allow you to force me to marry him?"

With a smile, Monique answered, "South Carolina. Welcome to the south. We do things differently here. Now keep your mouth shut or I swear to God what you got earlier will be nothing compared to what I'll do to you."

She stormed out of the room, but nothing she said made any sense. Why would they force me to marry Brock? I looked at him as he sat defeated in the chair and asked, "Why are you letting her do this to me? To us?"

"I won't let her hurt you, I promise. Just do as she says and everything will be okay."

"What's happened to you, Brock? Where is the man who runs a multinational company and is a self-made millionaire?"

He hung his head and said quietly in a far less distinguished tone than he usually had, "My name isn't Brock. My name is Justin. Justin Archer." Looking up at me, he added, "And I meant what I said. I did fall for you and you are a sweet girl. I'm sorry for all of this."

"What happened to your voice? Why do you sound like that? What do you mean your name isn't Brock Hannon? Who are you?"

He shook his quickly left and right and pressed his lips together. "I shouldn't have said anything. Just do as she wants and I promise you'll be okay. I won't let her hurt you."

"Brock, answer me! What is this all about?"

Just then, a minister and two more people entered the room followed by Monique pretending to be the supportive sister of the groom. "We'll be having the ceremony out on the deck since the sunset is going to be just perfect tonight. Please feel free to walk straight through to outside and the three of us will be joining you momentarily. Just give the lovebirds a few minutes to get ready."

They walked past me with smiles on their faces, and I sat too stunned to tell them the truth of what was going on. As the door to the deck closed, Monique walked up to in front of the couch and glared down at me.

"Play this right and the worst you'll be able to say is that you're married to this man. Play it wrong and you'll be dead, but not before you're married to him. Either way, you're about to become his wife. The choice of what happens after that is up to you."

She turned to say something to Brock or Justin or whoever he was, and all I could think was I was about to be forced to marry this man who wasn't even Brock Hannon and there was nobody who could save me from Monique and her awful plan.

Closing my eyes, I let the tears come as an even worse reality filled my mind. The man I loved thought I'd betrayed him and had no idea where I was to stop this madness.

CHAPTER TWENTY

GAGE

THE STONE WORLDWIDE BUILDING SECURITY guard quickly waved me in as Tristan's assistant waited for me on the other side of the metal detector to escort me up to his office. Michelle and I said nothing as we walked toward the elevator, her shoes making a sound that reminded me of my mother's metronome that used to sit on top of her piano as my sisters took turns practicing their playing. So measured and regular, the tapping of her shoes as they hit the white marble floor strangely calmed me.

At least for a few moments. But as soon as those elevator doors closed and we stood still facing those dull metal doors, all my fears about what might happening to Jordan at that very moment came rushing back.

Fucking Brock and Monique!

We reached the top floor and exited into the executive suite where Tristan was waiting for me in his office. Michelle gave me a gentle pat on the upper arm as she left me to return to her desk, and I walked into the CEO of Stone Worldwide's office hoping to God he could help me rescue the woman I loved from whatever Brock was up to.

Tristan Stone never failed to surprise me. Wealthier than most men his age, he always seemed far more down to earth than his peers who shared his social level with him. This afternoon he looked the same as he always did when I saw him in his office. He wore a dark suit, striking dress shirt and tie, and a look on his face that said he had a lot of money and knew how to wield the power that came from that fact.

But in his brown eyes I saw the familiar warmth he showed those of us he called friends.

Extending his hand, he offered me a seat. "Gage, it's good to see you again, although I wish it were for far more pleasant reasons."

"Thanks for seeing me, Tristan. You're the only person I knew to call once this all began to unravel."

He leaned forward in his office chair and took a deep breath. "I never felt good about that Brock Hannon. Nina and I both had a feeling about him that something was wrong, but I never could put my finger on it. I regret not telling Daryl to check him out for me months ago."

I nodded. "I'm not sure it would have mattered. Brock seems to have hidden all his dirt better than anyone Daryl's ever seen. His sister is a different story, though. I'm sure she's involved in whatever's going on."

Tristan's face contorted into a look of disgust. "Nina's told me all about her. They sound like real winners."

His cell phone rang and looking down at the screen, he said, "I asked Nina to call me when you got here so she could tell us if she remembered anything Jordan told her that might be able to help us."

"Hey, honey. I have Gage in my office right now. I'm hoping between the three of us, we can figure out where Walker should take him. He's got the plane ready, but we need to know where to go."

"Tristan, I have no idea," she said in a frantic voice full of fear. "Gage, I'm so sorry this happened. I told her I didn't think she should marry Brock and when she finally agreed, I was so happy. What do you think happened when she went to see him?"

"I have no idea," I said, trying to remain positive but worried that every minute that went by and I hadn't found her was one that could be her last. "I never dreamed the guy would do anything other than try to convince her to change her mind. I can't believe she did, though."

"She didn't!" Nina said in tears. "I know she didn't. She didn't love him. She knew it. And she loves you. Of that, I'm certain. Please don't doubt that."

"Nina, did Jordan ever say anything about where he has homes or somewhere they might go to get away? I've got men checking his home and office in Dallas, but they aren't there. So where would they go if not there?" Tristan asked.

The phone remained silent for a long moment as Tristan and I sat there staring at each other, and then Nina made a noise that sounded like she'd clapped her hands together.

"Honey, what is it? Did you remember something?"

"Yeah, but I don't know if it's anything. Right after they got engaged, Brock told Jordan he had to stay away from her for two weeks."

Tristan's expression turned to confusion, and I leaned

forward toward the phone on his desk. "Yeah, I thought that was weird too. Right after they got engaged he doesn't spend time with her? Do you know why?"

"He said he needed to catch up on work so they could elope. He didn't want to wait until the real wedding, so they were going to elope. She told me the day Cara and I took the kids to the Staten Island Zoo."

"Elope? Are you sure? She never said anything about that to me."

"She probably didn't want you to know, Gage, but she told me he had said to her he didn't want to wait. She thought it was romantic at the time, but I thought something might be wrong. I mean, why not just wait? She wasn't going anywhere, as far as he knew."

"Nina, honey, did she say where they were going to elope to? Dallas?" Tristan asked.

"I'm trying to remember. We were looking at the animals and she was talking about them eloping. Oh God! Why can't I remember? And I can't even ask Cara because Jordan whispered it to me. I'm sorry, Gage. I know she told me, but I can't remember."

Disappointed, I sat back in my chair and tried not to let myself get lost in the despair that threatened to take me over. Jordan had been gone for hours, and God only knew what had happened to her by now.

"Nina, do you think it was out of the country?"

"No. Well, I don't know, but I want to say it wasn't out of the country. God, why can't I remember this, Tristan? She's my best friend and I'm the person who can help her and all I have is mommy brain all muddled with kids' cartoons and what I need to make them for dinner!"

"Don't get upset, honey. Maybe if we just talk for a little bit it will come back to you. If they weren't going to his home in Texas, what about hers? Do you think they'd go to her hometown in Connecticut?"

"I don't think so. Her parents wouldn't be happy about not being at their wedding, and if her grandmother ever found out about her eloping, she'd flip her wig. Her grandmother might be old, but she's spunky and she'd tell Jordan in no uncertain terms what she thought about not being there when she got married."

I was beginning to get antsy just sitting there. Never before in my life had I felt so useless. The woman I loved was out there somewhere with Brock and probably his manipulative sister too, but for what reason? Was he planning to force her to marry him? Because I couldn't believe she truly had changed her mind and wanted to be with him.

Jesus, maybe she was right when she accused me of being nothing but bad for her. First, I left her without even a decent excuse for why I didn't want to be with her anymore and broke her heart, even though I thought I had to do that to protect her. And now, here I sat unable to do anything to save her because I didn't even know where the fuck she might be.

All I knew was that she needed me and I couldn't let her down this time.

"Oh my God! That's it! Her grandmother. That's the answer!" Nina exclaimed into the phone. "I said to her that her grandmother would have a coronary if she wasn't there to see her granddaughter walk down the aisle, but right before that we were hanging out in front of the leopard cages and Jordan said she and Brock were eloping to Hilton Head that weekend. That's it! Hilton Head!"

I looked at the phone like it was something magical I couldn't believe. "Hilton Head? Are you sure, Nina?"

"Yes! I'm sure, Gage. That's where she said they were going. Do you think that's where she could be?"

Tristan already had his office phone in his hand and was dialing a number. "We won't know if we don't try. I'm calling the pilot right now to tell him to take Gage to Hilton Head Island. Once I do that, I'll be home. Love you."

"I love you too, baby. And Gage, go get our girl back."

I practically jumped out of my chair. "I will. Thanks so much for your help, Nina. We couldn't have done it without you."

"Just go get her and bring her back so we can all sit out at the pool real soon and laugh about all this, okay? Get her away from those people and back where she belongs."

"I will."

Tristan put down the receiver and stood to walk me out. "Walker will be waiting for you at Teterboro Airport. He's filing the flight plan right now. Once you get down there, you can use the suite at The Richmont for when you find her. My security chief down there knows everything about the island, so I'll tell him to be at your disposal. Whatever you need—transportation, help locating places there—he's the one who I'll make sure takes care of you."

I stopped at his office door and put my hand out to shake

his. "I can't thank you enough, Tristan. I don't know what I would have done without your help. You and Nina."

"Jordan's a good person, and I don't want to see her hurt by the likes of Brock Hannon. Plus, my wife would never forgive me if I didn't do everything I possibly could to help find her best friend, and her happiness means the world to me. Remember, call me if you need anything."

"Can you tell Daryl what's going on? He might have found out something else that could help me find her."

Tristan nodded and flashed me that confident smile of his. "I will. And don't worry. You're going to find her and she's going to be okay."

"Thanks, Tristan. I'll let you know what happens. And thanks for everything."

As I prepared to leave, my phone rang with a call from Daryl. Looking at Tristan, I showed him my cell. "Speak of the Devil."

I pressed the speakerphone button and said, "Hey, Daryl. I'm at Tristan's office. I think Brock and Monique took Jordan to Hilton Head. Why I have no idea, but I'm sure she's in danger."

"It's even worse than that, Gage," Daryl said frantically. "We were all wrong about Brock not knowing about who Monique really is. I just found out he knew his sister was dead. He paid for her funeral, for Christ's sake! Hailey or Monique or whoever the fuck she is isn't playing him. They're in this together, whatever it is!"

Daryl's news shook me to my bones. This was even worse than we'd thought. I took off like a shot toward the elevator to get to Teterboro Airport as quickly as possible. I just prayed I wasn't too late.

TRISTAN'S PILOT'S VOICE CAME OVER the plane's speaker, startling me out of the nightmare that had filled my head the entire flight. Over and over, I saw Jordan being harmed by Brock and Hailey, threatened by her and forced to marry him as witnesses stood by and did nothing but watch. The terrified look in her beautiful green eyes stayed in my mind even now as I began to hear Walker explain we were almost to Hilton Head.

"Mr. Stone has arranged for a car to be waiting for you when we arrive. I expect we'll be there within ten minutes, so fasten your seat belt and prepare for landing. The weather's good, so I expect it to be a smooth one."

I nodded, silently thanking him for helping me get to this point. As I sat there alone waiting for the chance to bolt off that plane and begin searching for Jordan, I tried to remind myself of how much Tristan and Nina had gone through and how well things had turned out for them. She'd run all the way to Italy, and he'd found her. That bastard Karl had done everything in his power to hurt them, even trying to kill Tristan in the end, and still they'd come out the other side stronger and better.

If only that could happen for Jordan and me.

I had to believe I could find her, or I'd go out of my mind. I had no idea where to go once we landed at Hilton

Head since I'd never been there before. What if I chose the wrong part of the island to search for her, wasting valuable time while Brock and Hailey did whatever horrible things they planned to do to her?

Sagging in my seat, I hung my head. All of this had happened because of me. Because of what I foolishly did. Back when I had a chance to be her protector—to truly be her protector—instead what did I do?

I left her. It didn't matter that I thought I was doing the right thing and that I never wanted to hurt her. I made a mistake and she did get hurt. But even worse, my choices then had set all of this into motion.

If I'd never broken up with Jordan, she never would have gotten involved with Brock Hannon. She wouldn't be in his grasp having God only knew what being done to her. And I wouldn't be getting ready to race off a plane in Hilton Head to drive like a madman to try to find her before it was too late.

Closing my eyes, I silently pledged to her I would find her in time. I wouldn't let her down again.

As the plane began its descent, a terrifying thought wormed its way into my brain, sending a chill down my spine. What if she had changed her mind? What if when she went to see Brock, he showed her the kind of life he could offer her and that desire to have the life she'd always dreamed of overpowered what she felt for me?

What if that text was how she really felt?

The sour taste of bile rose up in my throat at the mere thought that I'd lost her forever this time. I had to believe she loved me. No matter what, I had to have faith in that. Jordan hadn't changed her mind.

But that truth only lead to a more frightening one. If Jordan hadn't changed her mind, had Brock taken her by force and brought her here to marry him? The disturbing thought of him harming her settled into my brain, and as the plane touched down and began its movement toward the hanger, I leaped from my seat, ready to go find her.

It took what seemed like forever to reach the hanger, but finally the plane rolled to a slow stop and the door lowered to allow me to leave. The car Tristan had arranged for me waited nearby, and I made a dash for it to get this rescue on the road. A luxury car, it had all the bells and whistles I'd expect from him.

Inside, the keys were in the ignition and a map of Hilton Head Island sat on the passenger side seat. That's all I needed. Circled in green, Tristan's hotel was located in the Folly Field Beach area not far from the airport, and other parts of the map were outlined in red and blue, along with the main road BUS 278/William Hilton Parkway outlined in black. I looked at it unsure of where to begin, but at the very top of the page I saw a yellow sticky note that read, "Red is residential and blue is commercial."

Now I just hoped I chose the right part to search for her. But I didn't know which one to choose. My gut told me whatever Brock was up to, he hadn't brought her to a hotel. Likely, he owned a home here, so I needed to focus on the blue areas.

I headed out onto the parkway toward Burkes Beach, the

closest area of the island to me where I could find residential homes. Like a stranger in a foreign land, I felt like I didn't even have my bearings yet, but I couldn't wait to get acclimated to the area.

Jordan couldn't wait.

Burkes Beach had a mix of hotels and residences, and with each vacation home I passed, I slowed down and tried to make out if anyone who looked like Jordan stood on the porches or near a window, but I saw no one.

This was like looking for a needle in a haystack. How was I ever going to find her? Even on a small island like Hilton Head, finding her would be next to impossible.

And every moment I spent staring into strangers' homes and not seeing her was another moment she was in danger.

Or worse.

I couldn't give up. I'd done that once before with her because I thought her life would be better, and it was the biggest mistake of my life. I wouldn't give up on her again.

CHAPTER TWENTY-ONE

JORDAN

EVERYONE AROUND ME ACTED LIKE forcing a young woman to marry someone was perfectly normal, like something that happened every day in their world. Had I been transported back in time to the Middle Ages?

Brock gently held my hand, and for every time that I yanked it away, he looked down at it and said nothing, just slipping his fingers through mine once again. Over and over he repeated this until I exploded and barked, "Stop holding my hand! Stop acting like this is normal! Does no one have a problem with the fact that I don't want to marry this man?"

I looked around to see that truly no one cared. Monique just shot me an angry look, a clear threat that if I kept it up, she'd make my life a living hell and likely a very short one at that. Brock simply gave me a sad, impotent look that told me once again that he wouldn't be the one to save me from this and lowered his gaze so he didn't have to face my growing hatred for him. The witnesses behind me looked away when I turned around, a look of discomfort on both their faces as they avoided my desperate stare.

The minister seemed to be the only person around who I

saw truly wasn't okay with what was happening, but before I could appeal directly to him, Monique pulled him into another room. When he returned, all I saw was a look of pure fear in his eyes.

He wouldn't be able to help me either.

My heart sank even further as he began to speak the words of the marriage ceremony. Dearly beloved? Beloved my ass! How could this be happening? And why? Why on earth was Monique so eager to see me married to her half-brother? I had nothing more than a decent job teaching third graders and a slightly better than mediocre apartment in Brooklyn, a place she equated with some kind of slum.

I had nothing, so why would Brock's marrying me be so important?

As the minister continued to recite the marriage vows, I turned to look at Brock and whispered, "Please don't do this. I don't know what's going on, but you don't have to do this. You can put a stop to this whole madness right now."

He turned to look at me and gave me a meek smile before he whimpered, "I do."

Coward.

The words coming out of the minister's mouth flowed into my ears, but all I could do was shake my head. No, I did not take this man for anything. I didn't love him enough to even help him if Gage busted in right now and kicked his ass for doing this to me.

Gage. Oh my God, if I married Brock, there would be no way Gage would ever forgive me. Why should he? What kind of person was I that I couldn't see there was something just not right about Brock and his sister? How many times had he said he didn't trust him or her, and I just brushed his worries off?

"Miss, you need to answer," the minister said softly.

He looked at me with true concern in his soft brown eyes, the bushy eyebrows above them making it almost impossible to see how much he didn't want to do what he was doing. While his eyes told the truth, everything else about him showed how terrified he was. His shoulders had risen to just below his ears, nearly touching his frizzy, grey hair, and his entire posture looked tight and fearful.

"No. I do not take this man to be my lawfully wedded husband. I'm being forced to marry this man, and even here wherever the hell I am, if this is still the United States, it's not legal to make me marry anyone."

For a long moment, the room seemed to freeze and everyone around me appeared to hold their breath. Everyone but Monique. Nothing on her froze, and as I watched, her eyes flashed the purest look of hate I'd ever seen in my life.

Then everything began to move in slow motion, and the next thing I knew she lunged at me with her hands going for my neck. Brock let go of my hand and backed away as she tightened her fingers around my throat and squeezed. I flailed my arms as her thumbs pressed into my flesh, my strength fading with each passing moment.

"You aren't going to ruin this!" she screamed as she violently shook me. "No fucking way!"

I thrashed from side to side, grasping at her forearms to escape her hold, but it was no use. No one would stop her and in just a few more seconds, I'd be strangled to death.

"You're going to kill her! We're not married yet!"

Brock's words echoed in my ears, and as my eyes closed and everything slipped away, Monique suddenly released me and I fell to the floor. Choking and gasping for air, I coughed until my chest hurt as everyone watched me lie there. I wanted to scream at the top of my lungs and demand to know what kind of people they were letting all this happen right in front of their eyes.

They had other ideas. I wasn't there for any reason other than to be Brock's bride, so even before I was finished coughing and gasping for air, he picked me up and stood me on my feet. Monique stood next to me, and when the minister repeated his question if I would take Brock as my lawfully wedded husband, the room fell silent as they all waited for me to speak.

But I couldn't speak. I could barely swallow without my throat feeling like Monique's hands were back around my neck squeezing tighter with every moment that ticked by. I opened my mouth, but no words came out. All I could do is croak noises as I tried over and over to say no.

"I think you know her answer," Monique said in a low, angry voice. "Finish the ceremony now."

The minister gave me one more pathetic look and took a deep breath. In a shaky voice, he said, "By the power vested in me by the state of South Carolina, I know pronounce you husband and wife."

I looked at Brock in horror, realizing the awful truth written all over his face. I was married to him, and now I'd find

out the terrible reason why he and Monique had drugged and
kidnapped me to force me into a marriage that meant something only to them.

FORCED INTO ONE OF THE house's tiny bedrooms, I watched
Monique and one of the witnesses take one last look at me
before they closed the door, and then I dashed to the windows
to see if I could escape. They'd been left unlocked, but one
look out toward the ground below told me I'd never survive
jumping the two floors and there were no eaves or ledges to
hang on to on this side of the house.

I was trapped.

Sitting down on the bed, I took a deep breath and tried to
keep the horrible thoughts that entered my head at bay.
Would they kill me now that I'd married Brock? I still had no
idea why us marrying was so important, but since neither one
of them had mentioned anything besides the marriage I
couldn't help but think that now that they'd gotten that taken
care of I served little purpose.

But why had they wanted me to marry him in the first
place?

None of it made any sense, and I was quickly becoming
exhausted from thinking of it. Part of me wanted to cry, but
another part of me kept telling the weepy part to shut up.
That part wasn't ready to give up, even though the whole
marriage thing had happened already.

That part of me had no intention of giving up and shed-
ding any tears just yet.

The sound of the doorknob turning made my head snap

to look toward the door, and I saw Brock quickly come in and close it, as if he was escaping from someone chasing him. Confused as to what he could possibly think we might have to talk about, I stood from the bed and folded my arms across my chest.

"Whatever you think you're doing here, forget it. You had your chance to do the right thing out there before that minister married us."

He didn't say a thing, but for a moment I thought I saw a look in his eyes that made me think he had plans to use this bedroom for its most romantic purpose. I backed up toward the far wall, shaking my head.

"No fucking way. Are you going to now tell me you need to have me give you a child too? Forget it. Every ounce of my being hates you, whoever you are, and I'm sure even my uterus would fight with all its strength to expel your sperm, you cowardly son of a bitch!"

Whatever that look in his eyes was, it disappeared when I told him my body would basically intentionally miscarry his child instead of doing what he wanted, and he frowned as he sat on the bed. "That's not what I'm here for."

"Oh yeah? Come to say you're sorry for forcing me into marrying you? Don't bother. I'm pretty sure whatever the hell that minister officiated out there isn't legal in any state in this country, not even this one, so as soon as I get the hell away from here, I'm going to make sure that gets erased from my life, along with you and that bitch sister of yours. If I have my way, the two of you will be living by the motto 'Three hots and a cot' for years to come."

His expression didn't change at my reference to him going to prison for all of this, though, and he just motioned for me to sit with him on the bed. "I don't have much time, so please listen, okay?"

But I wasn't about to budge from my spot next to the wall. "Listen to what? I'm not interested in any more of your excuses, so save your breath."

"Jordan, please listen. What I tell you might mean the difference between life and death for you."

"Life and death? Oh my God! Your crazy fucking sister is planning to kill me too?"

He shook his head and then stopped. "No. Well, I don't know. Just hear what I have to say, okay? I'm trying to help here."

"Help who? Yourself? Crazy Monique?"

His shoulders sagged, and he stared at me with a look of exhaustion in his hazel eyes. "You. Now please come here because I don't know how long before someone comes in. You already know I'm not Brock Hannon, so Monique obviously isn't my sister."

His words struck me like a slap to the face. In all the commotion, I hadn't even thought about who she really was. "Not your sister? Then who the hell is she and why was it so important for me to marry you, Justin?"

A noise outside the door startled him, and terror settled into his expression. "We don't have a lot of time. I was hired by Monique to impersonate Brock Hannon, but her real name is Hailey. She took him for a shit ton of money and then he died. That's her thing. She's a grifter. Her marks are usually old men, but Brock was different. He was a recluse, so he was the perfect target. He had tons of cash and a company he basically ran from his house. Pretty successfully too, from what I understand."

I moved toward the bed and sat on the end of the mattress. "Did she kill him?"

Justin opened his mouth to speak but nothing came out. Then he shrugged. "I don't know. I just know he was dead when I came into the picture."

"What was the point of all of this? You took over this guy's life for what?"

"To marry you."

The way he said it sounded so matter of fact, like it wasn't the most bizarre grouping of words he'd ever said. More confused than ever about why, I asked, "Why would she want to commit this whole fraud to get you to marry me? I'm nobody. I have no money she can steal, so why?"

He turned to look at the door and then back at me. "Yes, you do. She didn't tell me much, but she wouldn't be out to use you if you didn't have something she wanted, and that's always money."

Closing my eyes, I tried to keep my emotions in check, but they bubbled up to the surface and I began to cry. After all that had happened, I couldn't hold the tears back anymore. Somehow, this crazy woman whose real name I didn't know had gotten me confused with someone else, and now she'd orchestrated this whole forced marriage thing and I wasn't even the right person to scam!

Justin lightly touched my shoulder and whispered, "I'm

sorry. I never wanted to hurt you. All I had to do was impersonate this guy, but I really did fall for you. I know you don't care for me, and I get that, but let me try to help now, at least."

With my face buried in my hands, I sobbed, "She got the wrong person. I don't have the money you two think I have. I'm just an elementary teacher with a tiny apartment in Sunset Park. I'm nobody."

He lifted my chin so I had to look at him and shook his head. "We don't have time for this now. She's going to want you to sign something tonight. Do as she says and you might be okay. I'll do whatever I can to help you escape once you sign, okay?"

Wiping my eyes, I tried to understand what he was saying. "Sign what? What would she want me to sign? I just told you she got the wrong person. I'm just a nobody she got mixed up with the real person she wanted to scam. Why can't you get that?"

"Just do as she says, Jordan. Sign whatever she puts in front of you. Once you do that, I'll help you escape the first chance I see."

"Why am I signing anything? If she needs me to sign something so badly, then wouldn't that be my bargaining chip? Why give her what she wants?"

Justin sighed and shook his head. "She's not beyond hurting you, and nothing about this is worth being hurt or killed. You want to go back to your life as a school teacher with that guy Gage, right? So sign the papers she puts in front of you and then run away when I can find an opening."

Nothing he was talking about made sense. "And what's in it for you? I don't get the feeling you're doing this out of the kindness of your heart, fake Brock. So if I sign, what do you get?"

"I get what I was always going to get. Money. That's why I agreed to this whole thing. Twenty grand up front and twenty more when the deal is done."

"Where is she getting the money? From the real Brock Hannon?"

"We don't have a lot of time left, Jordan. Just listen to me and do as she says. Once you sign, you get your life back and I get paid."

"And she gets what? That's my problem here, pal. That crazy bitch out there is getting something huge out of this, or she wouldn't have designed this whole scheme and ended up drugging me to get me here for our sham marriage. So what does she get?"

He hesitated a moment and then leaned in next to me. "I don't know what Hailey gets, but it's got to be a hell of a lot more than the forty grand she paid me just to marry you."

Before his words could settle into my brain, the bedroom door flew open and there stood Monique or Hailey or whoever she was in all her fucked up glory, a look of pure madness in her eyes. "Time to get some work done, kids. Justin, you better have been able to convince her because I'm not in the mood for any more delays."

I jumped up off the bed and backed up toward the wall again. "I'm not signing anything, Hailey. I don't know what you think is going on here, but you got the wrong person.

Whatever you were trying to do, you failed. Your plan didn't work."

Her eyes opened wide for a second, like my bravado surprised her, and then she looked over at Justin still sitting on the bed but now cowering in front of her. "I didn't think I'd be able to trust you, but you didn't let me down. Go out into the living room and wait for us."

The words had barely left her mouth and he was bolting out into the hallway. Pleased with something he'd done, she took two steps toward me and then stopped. "I bet you have a lot of questions, Jordan. In that way, we're quite similar. I love questions, and I love finding out the answers even more. There's nothing like piecing together a puzzle, right?"

"We're nothing alike, so don't flatter yourself. I don't know what you think you've done, but you're wrong. You made a mistake and whatever this is, I'm not the person you thought I was."

She took another step and stopped less than a foot away from me. Reaching out, she wrapped the ends of my hair around her forefinger and stared at me with the same crazy look she'd worn so often around me.

"I always wanted blond hair like yours, Jordan. Ever since I was a little girl, I wanted hair like this. But I got my mother's hair instead."

Something told me if I didn't try to speak to her now that she might go completely off the rails and try to strangle me again, so I smiled and said, "You have very beautiful hair. I'm sure your mother's was nice too."

My words seemed to calm her for the time being, and she

smiled back at me. "You know, I think under different circumstances we might have been able to be good friends. I always wanted a sister, and we could have been like that."

I had no idea what to say to that. She wasn't anyone I'd ever want to spend time with, no matter what the circumstances. Even before I knew she was an out of her mind crazy woman, I didn't like her. My gut had told me something was off with this one.

As always, I should have listened to it.

My gut had also told me she had feelings for Justin too, so despite the fact that I likely shouldn't have asked, I let my curiosity get the best of me. "Are you and Justin together?"

Her smile spread across her face. "Yes, he's mine. Why?"

Trying to keep calm, I shrugged. "Just wondering. I had a feeling that you cared for him more than a sister should, even a stepsister, but I wasn't sure."

She twirled my hair around her finger again, this time tugging lightly as she said, "Yes, Justin is mine, and once we get finished here, he and I are going to ride off into the sunset. You can go back to your life with Mr. V and enjoy teaching those little kiddies their ABCs and colors and all that cute stuff you do, and everyone will be happy."

I had to stifle my urge to correct her ideas about what a third grade teacher taught. What a bitch! Instead, I just smiled and hoped Justin had told the truth because the sooner I got away from the two of them, the better my life would instantly be.

Hailey tugged me by the arm to follow her. "Time to get going, Jordan."

We got out to the living room and I saw Justin sitting on the couch waiting for us with a sheet of paper on the coffee table in front of him. He smiled meekly at me and then looked away as Hailey sat me down next to him.

"Sign on the bottom line and all this ends."

I picked up the paper and saw nothing but my name and Justin's name. No other words appeared on the page. Confused, I turned it over and saw a completely blank page on the back too.

"What is this? What am I signing?"

"Your name. That's it. All you have to do is sign your name and this ends with you returning to your little life with schoolchildren and a seedy little apartment in Brooklyn."

"But I don't know what I'm signing. I could be signing my death warrant for all I know. I could be signing a confession to a crime. I won't sign this."

Justin gently touched my arm. "Just sign it, Jordan. You aren't signing anything that will make you guilty of a crime. Sign it and be free."

I looked at him and wanted to believe what he was saying. I wanted to think that after all that time together that he wouldn't trick me into signing a paper that would hurt me in some way. But everything he'd done at this house told me I couldn't rely on him.

Shaking my head, I turned back to look up at Hailey. "No. You won't get me to sign this, unless you tell me what this is about."

I knew that wasn't she wanted to hear, but surprisingly, she didn't explode with anger. Instead, she just stood there for a moment looking at me and then said, "What you're signing will eventually be a legal document showing that you and Justin are officially married. That's it."

Was she telling the truth? I looked to my left at Justin and saw his expression hadn't changed, so maybe she had. Since I planned on getting this whole sham marriage declared null and void, what harm could come from signing her paper?

"Okay, but with one condition," I said, knowing at any moment this crazy woman might lose her mind and I might lose my life. "I get to go free without any problems from you two."

I carefully watched Justin's face for any sign that he had lied earlier when he told me he'd help me escape, but nothing in his expression told me he wouldn't. Turning to look up at Hailey, I saw her smile and nod.

"Okay."

My gut told me nothing about this was going to end the way I wanted it to, but I didn't have many choices. I could sign her paper and then hope that some slick lawyer could get me out of whatever came from it, or I could refuse to sign it and likely see just how crazy Hailey could get.

Hands shaking, I picked up the pen and felt both Justin and Hailey staring at me as I signed my name. Justin signed his name too and handed the paper to her.

Whatever it was, it was done.

"Now I can go, right?"

Hailey looked up from the paper and shook her head. From behind her back, she pulled out a gun and pointed it at my head. "I don't think so, Jordan. This is where this ends.

"You don't have to do this," I pleaded, silently praying to God to get me out of this terrible mess. "I won't say a thing. Just let me go."

Justin didn't give her a chance to answer and lunged at her, taking her down to the floor, so I grabbed the gun and with my hands shaking so hard I thought it might fall from my grasp, I pointed it at her.

"I don't want to use this, so please don't make me. I just want to leave and forget this ever happened."

Justin pinned her to the floor and looked up at me. "Get out of here! Run!"

Scared out of my mind and unsure what to do, I did as he said and dropped the gun before making a mad dash to the nearest door.

Taking the stairs by two toward the ground floor, I lost my footing and tumbled down them until I hit the last step and landed hard on my back, knocking the wind out of me. Everything in front of me appeared double and I couldn't get a full breath of air into my lungs, but I had to get to my feet and run to the main road before she made it down the stairs to get me.

It took every ounce of strength I possessed, but I grabbed onto a wooden post and pulled myself up. Barely able to stand, much less run, I still had to try and slowly I stumbled step by step toward the road.

Just as I reached the curb, I heard a gunshot from the house and turned to see Hailey running down the stairs like a madwoman. Adrenaline raced through me as I saw her hit that last stair and begin running toward me, her face the picture of rage. I had nowhere to hide and barely enough strength to walk, but I had to keep going.

A car slowly came around the bend just as I stepped onto the pavement, and then everything went dark.

CHAPTER TWENTY-TWO

GAGE

THE HEADLIGHTS SHINED ON SOMEONE stumbling into the road ahead of me, and in a flash I recognized Jordan's long blond hair as she fell to the ground in front of the car. I skidded to a hard stop and jumped out, dreading what I'd find when I reached her.

She lay on the ground, her eyes closed. Terrified she might be dead, I quickly pressed my fingertips to her neck to check her pulse as someone ran toward us in the darkness. It was faint but there, so I scooped her up in my arms and ran back to the car. As I pressed the gas pedal to the floor, I looked in the rearview mirror and saw the person running toward the car was that shopaholic bitch Monique.

I floored the gas, and Jordan slammed back against the seat as we took off down the street. Startled, she sat up frightened and confused. "What's going on?"

"It's okay. Monique was chasing us, but I left her in the dust back there. How the hell did you get away from them?" I asked as I tried to keep the car on the road at the same time as I looked to see if she was okay.

"Justin attacked her after I signed the paper and that gave

me enough time to escape."

Jordan slumped against the seat and closed her eyes, so I didn't bother to ask who the hell Justin was. I just took her hand in mine and held it tightly as I drove way too fast over the island's roads toward Tristan's hotel.

As long as we reached the Richmont, we'd be safe.

Brock and Monique may have been able to do as they pleased when it was just Jordan they were dealing with, but I wasn't going to let them hurt her again.

It only took a few minutes to drive to the hotel, and true to his word, Tristan had made sure everything was taken care of. Concierge was waiting to escort us up to our room, and when we got there, a full meal waited for us. I couldn't tell if Jordan was injured and that's why she'd collapsed in front of the car or if she'd just been unable to run anymore.

She sat on the bed and looked like she'd lost her will to live. Hanging her head, she said quietly, "How did you know where to find me?"

"Nina. She remembered you saying you and Brock planned to elope down here, so I took a chance and got here as soon as I could."

Jordan looked up at me and shook her head. "Did you search the whole island? That would be like finding a needle in a haystack."

Sitting down next to her, I slipped my arm around her and pulled her close to me. "I'd hoped I wouldn't have to or I might be too late for whatever they planned to do to you. I'm just glad I picked the right part of the island to search first."

She began to cry and buried her face in my chest, sobbing, "You were too late. I'm so sorry."

What did she mean I was too late? What had they done to her? It took every ounce of strength I had inside me not to let my rage get the better of me and drive right back to that house to punish the two of them for what they'd done to her.

"It's okay. They're gone now and I'm not going to let them hurt you again, Jordan. Tomorrow we'll leave here and go someplace safe for a while."

Her crying stopped for a moment but then began again harder, as if something I'd said had upset her even more. I didn't know what had happened with Brock and Hailey, but it wasn't good.

Looking up at me, she wiped her eyes and looked away. "I'm going to take a bath."

"Okay. I'll put off calling the police until you get out."

She stood bolt upright and shook her head. "No! No police! I don't want to deal with that."

Before I could say anything else, she walked into the bathroom and closed the door. I wanted to go back to that house and beat the fuck out of Brock Hannon for doing this to her. And Hailey? I'd never wanted to hit a woman before in my life, but if she'd been standing anywhere nearby me, I would have taken a shot at her too.

I stood by the bathroom door and quietly beneath the sound of the water running into the tub I heard Jordan's crying. Thoughts of Hannon raping her and every other heinous thing I could think of passed through my mind, and all I could do was stand there because I didn't want to let her out of my sight again.

I'd made that mistake and look what had happened.

After about fifteen minutes of blaming myself, I knocked on the door unsure of what to say or if there was anything I could say to make things better. She didn't reply, so I slowly opened the door and saw her sitting hunched over in the water, her arms, shoulders, and neck showing bruises from someone's hands hurting her.

"I just wanted to see if you needed anything."

She looked up at me and pleaded, "Don't go. Please don't go."

Forcing a smile, I stepped into the bathroom and sat down beside the tub. "I'm not going anywhere. It's okay. I'm here now."

Her long blond hair hung in wet clumps down her back, and just the sight of her made me want to take her into my arms and never let go. I couldn't fight the urge to show her how much seeing her like this broke my heart, so I kissed the top of her head and whispered the only words I could think of at that moment.

"It's going to be okay, Jordan. I won't let them hurt you again."

She began to cry again, quiet sobs that echoed off the beige marble tile all around us. God, it was tearing me apart not knowing what had happened to her. I wanted to ask a hundred questions, but the last thing Jordan needed at that moment was me acting like myself.

We'd never experienced anything like this. Our time together had been fun and at the worst, passionate fighting that ended up in even more passionate lovemaking. I'd never seen her cry, and the only time I'd ever heard her cry was when I broke up with her.

God, would she never stop paying for that? Because that was the truth of the matter. If I'd never broken up with her, she wouldn't have been sitting there in that tub sobbing over what that fuck had done to her. She wouldn't be bruised and beaten.

"I'm sorry you have to see me like this. I should have listened to you when you told me you thought there was something wrong with Brock."

I'd never seen her look so defeated. Those green eyes I loved to get lost in now looked like they'd never lose the fear that had settled into them.

"You couldn't know, Jordan. He seemed like a normal guy," I said, hating how I had to practically defend him.

"His name isn't Brock, by the way. It's Justin."

Her words hung in the steamy air around us for a moment and then my brain processed them. "What? He's not Brock Hannon."

"No. He was just a guy playing him to get to me."

"I thought Monique was the one pretending to be someone else. Some Hailey girl who scams old guys out of money."

Jordan looked at me surprised. "You knew about that?"

"I just found out. I asked Daryl to check both of them out, but he only found out about Hailey by the time I realized you were gone."

Hanging her head, she covered her face with her hands. "I'm so sorry, Gage. She read me the text she sent to you. I can only imagine how much that hurt, and I'm sorry. I didn't have anything to do with it. I was drugged and she took my phone."

"Drugged?"

She lifted her head and nodded. "They put something in my water when I was at Brock's apartment telling him I couldn't marry him. She's crazy, Gage. I think she would have killed me if I didn't get away."

"What was all this about?" I asked, more confused than ever. If Brock wasn't Brock Hannon, and Monique wasn't really his sister, what was their story?

"I don't know. Nothing she said made sense. All I know is that it was paramount that he and I get married."

I gently touched her shoulder, lightly caressing the bruise forming there, and kissed the top of her head. "Well, thank God I found you in time so she didn't succeed with that part of her crazy plan."

Jordan fell silent, and as we sat there the only noise was the sound of the water gently lapping against the sides of the tub. I didn't know everything that had happened to her with them, but just seeing her so broken tore me up inside.

She turned away from me and mumbled, "Just give me a few minutes, okay?"

I stood from the tub and looked down at her bent over hugging her knees. I'd never seen her so frightened. I hated this.

"Okay. I'll be just out there if you need anything."

When she came out of the bathroom in her pink t-shirt and shorts and trying so hard to be strong in front of me, I wanted to take her into my arms and never let her go. She didn't have to pretend she wasn't shaken to the core after what had happened. The fuckers had drugged her and kidnapped her. She had every right to be coming apart.

Tugging on the bottom of her shirt, she looked down toward the floor and quietly said, "I hope you can forgive me, Gage."

Jesus, she was asking me for forgiveness when I was the one who'd messed everything up. I cradled her face and shook my head. "It's not you who needs to ask for forgiveness. It's me. If I'd never been so stupid to fall for those letters, we would have never broken up. This is all my fault."

"Oh, Gage, no! It's not your fault. We've both done things we wish we hadn't, but it's not your fault."

Jordan lay her head against my chest and hugged me tight, like she was afraid I might leave if she loosened her hold. I ran my hand over her damp hair, hating what had happened to her. To us.

If only I hadn't fucked up.

But I had to pretend to be strong for her now because she didn't need some guy with a self-loathing problem dumping his issues on her. When I got my hands on those two assholes, I'd let them deal with my shit.

I couldn't think about that, though. If I did, that would be just another thing between us, and we couldn't handle that now.

"It'll be okay. It will. I promise, Jordan."

She shook her head and sighed. "I don't understand how this could have happened. None of it was true. None of it."

Tilting her head back, I searched her eyes for answers.

"What do you mean none of it was true?"

She sighed again and sat down on the bed. Hanging her head, she said quietly, "The whole thing was a set up. This Hailey person wanted me to marry Justin, who was pretending to be Brock. She had us sign a blank piece of paper and then she planned on killing me. None of it makes any sense. Why me?"

"You signed something? What was it?"

"A blank sheet of paper," she mumbled covering her face with her hands.

"Jordan, why did you sign that? You have no idea how diabolical this woman is."

She dropped her hands and stood up to glare at me. "Like I had a fucking choice! I don't know how diabolical she is? She drugged me to make me marry someone and then planned to kill me! Trust me, Gage. I fucking know!"

I wanted to apologize, to tell her I didn't mean to focus on such trivial bullshit like whatever the hell she'd signed, but she spun around and headed toward the door.

"Jordan, where are you going? I don't want you out of my sight here."

She snapped her head back and flashed me an angry look. "This is one of Tristan's hotels, Gage. I'm sure I'm safe here."

The implication that I couldn't keep her safe but Tristan could hit me like a fist to the gut, and I stepped back as my self-loathing began to take me over. I hadn't kept her safe, no matter how much I wanted to. And it was written all over her face that she didn't believe I could either.

"I didn't mean it the way you're taking it, Gage."

I shook my head and tried to act like what she'd said hadn't hurt. "Yeah. You're right. Just be careful."

Jordan turned toward the door and stopped. "I really didn't mean it the way you took it. I just don't…I don't want to fight. I just need to clear my head after everything that happened."

As the door closed behind her, all I could think of was how much I loved her and how much I wanted to find Hailey and Justin and kill them for what they'd done.

My phone ringing saved me from wallowing in my own self-loathing and I answered it to hear Daryl's gruff voice already talking. "…I found out more about our girl Hailey. Tell me you already found Jordan. This Hailey bitch is definitely not someone she should be anywhere near."

"Daryl, I know. I got Jordan away from her, but not only wasn't she who she said she was but Brock wasn't who he said he was either. He was just some guy named Justin."

"What the fuck is going on with these people?"

"Jordan says that Hailey wanted her to marry this guy named Justin. Then she had her sign some blank sheet of paper. I'm sure she's up to something pretty fucking bad."

"No doubt. Thankfully, you got your lady away from those crazy bastards before something really bad happened."

I shuddered at the thought of what could have happened if I hadn't gotten to her in time. Daryl continued to talk about how happy he was to know Jordan was safe, but then he said, "This is all well and good, but we need to know what was behind all this. Who are these people and why did they want Jordan so badly?"

"No idea. She doesn't know either."

"You know what? Give me a minute to check something out, Gage. I've got a hunch I'd like to check out. I'll call you back in a few."

Daryl left me sitting there in the hotel room unsure about virtually everything that had happened. Not about how much I loved Jordan, though. Throughout all of this madness, that had been the only constant.

I had a second chance with her, and she needed me to be the man I promised her I'd be. And now that we were back together, it was time to make it official.

My phone rang as my mind filled with how I'd ask her to marry me. Looking at the screen, I saw it was Daryl again. Maybe his hunch hadn't panned out.

"Hey Daryl. No luck?"

More excited than I'd ever heard him, he said, "Exactly the opposite. Always trust the gut, my friend. It never steers you wrong. When you told me about the engagement party, you said you didn't think it had been planned for long, but the Royale Hotel doesn't do last minute. Not unless you have the bucks to back up your request."

"That makes sense. Hailey and this guy Justin can't have that kind of money, can they?"

"I didn't think so either, so I made a quick call to the Royale. I know one of the event planners there and asked her who paid for Brock Hannon's engagement party. Too say I'm surprised would be an understatement."

"There's someone behind this bankrolling it, sort of a mastermind?" I asked, stunned that there was more to this story.

"Not just someone. None other than Dalton Spear himself."

"Why would someone like him be involved in this?"

"I don't know yet, but you can bet I'm going to be looking into this. I'll call you as soon as I find something out."

The conversation with Daryl only made me more concerned for Jordan's safety. Knowing that Hailey and Justin had someone like Dalton Spear behind them meant their resources were practically limitless.

And people with no limits were the most dangerous kind of enemy.

Chapter Twenty-Three

Jordan

THE HILTON HEAD RICHMONT MAY have been the safest place for me on the island, but all I wanted to do was run away and never come back. Everything I'd been through that day had a surreal feel to it, and as I walked down the hallway I struggled to get my head around the idea that anyone in the world would bother to kidnap someone like me. I was a nobody—one of millions of souls who called themselves New Yorkers and lived day to day in the greatest city on earth but no one of consequence.

Yet there I was, newly rescued from being kidnapped and forced to marry a man who'd been impersonating a millionaire just to trick me into falling for him. Christ, when the hell did my life become such a mess?

And through all of this craziness, Gage had been the man I loved, even if I hadn't wanted to admit it for all those months. Now he sat in a hotel room after saving me waiting for me to return thinking he was to blame for all of this happening to me.

I didn't mean to act like he couldn't keep me safe. The last thing I wanted to do was make him feel unloved. After all the time we'd spent apart, all I wanted was to be back with the man I loved and start over again.

The elevator doors opened and I rode down to the lobby, needing to find a phone. There were only two people in the world I could talk to, and if it couldn't be Gage, then it needed to be Nina. Without my cell phone, I had to hope the concierge would allow me to use their phone to call her.

An older woman with dark skin and long straight black hair smiled at me as I approached the counter. "Can I help you, miss?"

"My name is Jordan Wright and I'm in room—" I stopped speaking as I tried to remember our room number. "I'm sorry. I can't remember my room number. I've had a hard night. I just want to use a phone to call my friend. She's the wife of the owner of the Richmont."

I was rambling, but that was where my head was at the moment. The concierge woman looked me up and down, likely thinking I didn't belong at this kind of hotel with my t-shirt and shorts stuck to my still damp skin and my wet hair hanging in stringy clumps around my face. But instead of turning me away, she smiled again and nodded.

"Ms. Wright, we're happy to help you. Please feel free to use the phone in our office behind me. Just come around the counter and I'll let you in."

A feeling of relief washed over me and I did as she said, hurrying into the room to call Nina. I closed the door behind me so she wouldn't hear about the madness that had been my day so far and dialed the phone. Thankfully, Nina answered on the second ring, as eager to speak to me as I was to talk to her.

"Oh my God, Jordan! Tell me you're safe. Tell me Gage got you out of whatever Brock and his awful sister were doing to you."

"It's okay, Nina. I'm fine. Gage rescued me before any real damage was done. Well, not exactly before, but I'm okay now."

"What happened? Are you sure you're okay? Are you at the hotel?"

"I am. I'm just exhausted from everything that happened, and then Gage and I had an argument and I had to get out of the room for a few minutes."

"Oh honey, you sound terrible. What did you fight about?"

I didn't want to tell Nina about how I had to marry Brock and how awful I felt lying to Gage about it. Just having to think about all that made me feel sick. All I needed at that moment was to hear her say things were going to be okay.

"It's not important. I'm going to head back up there in a minute and apologize for being such an ass."

"Jordan, I'm so happy to hear your voice. I was so worried that something bad had happened. Every minute that I couldn't remember where you said you and Brock were eloping to could have been…"

Nina let her sentence drift off, and I heard the sound of her quietly crying. "Oh sweetie, don't cry. Gage and I are safe, so it's fine."

"I know. I'm being weepy again. Don't listen to me. Now that you and Gage are back together, everything's going to be okay and you'll come back here so I can give you a big hug and the kids can jump all over you and cover you in kisses."

Swallowing hard, I admitted the truth to Nina that I couldn't to the man I loved. "They forced me to marry Brock."

"What do you mean?"

"Well, he really isn't Brock Hannon. I guess I should have known that no real millionaire would ever want to marry me. His name is Justin. And Monique isn't Monique. She's Hailey and she's not his sister. I know this sounds totally fucked up and I'm probably not sounding like I'm making any sense right now, but there was a gun and they forced me to marry him. Oh God, Nina, how am going to tell Gage that?"

She remained silent, likely trying to figure out everything I'd just dumped on her or if I'd received a blow to the head. Finally, when she spoke, I heard in her voice just how bad things were.

"Honey, I know it seems like everything's gone wrong, but it's going to be okay. Good things happen to good people. You always say that. Well, you're my best friend and one of the best people I've ever met, so I can't believe things aren't going to get better."

"Jesus, Nina, if you're giving me the good things happen to good people speech, it must be really bad. He's not going to forgive me, is he? I married another man. How can I expect him to forgive me for that?"

As the tears began to roll down over my cheeks, Nina softly said, "I don't believe for a second that Gage can't forgive you for that. You said they forced you to marry Brock and there was a gun. I bet the whole marriage isn't even legal because you didn't do it of your free will."

"This is why things never work out for me, isn't it? My life is a complete fucking mess. I'll be lucky if Gage is even in the room when I get back."

"Don't talk like that. You're a wonderful person. This isn't your fault, so anyone who wants to blame you is an ass and not worth your time. But Gage isn't that kind of guy. Just tell him the truth. I bet he'll be so supportive, like he always is."

I sagged against the upholstered back of the office chair and took a deep breath in, letting it out slowly in the hope that I'd feel better. It didn't work. I still felt like shit.

"I'm so tired, Nina. It might be the drugs they gave me when they kidnapped me. I don't know. I just know I wish we were all out at your house around the pool drinking some good wine and having some good laughs. Will that ever happen again?"

"Of course it will, honey. Just don't lose faith in Gage. He's a good guy. Tell him what happened. He'll stand by you."

How could I tell the man who'd warned me over and over about Brock that I was actually married to him now? If he told me he'd married some woman instead of me, even if it was under duress, it would eat me up inside. How could I expect him to accept it any better than I would?

"I tried to tell him. I did, but I can't do that to him. I can't. I hate to lay all of this on you, but I need you to help me find a way to get me out of this marriage so Gage never finds out."

"Just tell him, Jordan. He'll understand."

"No, he won't. Please, I need your help. You and Tristan must know lawyers. I need you to find out what I have to do to get this marriage annulled or get a divorce. Whatever it takes, but I can't let Gage know."

"Okay, honey. First thing in the morning, I'll find someone. I'll talk to Tristan tonight and find someone who can fix this."

Sagging against the desk, I closed my eyes and tried to believe things would be okay. "Thanks. I owe you big."

I heard Tristan say something to Nina, and then she said in a frantic voice, "Jordan, the police contacted Tristan's security chief at the hotel. Someone was shot."

"Shot? Who?"

"His man there didn't tell him, but they're looking for you. Why would they be looking for you?"

"I held the gun, but I didn't shoot anyone. Why would they think I did that?"

Instantly, I remembered the only time in my life I'd been fingerprinted—when I applied for my teacher certification in New York. That was how they had my fingerprints on file and how they connected me to the gun.

"Just tell them the truth, Jordan. You're the victim here."

My heart slammed against my ribs as I imagined how I'd explain the bizarre story I didn't even understand myself. There was no way anyone was going to believe me.

"Nina, I need your help. I can't talk to the police about this. My fingerprints are on that gun and they're never going to believe me when I tell them what Hailey and Justin did. And even worse, if I talk to them, Gage is going to find out about the marriage. Please, I can't let that happen!"

"What do you want me to do?"

"Gage and I need to get out of here right now. I need you to get Tristan to let us use the plane again. I don't know where we can go, but I can't deal with the police now."

"Jordan, that means we have to lie to them. Tristan will have to have his security man lie about you being there in the first place."

"Please, Nina! I wouldn't ask if I didn't really need you to do this. I hate having to get you in the middle of all this mess, but please do me this favor."

The phone fell silent, but I heard mumbling in the background. As they spoke, I walked in circles in the tiny concierge office, hoping to God the police hadn't already arrived and spoken to them about me.

Nina returned to the phone and spoke quickly. "Okay, but flying isn't going to be possible since the pilot has to file a flight plan and the police will be able to find out exactly where you're going."

"Then how do we get out of here?"

I waited for Nina to answer but heard Tristan's voice instead. "Jordan, I want you to listen to me. Gage was using one of the Richmont's cars. You can use that and I'll tell my security staff there that they aren't to say a word about that vehicle until the police ask about it. But it might not take them very long. Once that happens, we'll have to find another way to get you where you're going. I'll call Gage now, so by the time you get back up to the room, he'll be ready to leave."

"Thank you so much, Tristan. I'm so sorry you and Nina got wrapped up in all this. I never meant for that to happen."

"Save the apologies for another time. You need to get out of there right now. My guy said the police are on their way."

"Okay. Tell Nina I love her and thanks again."

I hung the phone up and ran out past the concierge toward the elevators. By the time I reached the room, Gage had already spoken to Tristan and stood ready to leave. I saw the questioning in his eyes. He wanted to know why I, the victim, didn't just tell the police everything.

If only I could.

In the few seconds we had, I tried to let him know how much I loved him. Cradling his face, I looked up into his dark blue eyes and said, "If you don't want to do this, you don't have to. You never signed on for this. I know that."

Gage leaned down and kissed me on the top of my head. "What kind of knight in shining armor would I be if I let you drive away from here all alone to deal with all of this craziness?"

Resting my head on his chest for just a moment, I took a deep breath in and sighed. As long as Nina found a lawyer who could get me out of that marriage, he'd never know how truly bad this craziness was.

"We need to go, Jordan. The cops are probably already here."

I looked up at him standing there so strong and protective. "Promise me no matter what happens we'll get through this?"

Gage nodded and smiled in that crooked way I loved. "I promise. Nothing's going to separate us again."

"Okay. Then let's do this. Any idea where we can go?"

"I think it's time to go home," he said as he closed the door behind us. "What do you think of mountains and fresh air for a change?"

"I love it! But I have to be back at school in just over a week."

"We'll deal with that when the time comes. Right now, we need to get out of here or the police are going to find us."

We hurried down the hallway to the nearest stairwell. Halfway down to the main floor, Gage stopped on the landing, a look of fear crossing his face. "I left my phone in the room. If the police find it, they'll know where we're heading because I texted my family we're coming. I have to go back to get it. Wait here. I'll be back in a minute."

I took one last look at him before he tore back up the stairs and knew I couldn't let him pay for my mistakes. Now his family would be involved, and I couldn't let that happen. As the door to the hallway clicked closed, I silently told him I was sorry and began walking down to the main floor.

Where I'd go I had no idea, but this mess was mine and I wouldn't make the man I love pay, possibly with his own freedom. Gage was too good a man for that.

I opened the heavy steel door to the outside and the humid Carolina air stopped me dead. Catching my breath, I stepped out into the summer heat and saw the flashing red lights of a police car. My heart raced as I quickly searched for a way to escape. To the rear of the hotel lay about fifty yards of grass and then marshland and to the front was the main road, but I didn't dare try to make it past the cops since they likely had a description of me and I'd be caught in a minute.

I had no choice but to head back toward the marshes.

The sidewalk around the hotel led me straight to the grass and the fence that marked the end of the property. In the distance I heard a police radio and raced toward the marshland to escape. Headlights shined on me as I tore across the lawn, and my heart sank at the thought that I'd been caught before I even had a chance.

"Jordan! Get back here!"

I recognized Gage's voice immediately and shook my head as I began to climb the metal fence. "No! Go away!"

Halfway up, I felt a hand grab my right ankle and looked down to see Gage staring up at me with a mixture of hurt and panic in his eyes.

"We have to get out of here now. Get down here!"

I tried to swat him away, but he wouldn't leave. "You need to go, Gage. I can't put you in danger too. Let me go!"

"No!"

Before I could get my footing and climb higher, he wrapped his arms around my waist and pulled me down. Throwing me over his shoulder, he marched back to the car. "Thought you'd get rid of me that easily, huh? Now stop doing stupid things so we can get the hell out of here."

He opened the passenger side door and sat me down in the seat. I wanted to tell him he didn't have to do this, but he just slammed the door and ran around the car. Sliding into the driver's seat, he pressed the gas pedal to the floor.

I regretted the hurt in his eyes when he found me and gently placed my hand on his as he drove. "I didn't want you to get hurt because of me."

As we raced out of the Richmont parking lot and hit the main road on Hilton Head Island, he turned to look at me and smiled. "I'd be more hurt being without you."

"I just couldn't bear the idea of your family being involved too. I never meant for any of this to happen, Gage."

Slowly, one of his sexy crooked smiles spread across his lips, and he turned back to face the road. "Don't worry about that. They'll love you because I love you. Fugitive from justice or not."

The way he said those words made my heart sink. I was now a fugitive from justice. How the hell had my life turned into this?

Gage slid his hand off the steering wheel and laced his fingers through mine. Looking down at where our hands met, I had to admit there wasn't another person in the world I'd feel safer with at that moment than him.

"Thank you for protecting me."

He smiled and nodded. "Always. And once we get to somewhere safe, I'm going to help you figure out what Monique and Brock or whatever the hell their names are were up to and why Dalton Spear was involved with all this."

"Dalton Spear, the billionaire?" I asked in amazement. What on earth would a billionaire like Dalton Spear have to do with petty criminals like them?

Gage brought my hand to his lips and kissed it softly. "One in the same. But for now, we need to figure out how the hell we're going to make it cross country without getting caught because now that I got you back, I'm not losing you again."

I leaned over and rested my head on his strong shoulder. My knight in shining armor. The man I'd loved since the first time he kissed me in my kitchen. The one who'd given me up to protect me.

"I love you, Gage."

As he kissed me tenderly on the top of my head and promised me everything would be alright, I wanted to believe that could be true. I knew he'd protect me with everything he was, and I'd do the same for him.

But as we drove west into the night, I had a feeling before all this was over that those two people who stood in my kitchen kissing for hours would never be the same again.

GAGE AND JORDAN'S STORY CONTINUES IN UNBREAKABLE (A HEART OF STONE SPINOFF #2) COMING SOON!

BLOOD CRAVING
(SONS OF NAVARUS #5)

I am everything you hunger for. I am vampire.

For Sion, his only solace comes from reason and logic. Since becoming vampire in the 1940s, he has shunned feelings, morphing into a being more machine than man. As a Son, he keeps his distance from the others, allowing only one soul in the world to stir his icy heart.

A vampire turned in ancient Greece, Kali is the only hope the Sons and the Order of Macaria have to decipher the prophecy now that Thane is gone. But her past hides a dark secret that has finally caught up with her. Demons she only barely controlled now threaten her very life and the safety of all dear to her.

The one vampire who can help her knows nothing of how to reach another's heart, but without him, they both may be lost along with any hope the Sons have of defeating the Archons.

BLOOD CRAVING EXCERPT

I am everything you hunger for.
I am everything you need.
I am ecstasy and agony.
I am vampire.

CHAPTER ONE

THE GREY SKIES OVER PRAGUE were shrouded in a thick cover of falling snow that had begun just as the barely visible sun had dipped below the horizon. The city's spires and towers stood hidden from view as the storm settled in for the night. On the Charles Bridge, the lights stubbornly shone through the white flakes, showing the way to anyone who braved the mid-November weather.

Turning up his collar, Sion bowed his head and stepped out onto the street in front of the tiny apartment he'd rented months earlier when he'd arrived in Prague. He'd never believed he'd still be there as winter moved in to make itself at home, but after eight weeks of searching, he still hadn't found Kali anywhere in the hundreds of bleeder dens the central European city offered.

Night after night, he trolled the ugly underside of Prague, seeing the worst of the vampire world but never the one he so desperately wished to find. Tonight he'd perform that same march through dank rooms filled with lost souls both human and vampire, hoping this time would be the last.

The icy wind smacked him in the face as he made his way toward the bridge, reminding him of the winter days of his youth in Germany. Being so close to his childhood home brought back many memories of that past he'd worked so hard to bury, with the biting winds of winter being the most pleasant. Shaking his head, he pushed them out of his mind and focused on the night's task.

A group of Order supporters had given him a tip about a den where it was believed Kali had been spending time as recently as two nights before, so he had hope that he was getting close. He shuddered at the idea of what shape she'd be in when he finally did find her. Hoping he was wrong, he'd tried to convince himself that the vampire she was now was really no different from the gentle female he'd fed for months in Romania.

But no amount of convincing could prevent the truth from penetrating his mind. Kali would be changed from when they'd known each other before.

He'd seen what the life of a bleeder looked like each night, and it sickened him. Now with Bliss addiction seeping into every corner of the vampire world, the dens teemed with junkies both human and vampire. If he'd thought his human past had prepared him for the true horrors of the world, that belief was shattered the first night he entered the seedy underworld of bleeders and Bliss months ago.

Women and men, naked and sprawled out on filthy floors waiting for the drug they craved to settle into their system and take them away from all their problems to deliver them into that haze of ecstasy, littered each place he visited. Some were vampires, already slaves to the Archons' new drug, and others were humans, bleeders who joined centuries of their predecessors in the quest to find some part in the vampire world so seductive to so many.

The image of Kali as one of those women repeatedly stole into his brain and made him cringe. With each group, he held his breath and prayed that every one he searched through didn't contain her. These were the saddest souls he'd ever seen—willing slaves to a feeling so fleeting yet so powerful.

There was no way Kali could be one of them. She was too strong. Too smart to let that life take hold of her. Not until he saw her in front of him like that would he ever believe she was the addicted vampire Nico had spoken of.

The snow fell heavier now, and he squinted to see his way. The place was just a few blocks from where he walked, and while he could simply transport there, he rarely used that vampire ability, preferring instead to walk as he had when he was human. He was in no hurry to see another group of lost souls anyway.

He liked to keep as close to human as possible, ignoring so many of the tricks his kind possessed. Except for the blood he drank to keep his connection to their world alive, he was every bit the man he'd been during his human life.

Well, not exactly.

That man had been quite different, in truth. What everyone saw in him now was more machine-like than human. He knew what they thought when they looked at him. All brain and no heart. No soul. A thinking creature capable of little else.

That was a far cry from the man he'd been when he was turned in the 1940s. Then he'd been a violent beast, given over to the baser instincts of man, one who would hurt another sooner than help them.

Becoming vampire had changed him into that Ice Man all around him believed he was. Turning vampire had saved him.

He stopped and looked up to see the address of the night's den scrawled in red paint on the old wooden door in front of him. Breathing deep, he inhaled the cold air into his lungs and closed his eyes. Inside him, the thought that tonight he'd finally find her warred with the desperate need to never see her again if she'd become what he feared. His heart in his throat, he knocked and waited in the falling snow.

The metal window in the center of the door opened and two bloodshot eyes peered out at him. "Vampire or human?" a thin voice asked.

"Vampire," he replied with less pride than he'd ever possessed as a member of the vampire race and one of the Sons of Navarus.

The metal slammed shut, once again covering the window and the door opened, revealing an emaciated creature with sunken cheeks and vacant eyes. The man's skin hung off his bones, a sure sign of his addiction to something that was slowly killing him. His frail voice matched his appearance, but at the sight of Sion, he instantly perked up.

"We've been waiting for you. We've got at least a dozen who need you."

Sion looked at him, disgusted by the implication of his

words. Like he would ever be a vampire who'd feed his own kind or humans the junk they craved.

"I'm not here for that. I'm looking for someone."

His enthusiasm for his visitor undeterred, the man nodded his head quickly. "Oh, I have that too. What's your type? Human? Vampire? Some of both?"

"Stop talking. Where are the vampires?"

"Ahh, a man after my own heart. I don't do the humans either. Too much trouble. I can see that in you. You're a man who hates the hassle. We have a lot in common."

Turning back to face the jittery scarecrow who didn't seem to understand the command to shut up, Sion stared down at him considering how many fingers he'd have to use to snap his neck.

"You say one more word that doesn't help me find the vampires and I'll kill you. Verstehst du?"

Sion's use of his native tongue had the exact effect he intended, and the scrawny creature's eyes opened wide in fear. Even he had to admit he was never more terrifying than when he slipped back into German.

"Got it." Extending his spindly arm, the man pointed down the hallway toward an open door. "Right down there."

Forgetting him immediately, Sion marched down the dark hall. Each room he passed showed one horror after the next. Filth covered the floors, with empty vials of blood and Bliss scattered everywhere he looked. The first room contained all humans, pathetic souls strung out on every kind of drug there was. Vampires weren't affected to any great extent by human drugs, but those of the race that enjoyed enslaving humans certainly got off on them begging for vampire blood filled with them.

By the time he reached the room with the vampires, Sion's stomach was twisted in knots. He scanned the room quickly for any sight of Kali, but she wasn't there. That behind him, he moved to the second worst part of his nights.

Crouching down, he shook the bony shoulder of a male sprawled out on the floor naked from the waist up. Pulling his own jacket tight around his neck, Sion sighed at the sight of the man, his breath frosty in front of him in the near freezing room. How old he was he couldn't imagine, but he was in bad shape.

"I'm looking for a female named Kali. Light brown hair, vampire, she's been seen here recently. Do you know her?"

The male turned his head slowly at the sound of Sion's words and stared vacantly into his eyes. "A girl?"

"Yes, a damn girl! Her name is Kali. Have you seen her?"

He seemed to understand the words, but he just stared off into space. Grabbing him by the neck, Sion shook him. "Pay attention! Her name is Kali. Have you seen her?"

The male slowly closed his eyes and faded off. Sion tried to get him to focus again, but behind him he heard someone say, "You're wasting your time with that one. He can't tell you anything."

Turning his head, he saw a tall, blond haired male standing behind him. He looked vampire but didn't seem to be a junkie like everyone else in the room. Pushing the addict away, Sion stood to face the new vampire.

"Can you tell me anything?"

"She's been here."

"Is she still here?"

Sion waited for the answer with his heart in his throat.

Shaking his head, the male answered, "No. Does she know you're looking for her?"

Disappointed, Sion sighed. "I don't know. I don't think so."

The blond sized him up and opened up a bit more. "You don't seem like you want to hurt her. What do you want with her?"

Something about this guy's questions made Sion feel like he definitely knew more than he was admitting about Kali's whereabouts. Taking a step closer to him, he stared directly into his pale blue eyes.

"If you know something about where she is, you need to tell me now. I don't have time to play games with another fucked up vampire."

"What is this Kali to you? Girlfriend? Mate? Bleeder?"

The idea of Kali as a bleeder sent a jolt of rage racing through his veins. Pushing against the blond's chest, he lunged at him, leveling him hard against the wall. "I told you I don't have time for this. If you know where she is, you need to tell me now."

Any semblance of calm slipped away quickly from the male and fear filled his eyes. "I saw her. She was here for a few days, but she left last night. I heard her say something about not being able to face some guy."

"Anything else?"

The blond said nothing and Sion repeated his question as

he pushed his forearm against his throat. "I said do you know anything else?"

He shook his head violently. "I told you everything I know. I swear."

Sion released him and took a step back before he turned toward the door. Another night of no real progress. Kali was running from him. He'd had a suspicion she was, but why? Their disagreement over what she'd done with Sasa wasn't enough to make her want to avoid him. Pushing that idea out of his head as ridiculous, he returned to the idea he'd been unwilling to accept since arriving in Prague.

Kali was a Bliss junkie and didn't want to face him like that.

He stepped over someone lying across his path. Passed out, the emaciated female had a thin line of blood trailing from the corner of her mouth. Her clothes hung in tatters off her skeletal body, and bruises marked the insides of her arms as if someone had held her against her will. Looking down, Sion tried to imagine the strong, intelligent female he knew beneath someone's feet like this soul.

Was she as lost as this one he stared at now?

From behind him, the blond said, "Hey, you need to know. She's bad."

Sion turned away from the pathetic creature at his feet. "Who?"

"Your friend. This one doesn't have anything on her. She's in it bad. Much longer, and you won't find much of anything if you ever find her at all."

As he left yet another failed lead behind him, Sion silently promised himself and Kali he wouldn't let that happen. If he had to spend every night searching these wretched places, he'd find her and save her from the Bliss.

AVAILABLE AT ALL MAJOR RETAILERS

ABOUT THE AUTHOR

K.M. Scott writes contemporary romance stories of sexy, intense, and unforgettable love. A New York Times and USA Today bestselling author, she's been in love with romance since reading her first romance novel in junior high (she was a very curious girl!). She lives in Pennsylvania with her teenage son and a herd of animals and when she's not writing can be found reading or feeding her TV addiction.

Be sure to visit K.M.'s Facebook page at **www.facebook.com/ kmscottauthor** for all the latest on her books, along with giveaways and other goodies! And to hear all the news on K.M. Scott books first, sign up for her newsletter today and be sure to visit her website at **www.kmscottbooks.com**

Visit Gabrielle's Facebook page and her website at **www. gabriellebisset.com** to find out about her books too!

BOOKS BY K.M. SCOTT:

Crash Into Me (Heart of Stone #1)
Fall Into Me (Heart of Stone #2)
Give In To Me (Heart of Stone #3)
The Heart of Stone Trilogy Box Set
Ever After (A Heart of Stone Novella)
A Heart of Stone Christmas
Unforgettable (A Heart of Stone Spinoff Novel #1)

Temptation (Club X #1)
Surrender (Club X #2)
Possession (Club X #3)
Satisfaction (Club X #4)

SILK (Volume One)
SILK (Volume Two)
SILK (Volume Three)
SILK (Volume Four)
The SILK Box Set

K.M.'S BOOKS ARE IN AUDIOBOOK TOO!

BOOKS BY GABRIELLE BISSET:

Vampire Dreams Revamped (A Sons of Navarus Prequel)
Blood Avenged (Sons of Navarus #1)
Blood Betrayed (Sons of Navarus #2)
Longing (A Sons of Navarus Short Story)
Blood Spirit (Sons of Navarus #3)
The Deepest Cut (A Sons of Navarus Short Story)
Blood Prophecy (Sons of Navarus #4)
Sons of Navarus Box Set #1
Sons of Navarus Box Set #2
Blood Craving (Sons of Navarus #5) COMING
NOVEMBER 12, 2015!

Love's Master
Masquerade
The Victorian Erotic Romance Trilogy

Destiny Redeemed

25048572R00204

Made in the USA
Middletown, DE
15 October 2015